MURDER IN MINT CONDITION

A POLLY PEPPER MYSTERY

RICHARD TYLER JORDAN

MURDER IN MINT CONDITION

A POLLY PEPPER MYSTERY

RICHARD TYLER JORDAN

FOR KEVIN HOWELL
(You've always been there for me. I am grateful.)

PROLOGUE

"*Welcome to another edition of* Relic or Rubbish—*the television series where ordinary people—just like you—bring their family heirlooms, long-forgotten attic treasures, and prized collectibles to be appraised by our antique experts.*"

That refined narration belonged to Rosalind Fenwick, the beloved host of *Relic or Rubbish*, England's long-running antique appraisal television show. For twenty-five years, she had guided viewers through dazzling discoveries, painful letdowns, and a few tongue-wagging scandals. But tonight was different. It was the final night of a week-long *live* broadcast celebrating the show's quarter-century anniversary. Each evening the program had offered real-time unveilings of nearly forgotten treasures.

Among those gathered inside the white marquee tent tonight was American comedy legend Polly Pepper. While the cameras captured the excitement of the show, Polly's attention shifted between admiration for Rosalind Fenwick's polished performance and the chaotic ballet of crew members dashing around behind the scenes. As an iconic TV star in the States, she knew better than most what it took to create a television program.

The tent was buzzing with anticipation. Whispers about a special item selected to be appraised had circulated all week. The show's publicist, always keen to add a dash of hype and intrigue, had hinted that the offering could prove surprisingly significant. Was it a long-lost treasure—or an elaborate fake? Viewers were about to find out.

The show's familiar theme music swelled as the logo and opening credits appeared on television screens nationwide. A drone camera offered sweeping aerial views of the English countryside—green hills, winding lanes, and fields dotted with sheep. The camera sailed over crumbling abbeys and grand estates before focusing on Thistlethorne Lodge, the ancient castle in Abbots Clover that Polly Pepper had inherited. The shot dissolved to Rosalind strolling toward the marquee tent, a silk scarf around her neck ruffling in a soft, summer-evening breeze.

Rosalind paused outside the entrance, the murmur of the production crew and audience inside seeping through the canvas walls. She'd presented this show a million times, but something unsettling tugged at her tonight. Unease crept beneath her calm exterior. A niggling sense that tonight might alter more than just someone's understanding of a family heirloom.

She exhaled before casting a final glance at the camera shadowing her. With a small shake of her head, Rosalind pushed aside her uneasy thoughts and stepped into the marquee, where bright lights reflected off polished treasures. Another hand-held camera zoomed in, catching the sparkle in her eyes. She smiled warmly as though about to share a delicious secret.

"Perhaps tonight someone will discover they've been sitting on a fortune," she continued, speaking to the television audience. "Some may walk away disappointed. And a few? They might just unearth a secret best left buried in the past. I'm your host, Rosalind Fenwick. Please join me for the next hour—*live*—as we discover: Is it *treasure or trash? Priceless or pointless?*"

For the next forty-five minutes, Rosalind interviewed heirloom owners and expert appraisers, discussing everything from weathered Roman coins to antique pearl earrings. As discoveries unfolded, the crowd gasped, sighed, and murmured, with Polly leading the applause. But something gnawed at Polly, too. Her new friend, Rosalind, usually so pulled together, seemed just a shade off tonight. She looked a tad unsettled.

Of course, it had been an exhausting day—indeed, an entire week—of remarkable finds and a handful of heartbreaks. And as the live broadcast neared its final valuation segment, anticipation rippled through the crowd. Rosalind Fenwick, ever poised, cast a knowing glance at the camera, her signature half-smile hinting at what was to come. "And now," she said, her voice rich with intrigue, "we have something truly special. Could it be the find of the decade...or just another cleverly crafted forgery? We're about to find out. But first, please stay tuned for these brief sponsored messages. I'll see you back here in just a moment. You won't want to miss a thing."

The show's theme music swelled again, echoing through the tent as the camera lingered on Rosalind's composed smile.

"And...we're out!" Director Chad Wescott's voice crackled through the crew's headsets.

In the production trailer just outside the tent, monitors flickered with feeds from multiple cameras as crew members called out time codes and adjusted audio levels. Chad leaned forward, eyes fixed on the main screen. "Camera three, stay tight for the reveal. We'll need that reaction shot. Janine—keep an eye on the guest's mic; levels were spiking."

Inside the marquee, the shift from on-air polish to backstage urgency was immediate. The overhead lights dimmed slightly, offering a brief respite from the glare and pressure of the live broadcast. Stagehands rushed to adjust props, while a makeup artist swooped in to touch up Rosalind's forehead with a powder puff. A production assistant handed her a bottle of water, from which she took a sip.

"Sixty seconds, people!" Chad's voice called again through the crew's headsets. "You're all doing great. Let's keep this smooth. Big moment coming up."

And then it happened—

Standing just off to the side, near the edge of the makeshift set, Polly saw Rosalind suddenly sway. The world tilted beneath her feet, the buzz of the crew and audience blurred into a confusing hum. She pressed a trembling hand to her temple, fingers splayed as if to anchor herself.

"I—I feel...sort of—" Her voice faltered, the words dissolving into breathless silence. The color drained from her face, leaving her skin ashen and her lips pale. Her gaze turned glassy as she struggled to focus.

"Rosalind!" Polly yelled as she sprang forward from the crowd, reaching her friend as she wavered and collapsed. "Rosalind! Somebody get help!"

The floor manager lunged in beside her, yelling frantically at the crew. "Get medical! Now!"

Chaos erupted. Crew members scrambled. And Polly, kneeling on the floor, pressed her hand to Rosalind's cheek as the *Relic or Rubbish* theme played in the background—its jaunty notes a bizarre soundtrack to the unfolding panic.

Chad Wescott bolted in from the control truck. "What the hell? We're seconds to air!"

"We're out of time!" the floor manager looked at her watch. "Thirty seconds! What do we do?!"

Chad's eyes landed on Polly. "You!" He snapped a finger.

"Polly—you have to take Rosalind's place! You hosted your own show—this is second nature to you."

Polly's heart pounded. This wasn't scripted. There was no rehearsal or preparation.

Rosalind, struggling to sit up, grasped Polly's arm weakly. Her breath hitched. "—I'm really sorry...please, you have to do it...Please..." she nearly begged, as the production nurse guided her away.

For a split second, Polly's mind whirled—*Not your problem! Walk away.* But Rosalind's plea echoed. Millions of people sat at home expecting the show to return from commercial break. And Polly Pepper? Polly Pepper never backed down from a challenge—especially not one with a spotlight and camera. "Get me a microphone!" she said. Someone shoved Rosalind's into her hand. "Makeup!" she barked. A powder puff appeared seemingly from nowhere, dabbing frantically at her nose and forehead.

"Ten seconds!" the floor manager shouted.

Polly drew a deep breath that seemed to scrape the bottom of her soul. She straightened, smoothed her skirt, and stepped into the harsh glow of the lights.

"Five...four...three..."

Her pulse roared in her ears. *No script. No net. What am I doing?*

The floor manager sliced a hand downward. "We're live!"

Polly's smile instantly slipped on like an old glove. "Good evening," she purred into the camera. "I'm Polly Pepper. I'm stepping in for the incomparable Rosalind Fenwick. Don't you just love her? Yes, we all adore Rosalind! Unfortunately, she's suddenly feeling a smidge under the weather. Not to worry—she'll be right as rain in no time. But tonight's final item is too extraordinary to delay revealing to you. It's been the talk of the *Relic or Rubbish* family all week. Shall we see what's had everybody buzzing?"

A hush fell over the tent as Polly and the camera took center stage with the final item of the night. At the main appraisal table, horology expert Arley Kingston sat poised, his boyish smile warm and friendly, eyes gleaming with genuine enthusiasm.

Though still in his early thirties, Arley Kingston had a confident, self-assured presence. A British transplant from Jamaica, his lean, athletic build was complemented by smooth, dark skin and short-cropped hair. His warm, Ultrabrite® toothpaste smile and expressive eyes had made him a swoon-worthy fan favorite. He'd quickly built a reputation for his encyclopedic knowledge of antiques and his especially infectious passion for timepieces. That passion had been sparked at the age of ten when his grandmother showed him her Victorian clock with a built-in music box. He was instantly captivated by the delicate gears, the craftsmanship, and the soft chime that played. From that moment, he knew he wanted to spend his life surrounded by vintage artifacts—especially clocks.

Now, two decades later, that childhood wonder still shone through as he rested his fingertips gently beside an ornate gilded clock perched on a gleaming, black-lacquered stand. The elaborate centuries-old timepiece gleamed under the lights, its tiny, ceramic figurines frozen in place. Arley's gaze flitted between the clock and the audience, his expression that of someone eager to share a fun secret.

"Hold right there—that's the frame," Chad murmured to the cameraman, eyes glued to his monitors in the trailer. "Now—back to Polly—cue her line in three—two—"

Polly leaned forward, her eyes fixed on the beautiful clock. "Arley, this piece is remarkable. It looks quite old. No doubt it carries the weight of many long-forgotten secrets."

Arley leaned in to examine the clock. "Yes. You're spot-on, Polly. It's what's called an 'automaton' clock. An automaton clock is a marvel of craftsmanship, blending precise timekeeping with mechanical scenes that stir to life on the hour. This one is late eighteenth-century. Parisian." His fingers traced the delicate enamel casing. "Gilt bronze with hand-painted inlays...a lovely pastoral scene here. And look—the dial's porcelain, with Roman numerals. Typical of the period."

He turned the clock slightly, revealing a small engraving. "Duval, Paris, 1783. Duval catered to the aristocracy—this piece wasn't made for just anyone. These automaton clocks were conversation pieces, status symbols in the grand salons of France."

As Arley spoke, Polly's eyes were drawn to the tiny mechanical figures on top. A lady holding a lute, a gentleman bowed, and a harlequin watched them. "This is a remarkable piece," Arley enthused with reverence. His voice, rich with appreciation, carried just enough warmth to keep the appraisal from sounding clinical. Next to him, the clock's owner sat rigid, his eyes darting between Arley and the camera operator framing the shot. A small microphone was clipped to his shirt, a silent reminder that every reaction—every flicker of hope or disappointment—was being transmitted to an audience of millions.

Arley ignored the camera and divided his attention between the clock and its owner. "Now," he said, fingers gently brushing the edge of the clock's base, "originally, there would have been a glass dome covering these charming figures, protecting them from dust and—well—overly curious fingers." He offered the owner a playful smile. "It's not uncommon for those domes to go missing over the centuries. They're fragile, easily broken or separated. And while the absence of it does affect overall value, it doesn't diminish the craftsmanship or the clock's historical significance. If anything, it's a testament to how well this piece has endured.

"Let's take a closer look, shall we?" Arley continued. The camera zoomed in as he delicately turned the clock, allowing viewers at home to admire the intricate enamel work and the precise mechanics of the frozen figurines. Under the bright lights, the gold filigree gleamed, every detail a testament to the artistry of the period. Arley flashed the owner a smile and asked, "How did you acquire this extraordinary piece?"

The owner, a tall man in his late fifties with the air of someone who didn't expect to be called on in class, cleared his throat. His fingers twitched slightly against the table's edge, but he quickly composed himself.

"Well," he began, his voice steady, though tinged with nervousness, "it belonged to my grandfather. He acquired it when a friend—an art dealer who worked with private collectors across Europe—died and left it to him in his will. Apparently, my grandfather had once admired it, and his friend knew it would be in good hands with him."

Arley nodded, listening raptly. "And it's remained in your family ever since?"

The owner hesitated, then offered a tight smile. "Not exactly. It was stolen from my grandfather's house the very day he died, over twenty years ago. We assumed we'd never see it again." He exhaled, shaking his head slightly as if still distressed by the memory. "It re-surfaced at an estate auction in Toulouse, last year. We just happened to be in France then, and when I saw the little figures, I knew it was my grandfather's."

Arley's eyebrows lifted slightly. "That must have been a happy discovery."

"You have no idea," the man said, his gaze dropping to the clock. "I outbid everyone in the room. I wasn't about to let it slip through my fingers again."

Arley tilted his head, considering. "And you never learned where it had been all those years?"

"No," the owner grimaced. "And to be honest...I'm not sure I want to. It was all too weird. There's some legend of a curse attached to it."

Arley chuckled skeptically, but something in the man's tone made the director instruct the camera operator to zoom in just a little closer as if sensing the weight of the moment.

"Well," Arley said, his voice slipping effortlessly back into its polished broadcast cadence, "let's see if your instincts were correct. Because if this is what I think it is, you may have reclaimed a true masterpiece."

He gently inserted the key into one of the winding holes in the clock's face. After a series of soft, measured clicks the mechanism whirred to life. Arley carefully moved the hands to the hour, and with a delicate chime, the automaton sprang into motion. Hidden gears engaged, setting a series of cams and levers into fluid action. The lady's porcelain arms lifted to strum her lute; the gentleman bowed with mechanical grace. Each movement carried a charm—as if the figures remembered a courtly dance from centuries ago.

Polly leaned in, marveling at the sheer ingenuity behind the clock's creation. In the gentle dance of the tiny figures, she could almost hear the soft rustle of silk gowns and the faint echo of courtly laughter. *How could a craftsman, armed only with tiny tools and raw skill, fashion such a wonder more than 250 years ago?* she wondered.

Arley smiled and offered a history lesson. "French automaton clocks of this caliber are incredibly rare. This one? A true masterpiece." He gave a knowing smile. "Now, here's where it can get more interesting. Some automaton clocks of this era contained hidden compartments—a little covert luxury for the nobility. Many were designed with places to hide love notes or jewels."

The camera zoomed in as Arley felt around the base of the clock. Suddenly, he stilled. His expression shifted, just slightly. "Oh…" he murmured. "Now that's interesting." He exchanged a glance with the clock's owner, as he carefully felt along the ornate base of the timepiece, his fingers finding something practically invisible to the untrained eye. With another soft click, a section of the clock's base popped open.

Gasps rippled through the audience. Even Arley seemed momentarily at a loss. "Well, that's quite a surprise," he said, his voice filled with excitement and curiosity as he peered inside.

He removed his cumbersome cotton glove to pinch a small, folded piece of parchment from inside the shallow box. The camera zoomed in as he carefully straightened out the slip of paper, his brow arching as he scanned the faded ink with a magnifying glass. "It seems this clock's been keeping a little secret for a couple of hundred years." He looked at the owner. "Do you speak French?"

"*Un peu*—a little," the man said, his fingers tensing slightly against the table's edge.

Arley handed him the parchment and a magnifying glass. "What do you think of this…"

"*Trust neither the Cardinal nor his secretary,*" the man translated.

"Sounds pretty sinister," Arley said. "Maybe even court-level intrigue. In the eighteenth century, ornate furniture and objects like clocks were often used to conceal documents or jewelry during periods of upheaval. I am quite confident that if this piece were to come up at auction, a conservative price for it would be around—"

He paused mid-sentence. For a heartbeat, the audience held its breath. Polly, too, leaned closer, her eyes growing wide with expectation. What value was Arley about to place on the clock? Her mind raced with possibilities.

But, after a fraction of a moment too long, Arley sharply inhaled, followed by slow, disbelieving blinks of his eyes. His fingers twitched as though no longer his own. And in that surreal instant, Polly's heart pounded with uncertainty. The air around the table seemed to tighten. Then, Arley swayed, his skin taking on an ashen pallor. His mouth parted, soundless. He braced himself against the table, knuckles whitening.

A ripple of unease passed through the gathered spectators.

Something was wrong. Terribly wrong! Polly's voice cut through the murmurs. "Arley? Arley! Are you...?"

Arley's breath hitched. His pupils dilated. A single bead of sweat traced its way down his temple. His fingers clawed at his chest. "I—I feel..." The words slurred. His lips fumbled for meaning, his mind untethering. His body sagged.

Then—like a marionette with its strings abruptly severed— he collapsed forward. His arms struck the table, sending the antique clock skittering sideways, caught by its owner in the nick of time before falling.

A woman shrieked. The camera lurched, unfocused; voices began shouting, and chaos erupted.

"Cut the feed! Cut the feed—*now*!" Chad's voice exploded through the technicians' headsets. "Roll the standby graphic! Go to commercial! Now!" On home television screens, the broadcast switched to the show's logo and theme music, masking the confusion.

"Lock the set down!" Chad barked. "Medical—where the hell is medical? Security! No phones! No filming! Keep this contained! We are not going viral for the wrong reason tonight."

On set, the floor manager shouted orders. Audience members gasped and craned their necks to see over those standing in front of them. Some raised their phone cameras despite the prohibition.

Polly dropped to her knees beside Arley. Her voice cracked with fear. "Arley, can you hear me?"

Silence.

His chest was still. His eyes were wide and sightless, gazing at nothing.

A heavy hush fell over the tent.

...Arley's life—faded away.

1

BEFORE ALL THAT MESS…

When American comedy legend and former TV darling Polly Pepper inherited a castle in Abbots Clover, England, she naturally assumed it came with a crown. After all, she was a queen, for crying out loud. At least, she used to be. The critics called her "the queen of comedy." Surely, along with this unexpected windfall, she'd wield a scepter and say regal things like: "You have my permission to withdraw." Or "Off with their heads!"

Polly pictured herself waving smugly from the balcony of Buckingham Palace, flanked by William and Kate, as they gossiped over tea and crumpets. She'd live in Windsor-like grandeur—or Balmoral, at the very least—where every room would be decorated with enormous oil portraits of herself in spectacular royal robes, ermine capes, coronation rings, and the occasional falcon perched on her gloved hand.

She would preside from a gilded throne in the great hall, where guests would be served champagne and cucumber sandwiches. And if anyone dared to cross her? Well, let's just say they'd find themselves "unexpectedly detained" in the Tower of

London, where they'd be forced to watch her low-budget horror movie, *Crawling Eyeballs II—The Vision Returns*, on 24/7 loop.

Yeah, right. So much for Polly Pepper's wild imagination.

The truth was, instead of inheriting some grand Downton Abbey-like estate, Polly's eccentric fan, Alastair Drake, had left her his crumbling Norman castle, Thistlethorne Lodge, situated in the tiny village of Abbots Clover. The front gates sagged, and the stone turrets had more cracks to fill than Polly's last Botox session.

Yes, a lovely manor house was tucked behind the fortified stone walls, but Mr. Drake's idea of preventative maintenance on the place had been little more than providing his handyman with a screwdriver and a roll of duct tape. He'd otherwise squandered his money collecting movie star memorabilia. Thus, Thistlethorne Lodge was one leaky roof away from being condemned. Even the gargoyles looked terrified.

The British Historical Society sent letters to Polly. But they weren't sweet "Welcome to the neighborhood," greetings. They were packed with legalese and phrases like "heritage preservation," "unauthorized alterations," and "ramifications for noncompliance." The castle was a nationally protected property, and therefore, even replacing a doorknob required mountains of paperwork and committee approvals. She had briefly toyed with the idea of hosting a masquerade ball fundraiser to cover the cost of repairs, but after a visit to the attic's cobwebbed rafters, she realized the ceiling might collapse right onto the guests. Nothing ruins a black-tie event quite like falling masonry.

And then—a minor miracle occurred. While scrutinizing a water stain on the ceiling in the library, Polly's cell phone rang. It was her unctuous agent, JJ Norton.

JJ was the sort of Hollywood phony who prefaced his greetings with air-kisses and phrases like, "Honey, baby, cookie, sweetie." And ended them with, "Love ya! Mean it! We'll do lunch." He had a file of meaningless catch phrases: "Darling, you're not just a star—you're *the* star. Kiddo, if I had a dollar for every time someone told me you're more talented than that overrated Meryl Streep…"

JJ rarely telephoned, but when he did, it was usually to snare Polly into appearing (gratis, of course) at some charitable fundraiser. Now he trilled, "Polly Pepper pumpkin pie! How the hell are you holding up over there in soggy old England this a.m.? Or is it p.m.? Time zones are as confusing as the *Days of Our Lives* family tree."

Polly rolled her eyes so hard she practically gave herself a headache. "Well, well, if it isn't my favorite showbiz nuisance. What's up, JJ?"

"Does anything have to be *up*, sweet cakes? I'm simply calling to remind you that you're the most glittering star in the cosmos! Oh, and that little castle of yours…"

Castle. Of course. Polly knew JJ would have an ulterior motive. "I'm not mortgaging Thistlethorne to give you an advance on your next commission."

"Polly-*wolly*! You wound me!" JJ gasped. "Never mind, cookie, you'll *wove* me for this. Ever hear of *Relic or Rubbish*?"

"Doesn't ring a bell. A reality show where influencers reassess the relevance of Cher's career?"

"Lamby chops, it's a reality show on 'telly'—as you say in Blighty. A very popular antique appraisal program. People raid their attics, drag out useless clutter, and then take their *s-h-i-t* to a bunch of snooty experts for valuation. Of course, most of its *rubbish*—hence, the title. A rusted can opener said to be from the galley of the Titanic. Mass-produced Princess Di commemorative ceramic figurines. Family keepsakes they're convinced belonged to Anne Boleyn. You get the drill."

Polly raised an eyebrow. "A televised flea market."

"Bingo! It's *de-lish*. I never miss the US version: *What*

Grandma Horded. Rosalind Fenwick is the host in England. She's divine. Think Cate Blanchett crossed with Emma Thompson and a pinch of Rachel Weisz."

Rosalind Fenwick was one of the most beloved presenters on British television. She was poised, elegant, and sophisticated. Admired for her intelligence, charm, and diplomatic demeanor, she appealed to everyone from Joe Schmoe to the Royals. Even with her posh accent, she still managed to exude the sense that she was someone you could meet up with at the pub and have a pint or two. Simply put, the public adored Rosalind Fenwick.

"And what, pray tell, does any of this have to do with *moi*," Polly said. "Unless they're sacking Rosalind and hiring me to be the patron saint of clutter collectors. I am sort of ready for a new TV gig. Although wading through dusty attics and dodging cobwebs isn't really my thing."

Polly's memory flashed. There she was starring on her very own television show—sheathed in a sparkling Bob Mackie gown, her hair perfectly coiffed. God, she longed for that glory and adoration again. "I miss being famous and raking in the big bucks."

"You and me both, princess!" JJ sighed. "But no, silly, they don't want *you*. They want your house. Thistlethorne Lodge. As the filming location for *Relic or Rubbish's* big twenty-fifth anniversary show. Doesn't that sound marvey? The producer called only a wee moment-*o* ago!"

Polly blinked. "Why Thistlethorne? Unless they're looking for a pile that's about to collapse."

"It's a *castle*, sweetie. Everybody loves *castles*. Apparently, they tried to get Sandringham, but Camilla was in a *mood*. Said, 'No way, Jose.' And here's the *funsi-est* part. They'll cough up a substantial rental fee."

Polly's mental cash register suddenly began *ker-ching-ing* to life, tallying up roof repairs, new windows, and oh, why not, something wildly indulgent—like heating. "How substantial?"

"A prime number with a bunch of zeroes behind it!" JJ's voice lowered as if sharing a state secret. "It'll be the easiest money we'll ever make! Play your cards right, they might even feature your place on *Love It or List It!*"

For the briefest moment, Polly's eyes lit up. But just as quickly, her face dropped like a soufflé in a thunderstorm. She knew that when JJ dangled the words *"easy money,"* it was usually code for *"just sign here and prepare to regret everything."*

"What's in the fine print? Am I being paid to appear and humiliate myself in period costume?"

JJ giggled. "Semi-full disclosure, pumpkin...I don't know how it is in England, but for the U.S. version, the guttersnipes who crawl out of the woodwork to be on the show are generally elite members of the Great Unwashed."

"Are we talking flea dip and carbolic soap?"

"Pretty much. Picture this: a garage sale in Rancho Cucamonga. Primitives wearing oil-stained sweatpants and baseball caps with ironic messages like *My IQ Test Came Back Negative.*"

"The MAGA hat-wearing crowd who believe January sixth was a sightseeing tour gone slightly awry? Good grief." Polly sighed, envisioning hordes of locals hauling their family's junk across her front garden and mingling with pretentious antique experts.

"But the even more fun part?" JJ continued. "I know you *live* for celebrity mud-slinging. *Relic or Rubbish* is notorious for its nest of in-house vipers. I've heard loads of gossip about the arrogant antiques appraisers. It's all polite smiles and polished opinions on camera, but turn your back, and it's *knives out*, baby. Passive-aggressive tea breaks explode into full-blown tantrums over who gets to appraise the next faux Fabergé egg."

Polly barely heard what JJ was saying as her gaze drifted

back to the water stain creeping across the library ceiling. Was it her imagination, or had it grown in the past five minutes? It was another reminder that Thistlethorne Lodge wasn't just crumbling—it was devouring her bank account. Hosting the *Relic or Rubbish* production could be the answer to her costly home repair problems.

"I'll do it!" Polly abruptly snapped, cutting JJ off mid-rant. "Besides, it's only for a week. What could possibly happen in a week, right? And maybe someone will bring in Henry VIII's missing codpiece. Send me the contract...and a check."

2

___

The *Relic or Rubbish* production crew arrived at Thistlethorne in a thunder of rumbling trucks, spilling out tents, canopies, and filmmaking equipment. Teams moved with the focused energy of television people who knew exactly how much time they *didn't* have.

An assistant director paced the castle's inner ward, headset pressed to his ear as he barked instructions. A lighting technician stood on a towering scaffold while cables below him snaked across the lawn. A segment producer stood with clipboard in hand, checking and re-checking the tightly packed schedule. Beside the topiary, a sound engineer crouched over a box of lapel microphones, untangling wires with the patient concentration of someone defusing a bomb.

From her vantage point by the window in the breakfast room, Polly observed the spectacle with more than mild curiosity. She took a measured sip of her morning energy drink—a Bloody Mary—and let her gaze drift across the chaotic scene. Her eyes narrowed as she spotted a young man dashing toward the catering van, likely armed with a list of specific coffee orders.

Oh, the memories, she thought with a pang of nostalgia. Her years on a television soundstage hosting *The Polly Pepper Play-house* weekly variety series were a distant memory, but she hadn't forgotten how much sweat and caffeine went into making TV magic. Audiences only saw the finished product—a glossy, polished production. Few knew the efforts behind it. They'd never see the gaffers and grips and audio engineers or producers agonizing over every second of air-time. Or the lighting crew balancing natural and artificial light. Or gofers sprinting to fetch whatever someone with a smidge more seniority demanded. The people behind the scenes carried the show's weight on their shoulders, ensuring every detail was perfect. Polly had learned that their work—invisible to viewers—was often the hardest.

The soft shuffle of slippered feet behind Polly pulled her from her reverie. Tim, her adult but-still-living-at-home son, drifted into the room, wearing rumpled jammies. His hair was sticking up as if he'd spent the night in a wind tunnel. He followed her gaze out the window and let out a world-weary sigh. "The circus has come to town?" He collapsed into his usual chair and popped open the Red Bull that Polly's maid and bestie, Tiara, had left at his place setting—evidence of the well-oiled machine that was the family's morning routine.

Polly turned from the window, taking another sip of her drink. "Yep. Send in the clowns—might as well throw in the lion-tamers and fire-eaters while they're at it. Don't bother; they're already here." She tittered at her own joke. "At this rate, they'll be laying down a runway for air support."

Tim opened his mouth to fire off a snarky comeback but was silenced by the sharp ping of Polly's phone. She glanced at the screen. "It's the ringmaster herself—Rosalind Fenwick. 'ETA: *Un momento.*'"

Polly barely had time to process the news before Tim, mid-sip, said. "Oh, goody. *La Fenwick* herself. Can't wait to meet the queen of antiques. I did a little digging." He grabbed his phone and checked his search history. "She's a pretty big deal here in the UK. Not quite Judi Dench level of national treasure, but still..." He took another sip from his can, then glanced up, eyes gleaming. "Google sourced up a couple of dozen photos of her ridiculously good-looking son, Ethan, too." He fanned his face, emitting a low growl of approval. "*Muy caliente, por favor!* Grayson and I are solid, but these baby blues aren't blind."

"Not all that glitters is twenty-four karat," Polly reminded him. "But just out of curiosity..." She snatched his phone and studied Ethan's image. "Good heavens. He looks like a soap star who never learned to button a shirt."

"As for his mother, apparently, some of her *Relic or Rubbish* colleagues think she's a bit...not quite what she presents to the public. They've hinted in interviews that the effortlessly charming queen of antiques might actually shed her skin at night."

Polly waved a dismissive hand. "Sweetums, those online rags are as bad as the *National Intruder* ever was—more creative writing than journalism. You know better than to believe everything on the internet. But you also know Mummy loves a showbiz cesspool. Read me the juicier ones."

Tim could hardly stifle an eager giggle. "Her middle initial stands for *Pretentious*. Rosalind Fenwick is the kind of woman who'd admire your grandmother's brooch, then suggest it would have a more dignified life in someone else's family.'"

"Meow!"

"My personal fave? 'Rosalind Fenwick, known in certain circles as *the Lizard of Roz,* might know the difference between a Georgian and Victorian sideboard at fifty paces, but she wouldn't recognize sincerity if it were engraved on a silver platter and hand-delivered by a footman.'" Tim let out a delighted gasp. "That's not shade—that's a total eclipse. But hell, the public adores her."

A sudden glint of reflected sunlight flashed through the window and caught Polly's eye. She glanced outside as a car rolled through the main gate. *A Prius?* She frowned. "Can't be the famous Rosalind Fenwick. Unless production budget cuts mean the on-air stars are reduced to riding in Ubers."

But it *was* the big, important TV star! When the driver's door swung open, out stepped Rosalind Fenwick, her polished elegance impossible to miss. From the trunk, she withdrew a suitcase. Then, adjusting the strap of a leather satchel slung over her shoulder, she strode toward the house.

Suitcase? Polly frowned, watching as Rosalind moved across the gravel drive. Even from a distance, she could see Rosalind Fenwick exuded the effortless composure of someone accustomed to being in the public eye. As if sensing Polly's gaze, she glanced toward the window. Their eyes met, and she lifted a hand in a casual finger wave. The gesture was smooth and friendly. There was no urgency in her movements, no attempt to rush—only the quiet self-assurance of a woman entirely at home in her own celebrity skin.

For a fleeting moment, Polly felt a pang of something close to envy mingled with admiration. Rosalind was a British television star. She radiated unforced charisma, and reminded Polly of her friend and comedy idol, Carol Burnett—not just for her poise, but for the way she commanded attention without demanding it. Carol had that type of grace. She made people gravitate toward her, as if waiting for a punchline. Whether Rosalind was oblivious to her fame or simply at peace with it, Polly couldn't decide. Either way, she was magnetic.

A heavy rap echoed through the house as the front-door knocker delivered its commanding thud. Ordinarily, Polly would have left the task of greeting a visitor to Tiara—a subtle declaration that she was above the mundane business of answering doors. But not today. "I'll get it!" she called out, cutting Tiara off as their paths converged in the main hallway.

Rosalind was a big deal in England, and Polly had no intention of being dismissed as just another overindulged American TV legend lounging around in her castle. Nope. She'd take control and let Rosalind see that Polly Pepper was just as grounded as any British celebrity. Ideally, more so.

Polly waited behind the door for a fraction of a nano-second. She smoothed her blouse, touched an errant strand of hair, and summoned an expression of casual warmth. Then, with a theatrical flourish, she pulled open the heavy door. She hoped her smile was bright but not too eager, as though she were simply greeting a person of fame less stellar than her own. "Rosalind Fenwick! Welcome to Thistlethorne Lodge! I'm Polly Pepper! Delighted to meet you!"

Rosalind's face lit up, and she let out a small, unguarded squeal. "Polly Pepper! The pleasure is entirely mine!" She stepped inside and offered quick, affectionate air-kisses to Polly's cheeks in that effortlessly informal European way. She rolled her suitcase aside and parked it next to an eighteenth-century mahogany console table. "I've done my homework. Your television career in America? *Iconic!* I've watched *The Polly Pepper Playhouse* over and over on YouTube. All those hilarious comedy sketches? And your famous guest stars? *Tres magnifique!* There'll never be anything like it again. *Ev-er.*"

"I've seen your *Rubbish*, too," Polly said. "I mean *Relic or Rubbish*. It's practically compulsory viewing," she lied, having nodded off halfway through the only episode she'd tried to watch. Polly felt the tiniest flicker of intimidation. Rosalind had effortless charm—the kind that let her glide into any room and command attention without even trying.

As Polly accepted Rosalind's coat and draped it over the hall tree, she saw her guest's gaze sweep the foyer with appreciation.

Rosalind's eyes tracked the elegant curve of the wide mahogany staircase, then drifted to a floor-to-ceiling portrait of an aristocratic lady in a blue satin gown. She stepped closer, studying the brushstrokes with the reverence of someone well-versed in art. Her fingers hovered just shy of the gilt frame, as though tempted to touch the painted silk and test the illusion. *"C'est d'une beauté rare."* Rosalind murmured. Then, with a soft, almost wistful sigh said, "Your home—I'd never leave!

"The *Relic or Rubbish* expert antiques appraisers would have a field day here," she continued. "But don't let them anywhere near this exquisite vase." She stepped closer to a delicate porcelain vessel set into a recessed niche. Her fingers grazed the air around it. *"Sèvres* or *Meissen?"* she mused, her brow furrowing slightly. "I always get my French and German porcelain confused."

Polly's own smile deepened, her posture straightening just a touch—as if Thistlethorne itself had drawn up to its full height of pride under Rosalind's admiration. She could tell her guest didn't just appreciate the house; she understood it.

Where Polly saw the superficial beauty, Rosalind seemed to see beneath it—provenance, craftsmanship, history. She spoke the language of antiques with effortless fluency, and Polly suddenly felt like a tourist in her own home. An impostor, almost—aware she knew less about Thistlethorne's treasures than Rosalind appeared to.

"Shall we migrate to the main reception room?" Polly said, with just a hint of hostess bravado—as if leading the way might reestablish who was meant to be doing the impressing.

When they arrived, Rosalind absorbed the surroundings with another approving gaze. "Oh, Polly, this is lovely." She stepped farther into the room and admired the dark, centuries-old oak paneling and crown molding. "The craftsmanship—just look at it. No one does work like this anymore."

She turned, taking in the portrait hanging above the fireplace. She looked intently at the subject—a corpulent man in a powdered wig, his expression frozen in an unmistakable sneer. "Who's the chap with the attitude?" she asked. "Looks like he's about to throw a tantrum."

"The Duke of Droitwich," Polly said, rolling her eyes. "He built this house in the 1700s and, by all accounts, considered himself God's final draft—perfection in a powdered wig. Legend has it he once tried to commission a stained-glass window of himself for the village church, claiming it would 'uplift the commoners to gaze upon his countenance during worship.'"

Polly moved to the fireplace, letting her fingers trail along the carved stone mantel. "My favorite story is the one about his flatulent dog, Loki. One afternoon, Loki snatched the duke's robe—some grotesque monstrosity trimmed in ermine and pure egomania—and dragged it through the mud all the way to the stables. By the time the servants retrieved it, the thing was matted with manure and beyond salvation. Loki became an instant hero to the servants. From then on they treated him like visiting royalty and giggled about the incident behind the duke's back."

Rhythmic footsteps echoed down the staircase, growing louder until Tim bounded into the room. Polly turned with a smile. "And here's my own crown prince—my darling son, Tim. Stylish. Sharp-witted. And only marginally less high maintenance than the duke." She gave him a look of unabashed affection. "Tim, this is Rosalind—"

"—Fenwick! I know," Tim finished his mother's sentence. "Television *royalty*. I've seen your show. How's your son, Ethan? He seems to be all over Instagram."

"Ethan?" Rosalind blinked, then smiled with the amused knowing of someone who'd answered that question far too often. "Ethan...Twenty-eight and still living at home, determined to be a TikTok influencer when he *never* grows up. He's convinced I'm just here to admire his brilliance. Much like the duke up there."

She glanced at Polly. "Parenthood—where applause is mandatory and your opinion irrelevant." Then, turning back to Tim with a smile, she said, "But I suspect what you *really* want to know is his relationship status. Single. But straight, I'm afraid. Sorry. Though he does give off a different vibe when it suits him."

Before Tim could comment, Tiara swept into the room, leading the new maid, Elara, who carefully steered a rolling trolley laden with a gleaming silver tea service and plates of lemon drizzle cake. The rich scent of tea and fresh citrus quickly filled the room.

"Rosalind Fenwick," Tiara said, handing their guest the first cup and saucer. "I love your show. Lemon drizzle?" She gestured toward the perfectly arranged slices. Tiara settled beside Polly on the settee, her expression bright with curiosity. "I still remember that episode where a woman brought in what she swore was Napoleon's chamber pot—turned out to be a Victorian soup tureen. I'll bet you've had your fair share of oddities on *Relic or Rubbish*."

Rosalind took a sip of her tea, the picture of unflappable poise. "You wouldn't believe some of the things that have turned up over the years. There was a woman who'd been using what she thought was a rather ugly little plate as a bird feeder in her garden. Turns out it was a Picasso ceramic. She'd been letting pigeons eat off a thirty-thousand pound masterpiece for years. And then there was the retired schoolteacher who walked in with an odd painting she'd picked up for a fiver at a car boot sale. Turns out it was a lost Jackson Pollock."

Rosalind set her tea-cup down and turned to Polly. "I'm so delighted you're opening up Thistlethorne Lodge to *Relic or*

Rubbish. It's the perfect backdrop. The history. The charm. Everything about this place embodies what our show is about." She settled back into her chair with an air of satisfaction. "Honestly, we've been to so many castles—Alnwick, Carrickfergus, Rookhaven." She waved a hand as if brushing aside the grander strongholds. "Those places are in a league of their own—true feats of architecture, the kind of castles that define their eras. But your place is far more practical." She let the words hang for just a moment before offering Polly a perfectly polished smile, "Thistlethorne...well, it has a sort of *humble* elegance. *Intimate. Unpretentious.* You can tell it was meant to be lived in rather than, you know, just *admired*."

Polly nodded but wondered, *Is that a velvet-glove slap? Is Thistlethorne being insulted as less-than?*

"I'll have so much fun exploring Thistlethorne during my weeklong stay with you. I promise not to be any bother. I'm quite capable of making my own bed."

Stay? Bed? Of course, there would be one teensy-weensy bit of info dear JJ had failed to mention. "So that's why the suitcase."

Rosalind's expression flushed with embarrassment. "Oh, good grief! Has there been a misunderstanding? Your agent said he'd arranged everything. He assured my producer that *you* were the one who suggested the idea in the first place. You wouldn't have it any other way, he said. I'm really sorry, Polly..." Her voice trailed off, her confidence slipping. "I'm sure I can maybe get an Airbnb in the village."

Polly's thoughts raced. She vaguely recalled agreeing to let the production use the library for meetings—that was no biggie. But hosting the show's star? "Of course you'll stay! I should have thought of that myself, for real! It'll be a celebrity slumber party!"

Tiara lit up. "Finally! Someone interesting under this roof. In

Hollywood, we were *swimming* in fascinating people—directors, actors, even the odd politician hiding out. There was always drama. Always gossip. Exhausting—but wildly entertaining. These days...?" She waved a hand, all mock despair.

Tim added, "Since you'll be staying with us, maybe invite Ethan down?"

Rosalind relaxed, relief washing over her face. "You're all proof of what I've always suspected: Americans are among the most gracious people on the planet."

"We can be," Polly affirmed. "Just ignore the red-capped crazies shouting about biblical literalism and insisting Jesus voted Republican. Ha-ha!"

Groans of agreement rippled around the room and Polly seized the moment. "So tell us—what should we expect from the week ahead?"

Rosalind shifted gears without missing a beat. "Have you seen *Antiques Roadshow*? The format's similar. People bring in things they had tucked away for years or passed down with scraps of family lore. But what sets *Relic or Rubbish* apart is the emotional connection. We don't just slap on a value and send them packing. We dig into the backstory—what the item means to its owner, where it came from. It's as much about family history. That's largely thanks to our provenance research department, headed by Isla Morton. Very thorough. Intense, even. Ethan dated her for a while—which, in hindsight, might not have been his most inspired decision."

Rosalind described the upcoming week in terms of a well-oiled production machine. "The early morning setup with cameras and lighting tests will be the easy part," she said. "Then comes the flood of villagers and out-of-towners, carrying everything from a tennis racket once swung by Fred Perry to grand family heirlooms like Great-Aunt Beryl's ruby-studded brooch that's been missing since the Queen's Silver Jubilee.

"Then, on Friday we'll wrap it all up with the grand show-case, featuring the standout pieces from the week. Hopefully we'll have some jaw-dropping discoveries. Maybe a moment when an owner faints from disbelief, and the experts struggle to maintain composure while revealing something is worth a fortune—or not."

She leaned back, the glow of anticipation in her eyes. "So, my dear Polly, for the next week, expect a parade of history buffs, eccentrics, dreamers, and the occasional schemer or scammer."

"What are you hoping to find in Abbots Clover? A Rembrandt that's been stuffed under someone's bed?" Polly asked.

"Oh, we've seen it all. But it would be lovely to find something different and surprising. A Stradivarius violin? Anything with name-value history. You never know what a sleepy village like yours will reveal."

Then, with a jolt of panic, Rosalind glanced at her watch. "Oh, shoot! Speaking of surprising finds...our first production meeting is at noon, and it's nearly that now. You did tell my producer it was okay to use your library, right? Let me get set up in there so I can look all settled and professional when the *vipers* —I mean, expert appraisers—*slither* in. Please join us, Polly. They might have questions about the castle. Oh, and you do know the show will be broadcast live, right?"

Polly blinked. *Live? Classic JJ. Generous with charm, stingy with details.*

3
____

I t is a truth universally acknowledged that when a group of
antique appraisers gather under the same roof, the
daggers are never far behind—figuratively, of course.
Though history suggests the odd Victorian hat pin or letter
opener had made appearances. Add television cameras, national
exposure, and a viewing public that treats antiques appraisers
like minor celebrities, and you've got the perfect storm for
dysfunction. Every expert wants the spotlight, the prestige, the
big reveal. And when someone else gets it? Let's just say civility
is often clinging to life by the thinnest thread of professionalism."

The library at Thistlethorne was bathed in the amber glow
of midday light filtering through the French doors and
mullioned windows. Despite its name, there wasn't a single book
in the room. Instead, every inch of wall space was occupied by
autographed pictures of long-dead movie stars. A velvet rope
surrounded a cardboard cutout of Bette Davis. A battered director's chair was stenciled with Mr. Hitchcock in block letters on
the back. The castle's previous owner, Alistair Drake, had been

starstruck, and collected anything relating to Hollywood's golden era.

The room had the feel of a shrine—one part nostalgia, one part madness. Until the door eased open and broke the spell. In walked the director, Chad Westcott. Tall, lean, somewhere in his early thirties. He had the kind of careless good grooming that said, *Sure, I'm wearing jeans, but they're expensive jeans.* His dark hair did its own tousled thing, charmingly, and he had that very on-brand air of someone who worked in television.

A takeaway coffee cup in one hand, cell phone in the other, and a weathered leather messenger bag strapped across his chest, Chad stopped just inside the room and scanned the scene. And then—there it was—the grin. Big, warm, contagious.

His eyes landed on Rosalind Fenwick. "Oh wow—I *know* you!" he blurted, his voice full of sincerity. "I mean—I know who you *are*. Obviously. Sorry, that sounded weird. I don't mean to gush. But I'm sort of a big fan." He was endearingly flustered.

"And I'm a fan of *yours!*" Rosalind smiled as she extended her hand. "The minute the producers told me who'd be directing this season, I did some research. I *loved* those short-form history videos you did on YouTube. You've got a brilliant way of making the past feel fresh—and that charm of yours doesn't hurt either." She gave him a playful wink.

Chad laughed softly. "Honestly, like most TV directors these days, I sort of fell into it by just doing my own thing, making web videos in my flat. Short historical reels, the occasional ghost story, whatever got clicks. Turns out, if you wear glasses and a blazer and speak with enough conviction, people think you know what you're talking about. Ha-ha!"

Then his gaze shifted to Polly, his smile widening. "And *you* must be Polly Pepper—American TV legend and the lady of the manor." He extended a hand. "Chad Westcott. Chaos coordinator. Wikipedia gave me the highlight reel of your career. Impressive stuff."

Polly's face lit up. "I never object to a bit of flattery," she said, shaking his hand. "Welcome to Thistlethorne."

"Considering all I've heard about this show, I'd say I was hired to be a magician," Chad smiled. "Even though I can't make egos disappear. Ha-ha! I heard the last director barely survived. Word is, the bloke left for lunch one afternoon and never came back. So here I am, to make sure *Relic or Rubbish* doesn't end in actual bloodshed."

"Poor Oswald." Rosalind recalled last season's director. "They chewed him up, spat him out, and picked their teeth with his spine."

"And here I was thinking antiques appraisers are like mild-mannered accountants," Polly said. "All tweed jackets and gentle *hmm-ing*, looking like they'd faint if someone raised a voice at them."

Rosalind scoffed. "Oh, Polly, you'd have an easier time kissing a cobra than getting this lot to behave. They sharpen their tongues in their off-hours, just waiting for the chance to correct each other—on camera, if possible. It's bloodsport."

There was a knock on the door and Ambrose Carouthers swept in, wrapped in an aubergine velvet waistcoat and a matching silk cravat. A signet ring gleamed on the pinky of his left hand. He paused just inside the doorway, eyes scanning the room with the pained expression of a man forced to endure inferior company. When he finally spoke his voice was low, each word saturated with a tone of superiority. "It's always a challenge to find true elegance outside the Continent."

Polly opened her mouth to offer a greeting, but he silenced it with a languid flick of his hand—an idle wave that seemed to translate as, *yes, yes, I see you. You'll have your moment when I'm ready.*

"Ah," Rosalind murmured, her voice like silk dipped in arsenic. "The only man I know who considers his own reflection the most suitable company."

Ambrose turned, his smile polished to a high shine. "Rosalind Fenwick. Still dazzling with that mix of charm and condescension. The camera adores you. Pity about the rest of us."

His gaze drifted to Chad, lingering just a beat longer than necessary as his appreciative eyes took in the sum of the man's attractive parts. "And you must be our new director," he said, his tone smooth and appraising. "Fascinating." The word hung in the air, teetering between compliment and desire. "I trust this season of *Relic or Rubbish* will demonstrate a firmer grip on quality control."

Rosalind didn't miss a beat. "Ambrose, your charm remains as genuine as a forged signature. Chad will survive us. He strikes me as the sort who can smile through tantrums, soothe distended egos, and mop up after a massacre."

Then, as if remembering there was someone else in the room, Ambrose finally turned to Polly. "Polly Pepper, is it? The name rings a faint bell. You're something of a minor sensation in the colonies, I'm told. How quaint."

The words had barely left his mouth when there was another knock on the door. Diedre Paige, the jewelry and gemstone expert, waltzed in, as tough as a diamond under pressure. Everything about her appearance—the severe sweep of her chignon, the rigid way she clutched her handbag—spoke of a woman who valued control. Her sharp gaze flicked over the room, assessing its contents—and its occupants—with the cold precision of an appraiser always searching for flaws. "Ambrose," she said coolly, her eyes landing on her colleague.

"Diedre." Ambrose responded with an equal lack of warmth. "How delightful."

"Save it," she replied flatly and turned her sharp eyes on Rosalind. "And here's darling Roz. You're looking...sturdy."

Rosalind let out a low, amused hum. "And you're looking... still alive. How persistent."

Polly suppressed a delighted grin. This was her kind of theater—velvet insults delivered with the precision of a scalpel. She had a soft spot for Hollywood-style egos, and now, Thistlethorne felt less like a castle and more like the set of a particularly savage soap opera.

"And you must be our new director," Diedre cooed, as her gaze swept over Chad. "You're markedly more attractive than that rather unfortunate headshot on the show's website. I hope your talent matches your bone structure."

She turned to Polly, her eyes narrowing slightly. "Forgive me, I don't believe we've met. Are you...anyone?"

Before Polly could answer, Rosalind stepped in, her smile cool and composed. "Our hostess," she said, her voice lifting just enough to signal a correction. "American television *royalty*— Polly Pepper. Without her generosity, we'd all be shooting in a draughty antiques barn off the M4." The undercurrent in her tone made it clear to Diedre that further ignorance would be not only gauche—but regrettable.

Diedre examined her nails, and before she could sputter a response, the library door opened yet again. Howard Kettering, the show's art consultant and oil painting expert, entered with a genial smile. His plaid trousers and paisley waistcoat clashed magnificently, as if chosen by a man more loyal to fun than fashion rules. With his salt-and-pepper whisper of a beard and quick, intelligent eyes, he looked like he'd just stepped out of a BBC special on British portraiture. "Lovely to see you all again," he said, clasping his hands together as if genuinely delighted. "And what a setting! You could hang a Turner here and do it justice.

"Rosalind, you look radiant as ever," he said with a respectful nod, his voice as smooth as oiled walnut. To Ambrose, he extended a hand and added warmly, "Still dazzling us with that waistcoat. A touch of Gainsborough, perhaps?" Diedre received a slight bow and a kind smile. "Lovely earrings," he said, with genuine appreciation. Then his gaze landed on the newcomer. "And you must be our director," he said, extending his hand to Chad with sincere warmth. "Howard Kettering. I specialize in eighteenth and nineteenth-century oils." His smile grew. "It's a pleasure. We're in capable hands, I'm sure.

"And you—" His gaze and smile landed on Polly, raking over her as though appreciating the brushstrokes of van Gough's *Starry Night* "—must be Polly Pepper. What an absolute *delight* to meet you."

Polly's smile warmed. "The delight is mutual. Though this is our first meeting, I feel I've already formed a positive opinion—and admiration."

Before Howard could offer a witty retort, the door flew open with the urgency of someone who'd arrived late—on purpose. Clara Montague, the show's authority on textiles and vintage couture, entered with brisk elegance. "Sorry to be tardy," she declared, breathless and clearly not sorry at all. "I've just escaped from that dreary annual employee health screening we all have to endure. Blood pressure, cholesterol, BMI. I haven't felt so judged since my last blind date!"

Chad stepped forward, hand outstretched. "Clara Montague, I presume. Chad Westcott. Director. A pleasure. I've admired your work—especially that piece on Edwardian mourning gowns. Chilling, but in the best way."

"Darling," Clara replied, slipping her hand into his, "you had me at 'mourning gowns.'" She gave Rosalind a kiss-kiss greeting, offered Howard an affectionate squeeze of the arm, and gave

Ambrose a glance that suggested shared history—best left undisturbed. To Diedre, she offered only a nod, before finally turning her attention to Polly. "And you must be our castle's *grande dame.* I recognize you from the television when I lived in the States. I adore a woman who opens her home to chaos and cameras. I hope you've triple-bolted the liquor cabinet from this lot."

Clara positioned herself neatly to the side, as the door opened once again, this time with the force of a battering ram. "Aha!" a baritone boomed into the room, as if the concept of an indoor voice had never once applied to him. "I was told I'd find you all in here! Have I missed anything? Are we still in the pretending-to-like-each-other phase?" It was Martin Hargrove, the militaria expert. He moved with the confidence of a man accustomed to taking up space. Even his clothing struggled to contain his personality.

"Ambrose!" Martin bellowed, clapping his colleague on the back with the force of a siege weapon. Ambrose stumbled forward half a step. "Still trying to convince the world that antique books are more valuable than a medieval poleaxe?"

Re-adjusting his spectacles, Ambrose sighed. "One of us, Martin, deals in objects of refined intelligence, and the other in" —he gestured vaguely at Martin's hulking frame—"blunt instruments."

Martin roared with laughter again. "Brilliant! God, I've missed all of you since last season!"

His gaze landed on Polly, his eyes bright with curiosity. "And you must be the iconic Polly Pepper! You've got quite the reputation."

Polly took his outstretched hand—which felt rather like clasping a bear paw—and flashed a dazzling smile. "Most of the rumors are only *half* true."

Martin let out another booming laugh before turning to

Chad. "And you must be the poor bastard hired to keep this lot in line. Good luck with that!"

Polly looked around the room, taking in the assembled cast of characters—each one a force unto themselves, each carrying the potential for drama...or disaster. The atmosphere hummed with a quiet undercurrent of competition lurking beneath the polished veneer of professionalism.

Then, Chad clapped his hands together, cutting through the introductions. "We're missing one more—Fabian Dupont—but we can't wait. Time to get to work!" His voice carried enough authority to command their attention. "You've all done this many times before, so I'll keep it brief. We start at 8:00 a.m. sharp tomorrow morning, so I expect everyone ready to roll then." He moved briskly through logistics, explaining key filming locations on the castle estate. Every detail had been considered—camera angles, crowd control, the delicate balance of authenticity and entertainment.

"I want insight and energy in equal measure," he continued. "Engage the guests, bring history to life, and of course, keep it *entertaining*." He covered what they already knew: how to handle unexpected finds, murky provenance, and the inevitable letdowns when hopeful owners discovered their cherished heirlooms weren't worth more than sentimental value. "Oh, and one last thing," he concluded, "don't forget this week marks our twenty-fifth anniversary, and each night's segment will be broadcast—*live*."

Silence.

The appraisers, and even Rosalind, exchanged nervous glances. *Live* meant no safety net, no do-overs—every flub, every awkward pause, every unexpected guest reaction would be aired in real time. "As in what you say is what you may be forever remembered for," Chad confirmed. "If you botch a valuation, misidentify an artifact, or insult someone's great-grandmother's plastic hula girl that wiggles on the car dashboard, you'll be doing it in front of a national audience. Heaven help us."

"Fab-u-*lous*," Diedre deadpanned. "Just as long as that know-it-all little pisher from last season, Arley Kingston, isn't lurking behind a curtain, waiting to correct me mid-valuation. Where *is* the little twit, anyway? Off stirring up trouble at Sotheby's or Christie's?"

"He'll be here on Wednesday," Chad said, referencing the young horology expert and thorn in the side of the other professional appraisers. "You're all professionals, so behave like ones. Now, let's make this a week to remember."

With that, the meeting adjourned.

Polly wasn't sure whether to be thrilled or terrified. Possibly both. She'd been in the entertainment business long enough to know that when you gathered talented, ambitious, and competitive people in a room, it wasn't a case of *if* sparks would fly—it was *when*. She gave it three days before someone lit the fuse.

Maybe three hours.

And whoever struck the match would be smiling when they did.

4

———

The first morning of appraisals and valuations unfolded beneath a sky as dull and moody as tarnished silver. A thin mist moved through the castle grounds, curling around the trunks of ancient trees and settling like ghostly breath over the damp ground.

Tim and Tiara had been unceremoniously wrested from the warm cocoons of their beds and thrust into the new day. Polly had insisted. "Reconnaissance!" she'd decreed, ignoring their sleepy suffering. "You're my eyes and ears. Keep 'em peeled. Report all juicy gossip! If it looks like daggers are about to be drawn by the antiques experts, call me. Rosalind says these people can be ruthless, and I want a front row seat!"

Now, grumbling and bleary-eyed, clutching takeaway coffee cups, the duo waded through the throng of antique owners, their expressions a silent protest against the indecency of being awake at such an hour. Then a familiar voice rang out. "Well, well—I never thought I'd live to see the day—Tim Pepper venturing into the abyss of pre-dawn."

It was Constable Grayson Jenkins—the sole officer of the Abbots Clover Police Department and the man who occupied

Tim's thoughts in the dead of night. His blue uniform—complete with a utility belt stocked with standard law enforcement gear—radio, handcuffs, and a baton—resting comfortably at his waist. Amusement twitched at the corner of his mouth as he surveyed the bleary-eyed duo.

Tim groaned, clutching his coffee closer to his chest. "You need to arrest someone right now! We were kidnapped! Dragged from our beds in the middle of the night! We're victims of Polly Pepper's foul play!"

Grayson snickered. "Oh, the inhumanity! Someone alert Amnesty International. Tim had to wake up before his moisturizer settled." He gave Tim a mock sympathetic pat on the shoulder. "Cry me a river, bro," he said as he turned to leave. "Give a holler if you see anyone being strangled with a strand of Edwardian pearls."

In the pale half-light, several Steadicams glided among the queue of antique owners. Although *Relic or Rubbish* would broadcast live, the crew were filming supplementary footage for behind-the-scenes features. The line, as it snaked toward the grand marquee event tent, evoked a religious pilgrimage. Eager attendees murmured amongst themselves, speculating about each other's treasures. Was that an Old Master painting hidden beneath a blanket? Could that portrait be an undiscovered Hogarth? Each person clung to the hope that their cherished possession was worth a fortune.

As Tim and Tiara weaved through the crowd, they spied an elderly man standing beside a large, framed landscape painting. Beside him, a woman cradled a gilt-framed painting wrapped in a beach towel. Nearby, a young couple held a moody Impressionist piece. Conversation bubbled up naturally among them, each casting sidelong glances at their neighbors and sizing up the competition. "An interesting landscape you've got there, mister," the woman with the beach-towel-wrapped canvas remarked, eyeing the elderly man holding on to his ornate frame.

"It's an original Constable!" he said. "Been in my family for over two hundred years. Could be worth a million." His voice held the kind of certainty that dared anyone to challenge it.

"Hmm," said the young man with the Impressionist painting, squinting at the work. "Looks a bit rough to me. Maybe just an old study piece." His girlfriend nudged him sharply in the ribs.

"And what have you got?" the older man shot back, eyeing the swirling colors in the young couple's painting with a look of barely concealed disdain.

"An *Artanis*, we hope," the young woman said proudly, her grip tightening protectively around the frame. "Handed down to my grandmother from her grandmother. Probably very valuable."

"Everybody thinks that." The elderly man sniffed.

"Well, at least it's a proper painting," a woman with a small still life of fruit in a bowl chimed in, tilting her carefully bundled painting slightly to allow the gold edge of the frame to catch the weak morning light. "Unlike some of those mid-century prints I've seen other people dragging in."

A man a few places ahead—holding what appeared to be a framed Elvis-on-velvet painting—shot her a look but said nothing.

Behind them, a middle-aged woman said smugly, "Well, I know exactly what I've got. It's a landscape by a student of Thomas Lawrence. I reckon it'll be valued well into the high four figures." She glanced around as if daring anyone to challenge her.

The line began to shuffle forward, falling into a temporary hush. Were they about to receive confirmation of their object's enormous value—or a painful reality check?

"A theater of delusion," Tim murmured. "Half of them expect to leave here richer than King Charles."

"And the other half are bracing for the moment they're told great-granny's 'original' *Keep Calm and Carry On* poster was mass-produced for Walmart," Tiara said with a smirk. "The value of their heirloom is directly proportional to their wishful thinking."

As each visitor stepped into the tent, the *Relic or Rubbish* staff efficiently logged their items, tagged them, and matched them with an expert appraiser. The whole process ran like a well-oiled machine—*most* of the time.

One woman approached the check-in table, her hands tightening around a Depression glass butter dish. "This is a real collector's item," she said. "Will the appraiser be qualified to assess something this rare?"

Unfazed by the scepticism, one of the research assistants offered a reassuring smile as she affixed a discreet label to the piece. "Our experts have worked with museums, auction houses, and some of the most distinguished private collections in the world. Your piece is in very good hands."

Another guest thrust a bundle of dog-eared postcards at an assistant. "Can you get a *special* specialist to authenticate these? They're all signed 'Victoria.' We're pretty sure it was Queen Victoria."

The assistant glanced at the signatures—each in blue ballpoint pen, complete with loopy hearts over the i's—and bravely resisted the urge to laugh-snort. "Our appraisers can certainly offer an expert opinion," she said. "Though authentication does require extensive research and documentation." *And in your case...divine intervention.*

Even the castle cat, Mr. Boots, had managed to insert himself into the proceedings with his ever-present air of entitlement and importance. He padded silently among the appraisal tables, his tail aloft, pausing occasionally to survey the offerings. Stopping before a large portrait of a woman wearing a tiara, he narrowed his eyes in feline contempt. *How tragic. All that sparkle and still no dignity. I'd simply die if I required such external embellishment to announce my worth.*

The day had been long, with an endless parade of paintings, bruised egos, and occasional dramatic sighs from owners learning their heirlooms were little more than glorified dust collectors. By the time six o'clock—Lush Hour—finally rolled around, Polly was anxious and fidgety. And yet, the work day still wasn't over. The *Relic or Rubbish* live broadcast wouldn't begin until seven—a full sixty minutes away. An entire arid hour stood between Polly and her first glass of champagne.

The hum of last-minute preparations for the live broadcast droned around her, a relentless symphony of microphone checks, lighting adjustments, and people fussing over things she no longer had the patience to care about. It was the cruelest form of limbo—too late to escape, too early to drink.

She wasn't the only one growing impatient. In the production trailer parked just beyond the tent, director Chad Wescott paced in tight, anxious loops, his headset clamped in place, eyes flicking nervously across the multi-screen monitor wall. "One minute to air," he announced, his voice calm but laced with the kind of tension that only a television broadcast could summon.

Around him, the technical crew worked with efficiency—confirming camera placements and ensuring the live uplink remained stable. The audio engineer adjusted levels one last time, making sure Rosalind and the appraisers could all be heard without interference from the ambient crowd noise.

Inside the tent, the set manager was giving her own instructions. "Cue positions!" she called. Rosalind took her place near the first featured table, smoothing her lapel mic as she exchanged a few last words with the antique expert beside her. Around them, appraisers did their final preparations, reviewing notes about the most exciting finds of the day. Some clutched iPads filled with provenance details, while others adjusted their posture, readying themselves for the moment they'd be ushered into the spotlight.

The camera operators, already locked on to their starting shots, gave thumbs-up signals to the control room. They had rehearsed their tracking movements earlier, ensuring that close-ups of artwork would be seamless. A Steadicam operator adjusted his rig, ready to follow Rosalind as she moved through the bustling appraisal area. The lighting crew made minor last-second tweaks to prevent harsh glares from bouncing off shiny canvases.

Beyond the cameras, the visitors shifted with anticipation. Others stood on tiptoe, angling for a better view. The *Relic or Rubbish* team worked the crowd, adjusting positions to ensure no one accidentally blocked the camera angles.

"Ten seconds," the director's voice crackled over the floor manager's earpiece.

"Five...four...three..."

The floor manager gave the signal.

Rosalind turned to the camera, beamed, and launched into her opening lines. "Welcome to *Relic or Rubbish*, where history comes alive—and family heirlooms finally reveal their secrets..."

And just like that, they were live. Even Mr. Boots took his cue and curled up quietly to watch.

5

____

The cameras were live, the lights were hot, and the stakes—at least for the hopeful owners of antiques—felt impossibly high. Inside the tent, paintings emerged from bubble wrap like relics from a tomb. Watercolors, oil portraits, charcoal sketches—each paraded before expert appraisers. Some were family treasures lovingly preserved; others were charity shop finds, now cradled with trembling hands in the hope of hidden fortune.

And then, it was time for the first night's grand finale item.

Earlier in the day, a striking nineteenth-century oil painting had emerged as the most intriguing submission: a moody seascape depicting a storm breaking over a craggy coastline. Its dramatic interplay of shadow and light bore all the hallmarks of a masterpiece.

Polly recognized the owner as a woman she'd seen waiting in the early morning queue. Now, under the bright lights, the canvas was even more impressive.

Rosalind Fenwick stood in the heart of the tent/makeshift television studio, microphone in hand. When Chad gave her cue, she broke into a wide smile and began presiding over the segment. "Earlier today, we were presented with something potentially extraordinary," she said to the camera and audience, her voice smooth but edged with a quiet thrill. "This breathtaking oil painting was brought in by Daphne Whitlow, whose family has long speculated about its origins. Our esteemed appraiser and art critic, Howard Kettering, has had an opportunity to examine the piece and has something interesting to say about it."

At Howard Kettering's side stood assistant researcher, Millie Travers, her sleek bob and tailored blazer projecting a cool professionalism that masked her nerves humming beneath the surface. For the past two years, she'd toiled behind the scenes in the provenance research department—fact-checking, digging through dusty archives, and piecing together the pedigrees of antiques. But what she really wanted was to be in front of the camera. And now, after diligently brown-nosing the producer and professional appraisers, here she was, her first on-air appearance on *Relic or Rubbish*. And she intended to make it count. Let the others scoff at her ambition. Millie wasn't here to make friends. She was here to make an impression.

It wasn't a solo appraisal. Not yet. But Millie knew how quickly reputations were built in the world of antiques. A sharp observation, the right historical fact dropped at the right moment—then the show's producer would recognize her value to the show. She wasn't about to waste her opportunity.

Attention remained riveted on Kettering and the painting. The weight of possibility hung in the air, taut as a violin string, stretching each second unbearably thin. At last, he cleared his throat, a small, deliberate sound. Everyone in the audience waited quietly, hanging on his next words. Kettering took his time, savoring the suspense. "This painting," he began, drawing out a pause for dramatic effect, "may be far more than a family heirloom. It's titled *Tempest Rising*. In my opinion, it is an original work by the renowned nineteenth-century artist Benedict Montrose."

A ripple of murmurs swept through the tent, spreading like the first tremors of an earthquake. Even Polly had to suppress a gasp, aware of its importance.

The owner blinked. "An *original* Montrose?" she echoed, gripping the edge of the table to steady herself. "Who's that?"

Kettering inclined his head, clearly relishing the moment to show off his knowledge of the artist. "Benedict Montrose was one of the most elusive painters of his era. Born in Scotland. The youngest son of a merchant family with ancestral ties to the Highlands. From an early age, he showed an aptitude for drawing the rugged coastline and rolling hills surrounding his home village. Encouraged by a schoolmaster, Montrose secured a place at the Glasgow School of Art, where he was influenced by the burgeoning Glasgow Boys movement." He turned to the woman beside him and graciously said, "Perhaps my colleague, Millie, would like to elaborate."

Millie blushed, but she quickly regained her composure and smiled. "Um...yes...Benedict Montrose. After completing his studies, Montrose spent several years traveling across France and Italy, absorbing Mediterranean landscapes and the techniques of the Impressionists. His time in Provence introduced him to the vibrant palettes of the French Post-Impressionists, which he blended with the moodier tones of Scottish scenery."

Kettering competitively interjected, "By the early nineteen-hundreds, Montrose had established himself in Edinburgh, exhibiting regularly at the Royal Scottish Academy and gaining a reputation for his evocative landscapes, moody seascapes, and intimate portraits of rural Scottish life. His brushwork, noted for its delicate balance between detail and impression, captured nature's grandeur and subtleties."

But then Millie reclaimed the spotlight. "Yes, Montrose was

known for his sweeping, tempestuous landscapes and his distinctive use of light. He was hailed as a visionary. Then, at the height of his career, he vanished mysteriously at sea—his body was never found. His paintings are exceedingly rare. Collectors fiercely covet his works, and at auction, they command staggering prices."

The owner's breath hitched. "Seriously?"

Kettering gave a knowing smile, tapping a finger lightly against the ornate frame. "The brushwork on this canvas, the layering of pigments, even the subtle detailing in the sky—all are hallmarks of Montrose's hand. And here"—he gestured toward a barely visible squiggle in the lower right-hand corner — "is his unmistakable mark." It was a barely discernible, easily overlooked, wave-like stroke nestled among the brushwork, mimicking a natural element in the composition.

"His signature was not meant for overt recognition but rather as a sort of Easter egg for those who understood his art." Millie added her two cents.

The camera zoomed in on the mark. The painting's owner, still reeling, shook her head. "I can't believe it. It's been hanging in my grandmother's sitting room for as long as I can remember. She always called it 'that stormy thing' and said it was handed down from her grandfather, but we never thought much of it."

Kettering, now eager, almost desperate, to cement his authority, adjusted his stance. "And do you know how he acquired it?"

The owner hesitated. "Not exactly. But I do know that someone in the family, way back when, was the captain of a ship. He sailed trade routes between England and the West Indies in the 1800s. My gran always said he had a habit of picking up 'souvenirs' in port—sometimes paying for them, sometimes...not." The owner let out a nervous laugh.

Kettering nodded, considering. "If he were a ship's captain

with access to trade hubs, he may have come across the painting through a private sale—or, indeed, dubious dealings. Given that Montrose vanished at sea, there's a real possibility that this piece was aboard the ship he was lost from. It's not out of the realm of possibility."

The owner swallowed, staring at the painting as though seeing it for the first time. The weight of its history—a vanished artist and whispered provenance—settled over the tent/television studio.

Then, cutting through the reverent hush, Millie added with an innocent laugh, "That's assuming Mr. Kettering's authentication holds up."

Polly made a face. *What the heck is Millie doing contradicting the expert on live television?*

Kettering turned to Millie with a patronizing chuckle, though irritation passed over his eyes. "I'm quite certain it will hold up."

"Are you?" Millie's tone was just a tad condescending. "Because, as you *should* know, there's been recent debate in academic circles about whether Montrose ever completed *Tempest Rising*, or if it was finished by a pupil after he went missing. If that's the case, well—" She tilted her head, her gaze drifting toward the cameras as if addressing the audience directly— "the valuation drops significantly."

A sharp silence followed, the shock at her words settling over the crowd like a heavy curtain.

Rosalind smoothly stepped in, turning her attention to Millie. "Are you suggesting it may *not* be an authentic Montrose?"

Kettering's jaw tightened, his fingers pressing against the bridge of his nose as he adjusted his glasses with an air of strained patience. "It *is* authentic," he stated, his voice clipped. "There is *no* question."

His eyes flicked to Millie, sharp as a scalpel. "I've spent a life-time studying Montrose's work—his brushstrokes, his techniques, the pigments he favored. Every element of this painting is consistent with his hand. To suggest otherwise is, frankly, absurd."

The air in the tent tensed, the gathered spectators sensing the undercurrents of a challenge. Millie held Kettering's glare for a beat longer than was wise. "Yes. Of course," she finally said, her tone now measured and softer. "I never intended to question your expertise, Mr. Kettering." She turned slightly, addressing Rosalind and the audience, "But you know as well as I do that the art world thrives on debate. Authentication isn't about blind certainty—it's about scrutiny, analysis, and sometimes uncomfortable questions...and answers." Millie stepped back, knowing she had to let Kettering have the final word. But she'd made her point and proved her knowledge.

Kettering cleared his throat and offered his final valuation. "If this were to come up at auction, I wouldn't be surprised if it sold for roughly three hundred thousand pounds."

For a heartbeat, the room seemed to tilt on its axis. Rosalind let out a low whistle, the sound slicing through the stunned silence. Recovering, she leveled a surprised look at Kettering. "That's astonishing," she added, her tone a perfect blend of disbelief and excitement, drawing the crowd into the delicious possibility of a hidden fortune uncovered.

Kettering, his posture stiff, seized the lifeline. "Easily," he said, his voice regaining its authority. "Given its rarity."

The moment had passed, and Rosalind turned toward the camera, her signature poise effortlessly intact. "What an extraordinary find," she said warmly. "And just one of the many remarkable pieces we'll be unveiling this week. Join us tomorrow as we continue to explore the fascinating world of antiques—their history, secrets, and the stories they still have to tell. Thank you all for watching, and we'll see you next time, on *Relic or Rubbish*."

"And...we're clear!" Chad called. Instantly, the space filled with the hum of chaos—camera operators, production assistants, all wrapping up their long day.

Amid the commotion, Kettering remained unnervingly still. A sound technician hovered, waiting to remove his lapel mic, but he waved him off without looking away from Millie. His jaw tightened; the polite façade he'd worn for the cameras disappeared. "You should have saved your theatrics for when we were *off* air," he snapped.

Still riding the high of fulfilling her dream of being on television, Millie barely had time to process his words.

"I don't know what stupid impulse compelled you to ambush me," Kettering spat. "Your little stunt made me look like a goddamn fool."

Millie scoffed, arms folding as she met his glare head-on. "Oh, please. You do that just fine all by yourself."

Kettering's nostrils flared. "You think this is funny? You think making baseless accusations in front of a national audience is some sort of game?"

"I think the audience deserves to know the truth—even if it's inconvenient for you," Millie said, holding her ground.

Kettering stepped closer, his posture even stiffer with barely restrained anger. "If you ever pull something like that again, I will personally see to it that your career in this industry is over. I should never have agreed to give you any on-air time."

A tense silence stretched between them. Millie lifted her chin, a saccharine smile curling her lips. "Mr. Kettering, I was just trying to help. I'm not that long out of uni and maybe more informed than you about the latest developments in the art world."

"Ah, youth. That great substitute for experience."

The sting in Kettering's words caught Millie off guard, and her smile faltered for a fraction of a second. "I wasn't contradicting you; I was adding to the conversation."

Kettering let out a laugh, one that was entirely devoid of humor. "Millie, you didn't *add* anything. You *grandstanded*. You seized the moment to put yourself in the spotlight regardless of the consequences to me!"

"I was simply doing what any *good* expert would—exploring every angle, making sure the audience understands the complexities of authentication. You seemed to forget that."

Polly studied her. She'd seen minor talent claw their way through years of auditions, backstage disputes, and infighting just to get an acting or singing role. And here was Millie, barely past thirty, speaking with the authority of someone much more experienced.

Kettering's voice dropped to a deadly whisper. "This show values *expertise*. Not ambition *masquerading* as insight."

Millie exhaled slowly. "I am sorry if I came across inappropriately, Mr. Kettering. I respect your work."

"No, you don't," he said, his tone smooth, almost amused now—but there was nothing warm in his eyes. "Mark my words, Millie Travers—you will regret this."

Kettering inhaled deeply and straightened his shoulders. "I hope you enjoyed your moment in the sun, my dear. I'll make sure you go back to your pathetic little research desk—never to be heard from again."

Polly and Rosalind grimaced at the exchange. "Oops," Polly said. "That sounded like the kind of remark people quote at your memorial."

6

———

For director Chad Wescott, the day was far from over. He'd spent the past fourteen hours wrangling a circus disguised as a television production—massaging egos, stamping out minor fires, and somehow keeping everything from shattering in a heap of broken antique vases and frayed tempers. His head throbbed with the dull ache of someone who'd spent the day babysitting both porcelain and people.

The expert appraisers had retreated to their rooms at the Fox & Hare in the village, and the crowd of hopefuls with their heirlooms and auction dreams had long since dispersed back to their natural habitats. But Chad knew better than to think his day was over. There were production notes to review, schedules to revise, and a flurry of e-mails from network executives, publicists, and at least one furious participant who hadn't appreciated his great-aunt's ceramic goose being described as "quaint."

And that was just the warm-up. The main camera had started glitching—an overnight replacement needed sourcing and shipping. The catering team was fuming about a flurry of "urgent" vegan demands. And to top it off, the local historian was threatening to write a negative review of the show after someone on-air referred to the village's folklore as "colorful, if wildly inaccurate."

Plus, he still needed to rebook travel for Arley Kingston—the show's horology expert—who was being flown in specifically to assess a rare French automaton clock that had been spotted. And then there was the matter of the appraiser who'd wandered back from the Fox & Hare after lunch with a cheerful swagger and breath reeking unmistakably of mid-shelf whiskey. Chad pinched the bridge of his nose and muttered, "I'm livin' the dream."

He'd been easily coaxed into joining Polly, Rosalind, Tim, and Tiara for a restorative drink in Thistlethorne's main reception room. Now, Chad held a glass of champagne, its bubbles rising steadily as he listened to the others' relaxed laughter. For the first time all day, the tension in his shoulders began to loosen. A bit.

He felt his phone buzz in his trouser pocket—a reminder that even moments of peace had a short shelf life. Chad didn't have to check the screen to know something had undoubtedly gone sideways. He took another sip, letting the chill of it dull the edges of his anxiety. "I can't decide what was more entertaining today, the parade of family 'treasures'...or the appraisers coming within inches of throttling one another over that mahogany sideboard," he said, his voice dry with exhaustion but mellowed by the drink.

"Delightful fun!" Polly mocked, lifting her glass in salute. "I counted at least three guests who seemed ready to duel at dawn for the sake of their family's honor." She gave a wry smile. "That old gentleman with the wooden chest? Swore it was Napoleonic? Nearly clobbered Ambrose with his walking stick when the modern hinges were pointed out. Honestly, by mid-afternoon, I was half expecting someone to challenge the experts to pistols at twenty paces—right there between the catering tent and the Porta-loos."

"Should we even mention the *incident*?" Tiara asked, her voice light but edged with curiosity.

"Which one? So many to choose from," Chad said, then took the last sip of his drink as though he needed every ounce of fortification.

"Well, not the one where Clara Montague flung that Regency-era snuffbox at Martin Hargrove's head," Rosalind chuckled. "Technically, she threw it *past* his head. It's not her fault his reflexes are atrocious."

"But it is her fault that the thing broke into three pieces when it hit the wall," Polly added. "Rather unfortunate, considering it had just been appraised at—what was it? Five hundred pounds?"

"Broken antiques aren't the only things that can lose value in an instant," Rosalind said. "Throughout my years on the show, I've discovered that sometimes, all it takes is the wrong comment at the right moment. Introduce a sliver of doubt about authenticity or provenance, and suddenly a masterpiece teeters on the edge of value and mediocrity." Her gaze lifted, meeting Chad's. "I'm referring, of course, to Millie Travers's contradiction of Howard's appraisal of the Montrose painting. It's one of the oldest tricks in the book—plant a seed of uncertainty and watch the price plummet. Probably lost half its value in seconds."

Rosalind's thoughts drifted through art history's cautionary tales—works once dismissed as imitations, only to be triumphantly reattributed to the masters. *Salvator Mundi*, for example: doubted for centuries, then crowned a da Vinci and sold to a Saudi prince for $450 million. A Van Gogh picked up at a garage sale for fifteen dollars, later authenticated and valued in the tens of millions. Or the disputed Caravaggio, *Judith and Holofernes*, that sparked years of debate before landing in the hands of an American billionaire. All it took was one expert's hesitation, a single well-placed question, and a painting's reputation could plummet like a stock in free fall. Was that what Millie was doing? Was she raising doubts under the guise of scholarly caution?

"Expert opinions," Rosalind said, her tone low but deliberate, "can resurrect—or ruin—everything."

Chad stretched and then rubbed the back of his neck. "And that's exactly what's going to keep me up tonight," he muttered as he set his glass down. "Millie pulling that stunt on air—especially against Howard Kettering, whose reputation is impeccable—creates a mess on multiple levels. Suppose Kettering is right, and Millie undermined him just to make a point. In that case, we've got internal politics bleeding into the broadcast, which is bad enough. But if Millie's right..." He trailed off, glancing at Rosalind. "Then we aired a segment praising a fake—or at least something with disputed provenance—and that's a PR nightmare waiting in the wings."

"Viewers love a scandal," Rosalind continued. "It's human nature, isn't it? People tune in for the antiques, but stay glued for the drama. One moment, you've got a lovely vase from someone's attic. The next, there's a full-blown controversy about it. Frankly, the whiff of something salacious tends to spike viewership. People can't help themselves; they love to gasp at someone else's misfortune. It's all fun and games—until it isn't."

"A celebrity spat is one thing," Chad said. "But this puts the show's credibility on the line. Sponsors don't like controversy unless it sells. And this? This could scare them off. If it turns out Howard was wrong, his reputation takes a big hit. He'll blame Millie for humiliating him on air, no matter what. And Millie..." He paused, considering. "If she challenged him without rock-solid evidence, she'll be in trouble. No one likes an appraiser who cries wolf. Either way, I'm stuck mediating the fallout between two people who can't stand each other."

Rosalind nodded. "It's a delicate balance—truth versus loyalty. Not everyone appreciates the difference when careers are on the line."

Chad's phone vibrated again—a reminder that his reprieve was over. With a sigh, he muttered about the next day's potential chaos. His words, laced with grim humor, marked the end of one tempestuous day—and the reluctant beginning of another.

7

———

Tuesday began the way Monday ended—behind schedule, a camera down, and at least one appraiser threatening to quit over the misplaced provenance of a first edition copy of *The Picture of Dorian Gray.*

On Wednesday, horology expert Arley Kingston arrived. When he wasn't drifting through the bustle like a curious ghost, he was cloistered in a side tent, poring over provenance documents and examining the clock he'd been flown in to assess. Polly passed by once and saw him hunched over the mechanism, utterly absorbed—as if it were whispering secrets only he could hear.

Thursday brought a crisis: a misplaced silver Regency-era calling card case and an all-out search involving a handheld metal detector and an intern in tears, insisting—between sobs—that she'd never touched the case. It turned up, eventually, under a folding chair.

Friday found Polly and Rosalind drawn to jewelry expert Diedre Paige's station, just as she was evaluating an elaborate necklace nestled in a velvet-lined box. Peering through her loupe, Diedre examined the central stone with clinical interest.

She turned it over in her gloved hands, murmuring observations with the calm focus of a surgeon.

The owner's voice, brimming with pride and nervous expectation, said, "It's been in my family for generations. We were always told it may have belonged to the Duchess of Windsor."

A ripple of curiosity passed through the surrounding onlookers. Polly saw Rosalind exchange a knowing glance with Diedre, who ran a fingertip over the back of the pendant, searching for hallmarks or maker's marks. "It's lovely," Diedre said at last, her tone carrying careful diplomacy, "but this is Edwardian—early twentieth century—before the Duchess of Windsor was even on the scene. And, more importantly, it wasn't custom-designed for royalty. It was mass-produced for the aspiring middle class."

The owner's face darkened. "Are you calling my grandmother a liar? She swore it was valuable. Said it'd been gifted by an aristocrat."

Diedre let out a measured breath, steeling herself against the pushback. "Provenance is crucial in establishing value," she said gently but firmly. "Without documentation or a verifiable history, it's impossible to confirm your claim. I understand the sentimental importance, but I assure you, this was a widely available design at the time. I've seen similar pieces at auction."

"I think you're wrong." The woman's voice took on a sharp edge. "Maybe you don't know everything. Maybe you've made a mistake."

Diedre, cool as ever, added, "If you're interested, I do know someone who would buy this now because it is rather pretty."

The woman hesitated, calculating. It wasn't the magnificent fortune she'd hoped for—but if she could sell it quickly, she might salvage a bit of pride. And if she bargained hard enough, maybe even have enough for a weekend away. Her hand closed protectively around the necklace, her indignation morphing into strategy.

From a few tables away, a fresh groan erupted. "Are you kidding me? It can't be worthless!" a man bellowed, the color of his cheeks deepening to an alarming shade of crimson as he clutched the gaudy porcelain figurine of a pouting cherub riding a swan. The appraiser had dismissed it as a mass-produced trinket—hardly worth the price tag it still boasted on its base. But the man was adamant. "I'm sure this is an original, one-of-a-kind piece!"

The figurine looked more like a novelty item than a masterpiece of craftsmanship. Yet in the owner's eyes it was a treasure beyond compare. The juxtaposition of the appraiser's clinical assessment and the man's fervent defense highlighted the absurdity and passion that often defined antique valuations—where even a piece that appeared utterly worthless could spark a riot of pride and indignation.

The appraiser, Fabian Dupont, folded his hands on the table and leaned forward. "Uniqueness doesn't always translate to value, sir," he said. "I once saw a pebble shaped like Winston Churchill's profile. One of a kind, yes, but no one was clamoring to outbid others for it."

"Don't patronize me! Just say it's junk," the man spat. "I know I could sell this on the internet for sure!"

"Then by all means, list it online," Fabian said with a polite smile. "Someone paid six figures for a banana duct-taped to a wall—so who knows? You might strike gold."

Day after day, item by item, Polly had shadowed Rosalind, drinking in the experience like someone granted backstage access to a rock concert. At Lydia Pinkham's decorative arts and fine objects table, they arrived just in time to hear the verdict on an item Polly had dismissed as pure kitsch: a shiny cocktail shaker shaped like a penguin, its polished silver body catching the overhead lights in a way that made it look absurd.

"A delightful piece," Lydia was saying, her voice holding a note of reverence as she handed it back to its beaming owner. "Early twentieth century. French. Highly collectible. I'd estimate at least fifteen hundred pounds at auction."

Polly resisted the urge to laugh. When she'd first laid eyes on the cocktail shaker, with its whimsical shape, she'd been certain it belonged in a novelty shop. But as Lydia spoke about the craftsmanship—the delicate silverwork, the careful enamel detailing—and explained how objects that once seemed like playful knick-knacks had become coveted pieces of design history, Polly felt her perspective shift. After a few days surrounded by experts, she'd begun to see art not just as decoration or investment, but as something with soul—a reflection of its time, its maker, even its owner.

The world of antiques, she was learning, wasn't just about gilded mirrors or oil paintings. Value wasn't always measured in obvious beauty or age. Sometimes it was in cultural significance or craftsmanship. She glanced at the cocktail shaker again. What she'd taken for kitsch was, in reality, a piece of art history.

Throughout the week, variations on the same emotional tides had played out—expectations soaring, then crashing with an unceremonious thud. Some guests clutched their newfound fortunes with breathless wonder, while others stormed off in frustration. The event unfolded with a rhythm of discovery and deflation, excitement and intrigue.

And then—just like that—*Relic or Rubbish's* week of broadcasting from Thistlethorne Lodge was nearly over. Only the grand Friday night showcase loomed. Horology expert Arley Kingston had been flown in expressly for this valuation. Now he was poised to wind the clock and unlock its mysteries.

8

AFTER THAT MESS…

The moment Arley Kingston crumpled forward onto the table, the marquee erupted into a surreal maelstrom. When his head hit the table with a sickening thud, the planet momentarily stopped revolving. The French automaton clock tipped dangerously. The owner's frantic hands shot out, fingers trembling as they lunged to catch it before it tumbled to the floor. For a split second, the entire *Relic or Rubbish* production unraveled into chaos. Crew members froze, not knowing what to do. All eyes were trained on Arley's motionless form.

Inside the control trailer, Chad Wescott's voice shattered the pandemonium. "Cut the feed! Cut the feed!" he yelled. "Roll the standby graphic—NOW!" His commands ricocheted off every surface. Every second was measured in pure, unbridled hysteria. The live broadcast was abruptly snapped away. Viewers' home screens went dark for a heartbeat before flickering to life with a stark, frozen standby graphic—an austere image of the *Relic or Rubbish* logo overlaying a backdrop of the lush English country-side. A low, tense hum of standby music filled the silence, leaving the audience in a state of suspense, wondering what technical difficulties had just taken place behind the scenes.

In the center of the chaos, Polly Pepper stood in wide-eyed disbelief as she stared at Arley's inert body. Then suddenly her muscle memory kicked in, and she launched into action. Polly had seen death before. Lots of times. Maybe not like this. Not on live television. But...

But a dead body was, well, a dead body—no matter where you found it. She pushed past her shock, her hands shaking slightly as she reached for the microphone she'd abandoned moments ago. "Medical!" she demanded, her voice cutting through the confusion. Every ounce of her experience as an amateur sleuth and a television host surged to the forefront—there was no room for hesitation in a moment like this.

Polly's eyes searched Arley's expressionless face as she took control in a way that filled the frantic air. The audience at home would never know the full extent of the unfolding catastrophe—but the crew heard her words. And they followed her direction.

The production nurse appeared quickly, her professional presence offering reassurance. A medical emergency vehicle siren wailed in the distance, growing louder until two uniformed medics burst through the marquee flaps, their expressions severe and focused.

Polly barely registered their arrival before one paramedic dropped to his knees and pressed two fingers on Arley's neck in search of a pulse. The other unzipped a black medical bag and began setting up a portable heart monitor. The harsh glare of the overhead lights bore down like an interrogation lamp, illuminating every frantic gesture—the snap of blue nitrile gloves, the flash of cold metal instruments, the clipped urgency in each exchanged instruction.

In that charged instant, Constable Grayson Jenkins, exploded into the tent. "Step back!" he thundered as he pushed through the crowd, forcing visitors and crew members to scatter as they vacated the space around Arley. He moved swiftly to confer with the paramedics.

Amid the upheaval, Polly remained close to Arley, her gaze fixed in disbelief on his unmoving form. Her heart raced, but she stayed rooted, unwilling to move away. Grayson could see the turmoil on her face. "What happened?"

Polly's voice was barely above a whisper. "I—I don't know. After Rosalind fell ill, I stepped in to host the program. One minute, Arley seemed fine, winding that clock and about to give his valuation. And the next...he just collapsed. I know he's dead," she whispered just loud enough for Grayson to hear.

"Go back to the house," Grayson instructed. "Find Tim and Tiara. Wait for me. I'll be there as soon as I can." He instantly shifted from protective friend to officer-in-charge, the weight of duty settling on his shoulders.

One paramedic looked up, and with a quiet shake of his head, ended any remaining hope.

9

———

Inside the main reception room of Thistlethorne Lodge, Polly and her troupe sat in tense silence. After what felt like an eternity, the door opened and Grayson entered with Chad Wescott, his professional demeanor resolute as his eyes swept over the group, taking in their stricken faces. "I called for support from the Bristol police. They're here now. They'll want to speak to each of you individually. But first—please—tell me what you saw."

Polly took a deep breath, her eyes distant as she began to recount the events. "Today was like every other day this week… until Rosalind became ill," she said. "The broadcast was almost over, and we'd gone to a commercial break. She was getting ready to introduce the final segment with Arley Kingston. I was a few feet away. I remember her laughing about something with one of the crew. Then suddenly…one moment she was her usual beaming self, and the next, she lost her balance and nearly collapsed. That's when Chad asked me to take over."

She paused, swallowing hard as she recalled the next moments. "I introduced Arley, who was supposed to appraise a French clock. Everything was going well. He was enthusiastic as he explained the clock's history to the audience. There was no hint of what was about to happen. No sign of distress, nothing unusual. He was calm, confident, charming. And then, he just—died."

Tim and Tiara exchanged glances as Polly's voice trailed off, and Constable Jenkins regarded her with a somber nod, his eyes reflecting concern and determination as he pieced together the events.

"I witnessed it all on my monitor in the control trailer," Chad added his tone low and reflective. "It's all on video, too. It's just as Polly said. When Arley began his segment, everything seemed perfectly normal. He was jovial—hyper, even—describing the clock's history with so much passion. I did notice a tremor in his hands—perhaps nerves, something I'd expect from anyone in the spotlight. And then, in one instant, he looked—stricken."

After a brief second, Tim looked around and said, "By the way, where is Rosalind? Is she okay?"

"I'll check her room," Tiara said, and within minutes, she returned with a frantic Rosalind Fenwick.

"Oh, my God! What happened?" Rosalind cried upon entering the reception room. "Tiara says Arley Kingston's dead!" Her voice pitched higher with each word, panic mounting. "But how? Why?" She pressed on, her voice trembling. "Heart attack? Stroke?" Her gaze ricocheted from one stunned face to the next, searching desperately for answers.

"We're doing everything we can to find answers, Ms. Fenwick," said Constable Jenkins, stepping forward to reassure her. "We need to piece together every detail, however small. What do you remember of the time leading up to Mr. Kingston's death?"

Rosalind could only shake her head. Her voice, when it came, was barely a whisper. "I wasn't there. I had one of my spells, and Polly had to take over for me." She drew a slow, trembling breath. "All I remember—it was during the commercial break—I was getting ready to introduce Arley for his segment. One moment, I was laughing with someone over some silly slip-up I'd made earlier, and the next, a wave of dizziness hit me from out of the blue. It happens from time to time. The room started spinning, the lights blurred into a haze, and I felt as if I were sinking into the floor. I remember the rush of voices coming to help me, but..."

She paused, her eyes distant with the weight of the memory. "It's all sort of a blur after that—I know I was with the nurse in the first aid station for a while. But I don't even remember how or when I got back here to the house and into bed."

Grayson leaned toward Rosalind, his tone measured yet probing. "So, Ms. Fenwick, you sometimes get dizzy spells? Was today's episode the same as the other times or more intense? Did you experience other symptoms—maybe fatigue, headaches? Anything that felt different? Were there any changes in your routine? Any unexpected stressors that might have triggered that reaction?"

Rosalind hesitated. "All I remember is suddenly feeling as if a wave were washing over me. I felt weak...disoriented."

Just as the tension in the room seemed to reach its peak, Chad's cell phone rang. He glanced at the caller ID. "The boss," he said, his tone wary. "This won't be good." He stepped out of the room for privacy. When he returned a few minutes later, his eyes glistened, and he seemed on the verge of tears.

"They're demanding answers—our producer Simon Belmore, and the network heads," Chad said. "I totally get it, but they're acting like I'm somehow on trial. They want a minute-by-minute account of everything that happened today—hell, all week. They're even questioning why Polly stepped in for Rosalind. They said I should've gotten written approval, had you sign a contract. Seriously? We didn't have time to take a breath!

"Every decision I've made this week will be under a microscope. It's like, because I'm the director, I'm responsible for the whole tragedy. But I followed policy to the letter—cut the live feed, switched to standby, immediately called for medical assistance. What more could I have done?"

He looked up, frustration flickering behind his eyes. "I'm not shirking accountability, but this was *live* television. Anything can happen. We all did everything we could. But that's not good enough."

It was clear that while Chad might have been following protocol, his role as director—and the authority that came with it—meant that, in the eyes of many, he bore responsibility for all had occurred. In that moment, the weight of accountability, tragedy, and the unforgiving glare of live television crushed down on him. He knew the search for answers and the quest for answerability was just beginning.

10

———

The following morning, the fallout from the tragedy was reverberating across the media and internet. In a swift, decisive move, senior broadcast executive Morris Harper announced that Chad Wescott and the show's presenter, Rosalind Fenwick, had been placed on administrative leave pending a full review and investigation into the death of Arley Kingston. Harper insisted it was standard procedure—while law enforcement and internal auditors pieced together every detail of the previous day's events.

Even Polly had found herself the subject of uncomfortable scrutiny. *Why had she been so close to the action?* It wasn't an accusation. Not yet. But the questions carried a quiet edge, a reminder that in a storm like this, even bystanders could find themselves caught in the undertow.

In a move that clearly signaled the network was also covering its own butt, an official press release from Harper emphasized that the personnel suspensions were necessary:

"We are deeply saddened by the death of our friend and colleague Arley Kingston, which transpired

during yesterday's live broadcast of *Relic or Rubbish*. In light of the tragedy, we have taken immediate steps to secure the highest standards of accountability within our broadcasting operations."

This was meant to reinforce their commitment to a thorough investigation, and shielded the network from scrutiny in what had instantly become a high-profile breaking news incident. But the statement only fanned the flames of speculation among fans of the show, each question intensifying the mystery behind Arley Kingston's sudden death.

The network's rapid-fire response immediately forced Chad back to London to face his bosses.

Rosalind, with her job suspended, accepted Polly's invitation to remain at Thistlethorne for at least a few more days—a temporary refuge from the storm of media attention. With her high-profile status as the face of *Relic or Rubbish*, being seen in public would only invite a relentless barrage of tabloid scrutiny.

The Bristol police had also moved swiftly. The medical examiner ordered an expedited autopsy, promising the examination would be completed within twenty-four hours. The rapid timeline was essential—not only to preserve crucial forensic evidence, but also to quell the growing media frenzy surrounding a death on live television. Every detail of that fateful day was under intense scrutiny.

Polly sat on the Chesterfield sofa in the reception room, nursing a mug of tea, her gaze distant as she stroked Mr. Boots's coat without really paying any attention. Tim was seated in an armchair opposite, looking forlorn. Tiara paced nearby, arms crossed, her usual buoyancy subdued.

"Well," Tim said, breaking the thick silence, "that was not how I thought the week would end."

"Poor Arley," Polly said, her voice faltering as she set down her mug. "He was so young. One minute he's waxing poetic about a stupid antique clock and the next...he's dead."

Tiara stopped pacing and perched on the arm of Polly's settee. "I can't get that look on his face out of my head. His expression—I don't know—surprise? Anger? Like Mr. Death snuck up on him and said, 'Gotcha!'"

A moment later, the door creaked open, and Rosalind entered, her usual polished composure softened by fatigue. A scarf hung haphazardly around her neck, and her posture had an uncharacteristic slump. "Morning," she said quietly. "Or—what's left of it." She gave a tired smile and sank into an armchair. "I thought I'd be relieved when this week wrapped up. I'd planned a short holiday in Scotland. Instead—" Her gaze drifted toward the window. "Instead, I'm awake in a nightmare."

Polly agreed, continuing to stroke Mr. Boots. "Arley seemed happy and healthy right up until..."

Rosalind's face softened into a bittersweet expression. "He loved his work. He once joked that he became interested in clocks, so he'd always have time on his hands. He thought that was funny. So did I."

"Everyone's hourglass eventually runs out of sand," Polly said sadly.

Rosalind folded her hands in her lap, not knowing what else to do with them. "In a field full of egos the size of Buckingham Palace, Arley was—unlike the others. No pretense. He didn't treat people like stepping stones or competition. There was nothing transactional. He just loved antiques—especially clocks."

Polly sighed. "It's always the good ones, isn't it? I didn't know him, but I instantly liked his sort of boyish charm. There was a freshness about him. He wasn't like the other old, stodgy appraisers. He had natural charisma."

Rosalind nodded in agreement. "He was genuine. He

remembered people's names. Like, everyone's. Not just the producers and big shots—he even knew the names of the runners, caterers, even assistants who only showed up occasionally when needed. He had a few detractors among the other appraisers, but viewers loved him. The network was offering him a full-time position on *Relic or Rubbish*. They were planning to make him a permanent member of the team next season."

"That makes this all the more heartbreaking." Polly sighed. "He was moving up."

"The full-time thing was a biggie. None of the others have that security," Rosalind said. "They're brought in on rotation, depending on what special items come through—furniture experts, silver specialists, textiles, you name it. They pop in and out, week to week. Keeps it flexible. Keeps costs down. Arley was going to be the first full-time expert appraiser. It would've been a huge step up for him.

"Not everyone was happy about that," she continued. "Ambrose, for one. He's been wrangling for a permanent spot for years—more airtime, more prestige. And Diedre—" Rosalind gave a weary sigh. "She pretended not to care, but I overheard her sniping about Arley 'getting handed a golden ticket just because he's good-looking.'"

"People can get nasty when a coveted job is on the line," Tiara muttered. "Especially when cameras and egos are involved."

"It's ironic, because Arley wasn't overly ambitious but still managed to rise," Rosalind added. "He didn't network or schmooze producers or suits. He just—did his work. And the right people noticed. That annoyed some of the others, I think."

A chill prickled at the back of Polly's neck as she realized that Arley possessed something his colleagues aspired to—a permanent high-profile well-paying job on television. Her thoughts drifted to a possibility—*No. No. No! Don't you dare go there, Polly Pepper!* She scolded herself. *Don't even think about the possibility of another murder to investigate! Hell, the autopsy report isn't even in! Plus, you promised Terrence you've given up playing amateur sleuth. Remember?* Polly reeled herself in with a reprimand for letting such thoughts even whisper in her head.

However, Tiara was pretty darn good at reading Polly's thoughts, and she reminded her that Arley died while millions of viewers saw the whole thing. "His death had to have been a sudden cardiac event—a heart attack or a fatal arrhythmia or a pulmonary embolism. I saw that on *Grey's Anatomy*."

Speculation soon gave way to certainty. In late afternoon, Constable Grayson Jenkins knocked on the door, carrying a copy of the autopsy report, his face etched with deep lines of sorrow and duty. He joined Polly and Co. in the reception room. With a grave and deliberate voice he said, "I'll get right to it. Arley's cause of death. While inconclusive, pending further toxicology and histology analysis, will be ruled—natural causes."

"Natural causes," Polly whispered. "But he was young. He'd barely started to live." Her words hung in the air, charged with disbelief.

Tim exchanged a supportive glance with Grayson, while Tiara and Rosalind looked on in silent acceptance.

Grayson shifted uncomfortably, his authoritative tone wavering slightly. "There were no visible injuries. No injection marks or external signs of drug use. No obvious venomous bites or stings. The lab will have the final results in a few days. But..."

After some effort setting a resistant Mr. Boots down from her lap, Polly stood and moved languidly around the room, a storm of thoughts racing with possibilities—none aligning with the coroner's conclusion. Her instincts refused to be placated by the coroner's sterile verdict. *Nope!* she said to herself, firm and resolute. *Arley was too young to die of natural causes.* "I just don't see it!" she said aloud.

In the gentle tone of a friend, Grayson said, "Yeah, I understand how you feel, Polly. But sometimes, even a young man's body can betray him. Fatal arrhythmias and undetected heart conditions can cause sudden death. As rare as that may be. We all share your disbelief, but nature can be cruel and unpredictable." He paused, his voice softening further. "I know it's hard to believe, but we need to trust the experts."

Polly was quiet for a long moment, Grayson's words settling over her like a slowly falling curtain. The defiant spark in her eyes dimmed, replaced by something quieter—something almost accepting, if still uncertain. Across the room, Rosalind sat still, her posture impeccable, but her eyes were glassy with resignation, as though a thread of hope had snapped. Tim looked down at his hands, brow furrowed, lips pressed together —lost in thought. Beside Polly, Tiara gave a small, solemn nod, her usual sparkle softened by the weight of confirmation.

Slowly, Polly allowed herself to consider the possibility that, despite her instincts, nature might indeed have taken its course —even in a young man like Arley Kingston. Finally, she said, "Life has ways of surprising us." Her words slipped over her lips as a grudging acceptance settled around the room. Polly's resolve wavered as she began to wrap her head around the grim reality that the coroner's conclusion was correct.

There was nothing more to say—at least, not yet.

By the time Lush Hour arrived, the mood at Thistlethorne had softened. The earlier tension gave way to quiet resignation. They all sat together—less for conversation, more for support.

There was a reflective tilt to Rosalind's posture, as though she were sorting through years of memories. When she spoke, her voice was low, and her words considered.

"It's strange," she began, "how a show about heirlooms can end up shaping your life." She glanced at Polly. "Like Arley, I never set out to be a television presenter—certainly not on a glorified reality show like *Relic or Rubbish*. I wanted to be a journalist—back when we still had print. That's where my real talent lies. I love writing. And I always imagined holding powerful people to account. As you've probably noticed, I'm pretty nosy.

"For twenty-five years, I've been the face of this show. I'm trusted by the public. And the network. I've even interviewed the prime minister and sometimes fill in for the nightly news when someone's ill or away on assignment. I make appearances on game shows and chat shows. It's a role that many would envy, but there's a price, and it's not always obvious." She paused, swallowing hard before continuing, "I've given so much of myself. I sometimes wonder what I've lost along the way."

As Polly listened, she felt an all-too-familiar ache deep within herself. *I know exactly what you mean*, she thought, recalling her own sacrifices at the altar of fame and public adoration. She thought of the missed moments at home, the absences from Tim's piano recitals and school plays. Polly's own doubts and regrets mingled with Rosalind's confession. The price of a life lived under a spotlight was steep. And as much as she admired Rosalind's success—and her own—Polly couldn't help but feel undefined losses.

Rosalind took another sip of champagne. "It's that age-old quandary for working mothers, isn't it?" she said quietly, her voice laced with something more complex than regret. "I wasn't always there when Ethan was growing up. I was building something, trying to make space for myself in a world that doesn't always welcome women with ambition and children."

She paused, swirling the champagne in her glass. "And now...he's chasing internet fame, as if going viral is the same as creating a real life. He calls it a career—this influencer thing— but I wonder what happens when the algorithms stop favoring him, when his youth fades and the world moves on to the next shiny distraction. Of course, I want him to do his own thing, if that makes him happy. But I also want him to be resilient. A mother worries. We always do. Always will."

A rueful smile tugged at the corners of her mouth. "I used to believe fame would make up for everything. But it's a sacrifice that no number of awards can justify. This past week I've been thinking...it might be time for me to move on. New faces—like Arley—are popping up. Not sure I can withstand the pressure."

11

———

Polly had always trusted her instincts. Without them, she wouldn't have achieved her elevated level of success in showbiz. And now—staring at the moonlit ceiling of her bedroom in the middle of the night—those instincts were screaming at her. No matter how many times she turned things over in her mind, she couldn't reconcile the coroner's conclusion about Arley's death. It was too neat. Too convenient. Arley Kingston—young and vibrant. Heart attack? At his age? Really? "It happens," she muttered into the darkness. But that didn't sit right.

She rolled onto her side as her body begged for sleep, but her mind refused to cooperate. Instead of drifting into her usual dreams of lounging on a white sand beach in the South Pacific, slathering Terrence Marks's chest with suntan lotion, Polly replayed the jarring events of Friday in her thoughts. The word "inconclusive" in the coroner's report nagged at her like a pebble in her shoe. If Arley's cause of death wasn't clear-cut, why had the medical examiner so quickly implied that the final determination would *probably* be natural causes? Was there pressure from the television executives to wrap things up and move on from their PR nightmare? Or—was there something else?

"Trust the experts," she repeated Grayson's words. Authorities were meant to be the final word, the guiding voices of truth. And yet, she had spent the entire week watching the experts on *Relic or Rubbish*—highly educated, deeply experienced professionals—make judgments that weren't always correct.

She thought of Ambrose Carouthers scoffing at a woman's silver tea set, dismissing it as a mass-produced knockoff, only for her to pull out a letter proving it had belonged to a duchess. Or Fabian gushing over a set of Georgian candlesticks that turned out to be Victorian-era replicas worth a fraction of his estimate.

And the antiques' owners themselves? How often had they fought back? How often had they insisted the experts were wrong, that their treasures were far more valuable than the appraisers claimed?

The coroner was an expert, too. Trained, experienced, and confident in his verdict. But wasn't it possible that, like an appraiser holding a beautiful but flawed antique, they had overlooked something vital? That they had rushed to an easy conclusion without considering every nuance?

Polly's thoughts turned back to Arley, his final moments flashing through her memory. His collapse. The confusion. The sickening realization that something horrible had happened. Could his death really be as straightforward as the coroner claimed?

It wasn't just the coroner's report that disturbed Polly. Rosalind's words, too, refused to fade. She had said Arley was about to get a permanent slot on *Relic or Rubbish*, and not everyone was happy about that. Jealousy, Polly knew from her years in showbiz, could spark ambition—or ignite something menacing.

Her mind drifted again to the appraisers. Ambrose Carouthers, with his easily bruised ego after Arley publicly dismissed his valuation of a copy of *Paradise Lost*. Then there was Diedre: soft-spoken, perpetually poised—and prone to casting lascivious glances Arley's way that were ignored. Polly had found it amusing when she'd first heard about it; the age difference made the notion seem harmless. But she knew spurned romantic feelings could curdle into resentment. Unrequited affection paired with professional rivalry? That was a cocktail strong enough to warrant suspicion.

Polly let out another sigh, pushing herself upright. Though tired, she tried to mentally retrace the entire timeline of Friday. Not just what she'd experienced inside the marquee tent—but every detail of the day, every odd glance or passing comment that had seemed trivial at the time. Had she overlooked something important?

The minutes ticked on, marked only by the distant hoot of an owl. Somewhere downstairs, Mr. Boots padded silently across the rooms in search of rodent prey, a muffled meow echoing faintly when he caught a mouse. Everyone else in the castle was asleep, lulled into slumber by the acceptance of the coroner's verdict—but not Polly.

Pulling the covers to her neck, she told herself that if the professionals weren't going to dig deeper, then she would have to do it herself. *But I have to be clever. Terrence especially can't suspect I'm going back on my word to not sniff around dead people.* But if there was one thing Polly Pepper had learned after years of navigating showbiz as well as murder cases, it was this: things aren't always as they appear to be—especially when everyone is determined to prove they are.

Whether anyone else agreed or not, she wasn't about to sit on her hands and let an "inconclusive" pronouncement close the book on Arley's life and death. To Polly, *inconclusive* meant unfinished—and unfinished meant it was time to investigate. After all, mistakes happen all the time. Even the most brilliant minds sometimes misjudge a treasure—or miss the telltale signs of—*murder*.

12

———

Morning finally arrived, casting a pale, golden light over Thistlethorne Lodge. It was just before nine when Polly arrived in the breakfast room. Rosalind was seated at the table, sipping tea with Tim and Tiara, describing a dream she'd had.

"My lovelies," Polly said, as she slipped into her chair and picked up her Bloody Mary. She took a long sip, then, drawn by activity beyond the window, looked outside. The *Relic or Rubbish* production site had become a hive of purposeful dismantling. The police had completed their investigation late the night before, after hours of collecting evidence. The crew was finally free to strike the remaining clutter.

"They come and go so quickly around here," Polly parroted Judy Garland as Dorothy Gayle observing the fast pace in Munchkinland. Her attention shifted back to her house guest, as she took another sip of her breakfast drink. "Rosalind," she said, "I've been remiss in offering genuine concern about your falling ill on Friday—the dizzy spell and all. I can only blame being wrapped up in Arley's death and the aftermath of it all. Does it happen often—the dizziness, I mean? Have you seen a doctor? Is there anything you can do to prevent it from happening again?"

Rosalind's teacup paused midway to her mouth. She waved a hand dismissively, letting Polly know her sudden indisposition had not been a big deal. "The whole thing pales in comparison to poor Arley, that's for sure."

"Not to be dramatic," Tim said, his tone light but edged with concern, "but dizzy spells don't usually just pop in for a social visit. I had a friend whose mum ignored hers, and...well, let's just say the outcome wasn't pretty."

Rosalind shrugged and offered a dismissive smile. "The nurse said it could have been hypoglycemia. Or an electrolyte imbalance. Personally, I think it was just a combination of nerves and hunger. The stress of a live show. Maybe it was exhaustion. Maybe I stood up too quickly. You know how it is— long hours, tight schedule, no time to sit and eat properly. I'm not worried. I feel completely fine now."

"If it had happened just ten minutes later, you would've collapsed on live television," Polly added. "They would have cut the live feed before millions of viewers saw Arley die right before their eyes."

Rosalind cleared her throat, her fingers fussing with the napkin in her lap. "I've thought about that. It's been looping in my head ever since. The whole sequence of events would have been different. Not that it would have changed the outcome for Arley. But the world would have been spared the spectacle."

It was a reasonable response—rational, pragmatic, dismissive. But Polly couldn't shake the feeling that, for all of Rosalind's self-assurance, something about her story didn't sit right. She noticed the tension in Rosalind's grip as she lifted her teacup, the way her fingers curled too tightly around the delicate porcelain.

Tiara, seated across the table, said, "I served you and Polly a late lunch Friday afternoon, so you had a meal. Veggie wraps. Remember? And you were already standing when it happened, so it wasn't from getting up too fast." Her voice softened with concern. "Rosalind, you really should get it checked out. It could be something serious."

"Right. And I appreciate your concern. I have an appointment scheduled with a doctor in a few weeks. It's on my calendar. When you live in England long enough, you'll discover seeing a specialist can take forever." Rosalind tried to scoff, but it came out more like a forced chuckle.

Polly continued to sip her Bloody Mary, enjoying the tang of tomato juice and Tabasco on her tongue as she studied Rosalind over the rim of her glass. Something about Rosalind's tone, her breezy dismissal of everyone's concern, struck a dissonant chord. Her words were right—but an undercurrent of tension beneath them was suspect.

The busybody in Polly—a part that never quite switched off —felt a prickle of suspicion. There was a hedging in Rosalind's words. On the surface her story held up: dizzy spell, upcoming doctor's appointment, the notoriously slow pace of the NHS. All perfectly plausible. Perfectly ordinary. And yet, Polly thought she detected vagueness. Inconsistencies. A sense that something lay just beneath the polished veneer, carefully protected.

And maybe that was it. Rosalind was just a private person when she wasn't in the public eye. Perhaps she simply held her cards close to her vest—especially when it came to personal matters like her health. Medical information is deeply personal, after all. It wasn't any of Polly's business to pry. She knew that. She did. Besides, plenty of working people are wary that an illness might jeopardize their career or lead to whispers behind their backs. Rosalind's position as a television presenter made that even more understandable; she couldn't appear fragile in a profession that required strength. But still—there was a sense that Rosalind wasn't just being reserved—she was being evasive. And Polly couldn't help but wonder about that.

Polly glanced out the window again. Crew members moved about, stacking folding chairs and dismantling lighting rigs. The grand illusion of *Relic or Rubbish* was vanishing, leaving behind only marker cones, ladders, and the empty shell of the mammoth tent.

A pang of something unexpected—nostalgia?—caught Polly. "Maybe it's silly," she mused, watching a production assistant haul away a prop lectern, "but I feel I need to say goodbye to *Relic or Rubbish* before it's completely gone. Just a quickie," she added, setting down her drink. "Back in a tick."

But this wasn't really about sentimentality. What Polly wanted was another look at the place where Arley Kingston had died. She stepped into the cool morning air. The hum of activity and the clatter of equipment surrounded her. It was organized chaos—a ballet of workers eager to wrap things up.

Polly wandered between cables and open crates. No one seemed to notice until she stepped directly in the path of a young woman hauling a lighting stand. The woman paused, breathless, her cheeks flushed from exertion. "Ma'am, you can't be here. Safety regulations. They're very strict." Her dark hair was tucked under a baseball cap, and a lanyard with an ID card —Riley—swung against her vest.

"No worries. If I step on a rusty nail I have oodles of insurance," Polly assured her with a breezy smile. "I live here. Just wanted to take one last look around before everything's gone. It was rather exciting having a TV production on the property." She sighed, letting her gaze drift over the event tent. "I can't help but feel a bit dewy-eyed, seeing it all going away. Thought I'd take a final stroll around before it's just another faulty memory." She paused just a moment before adding, "And, of course, it's where Arley Kingston died. Hardly something one can forget."

Riley's expression softened. "Yeah. I worked the lighting rig most of the day in the appraisal tent. I saw the whole thing. It scared the hell out of me. One minute, he's chatting live on-air with the owner of that fancy clock. The next..." She exhaled, shaking her head. "I mean, I've been on the crew for a couple of years now. I've seen my share of things going sideways—temper tantrums, technical malfunctions, diva fits—but this? Watching someone just die like that?" She shuddered. "It's not something I ever expected. Especially not to someone like him."

She hesitated as if trying to find the right words. "Arley was one of the good guys, you know? Genuinely nice. He made an effort. Always asked how my day was going. If he was heading to craft services for a coffee—he was always going for coffee: black, extra shots—he'd ask if anyone else wanted one." A small, sad smile flickered across her face. "Said he was always tired. Needed a boost. The coffee kept him sharper. I mean, none of it makes sense. He was young. Too young to die, for crying out loud."

Polly nodded, filing away the coffee-consumption detail. "Did he seem—at all off on Friday? Ill, maybe?"

Riley hesitated. "He seemed—thoughtful, I guess. Introspective maybe? But that wasn't unusual for him. He had to get into his professional headspace. Focused. You know? I did notice him on his phone a lot throughout the day. I don't know why I clocked that."

Polly's interest sharpened. "Any idea who he was talking to?"

"Not really," Riley said, glancing around as someone yelled for a roll of gaffer tape. "But we all check our phones a lot for messages. Okay, maybe I did notice him a little more than usual." A sheepish grin flickered across her face. "He was ridiculously good-looking, and my brother follows him on Instagram —he's sort of smitten. I figured I'd do a little re-con. I really didn't know hardly anything about Arley's private life. Wishful thinking, maybe."

Polly forced a smile in response. "That's one way to support your brother—scouting for eligible playmates."

Riley laughed. "Hey, just looking out for my baby bro. But yeah, that's probably why I noticed he was checking his phone so much. I kept half an eye on him."

"You've got good instincts, Riley. Was there anything else that made your radar ping?"

Riley considered, then shook her head. "I was pretty busy..."

"Hey, Riley!" a voice summoned from across the forecourt.

"Sorry. Gotta go," she said, offering Polly an apologetic shrug. "Watch your step around here. Nails and cables."

Polly barely registered the warning as Riley jogged off. Instead, she moved toward the tent and stepped inside. The quiet was a stark contrast to the electric energy from last week. But Arley's velvet-draped appraisal table still stood exactly where it had been when he died.

She moved carefully around the space, her gaze sweeping the floor. Here and there, traces of Friday's pandemonium lingered—a lapel mic lying limply on the ground, probably the one wrenched from Arley's blazer. A single latex glove, crumpled and forgotten by the paramedics. An empty takeaway coffee cup resting on its side.

Polly picked up the cup gingerly, turning it in her hands. It wasn't one of the generic cardboard cups from the craft services trailer where nearly everyone grabbed their java fix. This one had the logo of Bound to Read—the village bookshop-slash-coffeehouse. The shop's familiar emblem, a quill pen lying over an open book, was stamped on the sleeve.

It was a standard takeaway coffee cup—nothing remarkable. But Polly's eyes landed on a partially torn printed receipt sticker plastered to the side. It looked as though someone had tried to peel it off—one corner curled, the paper ripped jaggedly through the middle. The adhesive had fought back. Part of it remained: a partial line of custom drink instructions, and just enough of the billing reference to read *ROR Prods.*

Polly noticed something else. A casual doodle in black ink, drawn just above the sticker. Two triangles balancing precariously on each other, like a child's sketch of an hourglass. Someone had marked the cup with an identifier—not a name, but a symbol. In the middle of a busy production day, someone had obviously gone to the village for coffee even though a free and unlimited supply was just steps away. A slow, sad feeling settled over Polly. *Had this cup contained Arley's very last coffee?*

As her gaze continued to travel around the space, she spotted a foil packet—the kind that contains a single dose of aspirin—torn open and empty. She bent down and picked it up. The packaging was glossy and eye-catching—metallic red with bold black lettering across the front that screamed: *CRANK'D! Fast-Acting! Long-Lasting!* The warning strip along the bottom edge was bright yellow, like a caution sign. She stared at the empty packet, turning it over, running her thumb over the jagged edges where it had been torn open.

She pulled out her phone and snapped a few quick photos of the packet and the coffee cup. Then a shout from behind interrupted her. "Hey, lady! You can't be in here! This place is coming down!" A crewman in a headset gestured for her to leave.

13

The moment she stepped back into the house, Polly found Rosalind and announced, "We need a diversion. Fresh air! A change of scenery! Something to scrub the gloom from our thoughts and inject a little joy. We've been stewing in this house for days. A walk through the village, and a quiet cuppa at the coffee shop-slash-bookstore is positively medicinal at this point. Trust me, you'll fall head over heels for Abbots Clover."

Rosalind looked doubtful, but Polly pressed on. "Cobbled lanes, historic charm, the scent of freshly made bread wafting from the bakery. And a chance to soak up the kind of village life that novels are written about."

"What about reporters?" Rosalind asked. "They could be anywhere."

"Oh, please." Polly waved a dismissive hand. "If reporters were lurking about, I'd have heard the village gossip mill grinding away at full speed." She gave Rosalind a reassuring smile. "It's a quiet Monday morning. The vultures are probably still circling the *Relic or Rubbish* offices in London, waiting for another official statement. You've survived years of live television. I think you can handle a stroll down the village high street."

Mid-morning in Abbots Clover carried the soft rhythm of rural life. The sun cast a mellow glow over centuries-old cottages and shops, and a cyclist meandered through the foot traffic, his bell chiming like a greeting. Outside the butcher's, a spaniel gave a single, reproachful bark as its owner vanished inside.

They made their way to Bound to Read, tucked between the tailor and the Dusty Attic antique shop, its painted sign faded by time and the sun. When Polly pushed open the door, a brass bell gave a delicate jingle, and the gentle scent of ground coffee beans mixed with cinnamon and vanilla was immediate. The shop was divided into a jumble of bookshelves on one side and mismatched tables and chairs on the other.

In the center behind the counter, the shop's owner Sarah Rodgers looked up from the espresso machine, her blue eyes crinkling with delight when she saw Polly. "Well, look who's here," she said with a happy grin and wiped her hands on her apron. Then her eyes widened. "Wait a second—Rosalind Fenwick? No way. I know you from *Relic or Rubbish!* I love your show. This is wild. Welcome!"

Rosalind gave a warm smile, the kind that had been lavished on thousands of fans over the years. "You're very kind," she said.

Polly grinned as she stepped up to the counter. "Today, we're just two ordinary women in desperate need of caffeine," she declared. "A flat white for Rosalind. Black tea for me. And tell me you've got at least one slice of Victoria sponge left."

Sarah glanced at the pastry case. "Oh, darn. Just served the last slice. I'll find something equally yummy. Take a seat."

As Polly and Rosalind settled at a window-side table, the shop hummed with the low murmur of local gossip and the occasional indignant "woof" from a dog lying at its owner's feet.

Sarah returned with a tray and set down two steaming mugs. "If I'd known you'd be in I would have saved that Victoria sponge," she said apologetically. "Will these earn me forgiveness?" She offered a wink and slid a plate toward Polly with still-warm scones, a generous dollop of clotted cream, and a pot of ruby-hued jam.

Instead of returning behind the counter, Sarah pulled up a chair and joined them. "Ms. Fenwick," she began, her voice lined with genuine sympathy, "I'm so sorry about Arley Kingston. He must have been a friend. I was watching it live when it happened. It was awful. I can't stop thinking about it."

Rosalind gave a faint nod, her expression tightening as she tried to put words to the shock still lodged in her chest. "Thank you," she whispered. "Yeah, Arley was—he was someone worth knowing. He was smart, thoughtful—always two steps ahead of everybody. Always had the driest remark and piercing insight."

She paused, her gaze drifting toward the window, where the view of everyday life in the village seemed almost surreal. "One minute he was standing there—in his element, doing what he loved to do. And then—just gone. Like someone tore the page right out of his story."

Sensing that Rosalind's emotions were at a tipping point, Polly reached for a scone and split it in half, the clotted cream offering a small, comforting distraction. "We'll get through this," she said gently, her voice a steady balm.

Sarah nodded, then gave a wistful smile. "It's strange, isn't it, how life barrels on—even when it feels like everything should stop." She took a breath, sat up a little straighter, and added, "Anyway, not to make light of things, but we had a couple of your antique experts in here last week..."

She glanced at Polly. "From years of watching *Relic or Rubbish*, I knew the second they walked in they were Diedre

Montague and Fabian Dupont. And let me tell you, *they* knew it too. If you get my drift."

Rosalind let out a dry laugh. "Let me guess—charming, humble, and thoroughly unassuming?"

Sarah snorted. "Like a fox in a henhouse. They strolled in as if expecting applause and selfie chasers. Charlie, my part-time barista, was the only one unfazed—he's part of the TikTok generation and wouldn't recognize a TV celebrity unless they'd gone viral for something on YouTube. To him, fame lives on a phone screen, not on a slow-moving BBC program with harpsi-chord music and people gasping over porcelain.

"But poor Ellie Cottsman—one of my regulars. She'd come in for a cappuccino. When she saw Diedre, she just wanted a bit of expert insight into a ring she'd inherited. Nothing dramatic. Just 'Do you know what the stone is?' Fabian glanced at it and said, 'If you're asking about value, don't bother. Sentimental's all you've got.'"

Rosalind groaned. "Classic Fabian."

"Poor Ellie looked like she'd just been slapped." Sarah shook her head, her voice tinged with disapproval. "I mean, I under-stand Fabian's point. People shouldn't think just because some-one's an expert, they can hand out free advice. It's like cornering a doctor at a barbecue and asking them to diagnose your rash. But come on, there was no need to be rude."

"I'm sorry that happened," Rosalind said. "Fabian can be remarkably efficient at offending people—but he rarely notices. Or cares."

Sarah nodded. "Some of the antique owners came in during the week too. Honestly, they weren't much better. You wouldn't believe—oh, I guess you probably would—the people who are convinced they own some long-lost treasure. You probably see it all the time. One man—an older guy, very serious—who sat at that table, said he was waiting for his appraisal time slot. He was certain his clock was worth a fortune."

Polly's ears perked up. "Clock?" The word left her lips a beat too quickly. She tried to sound casual, but her mind was already flipping through mental notes. "Do you remember what kind of clock? Anything special about the guy?"

"He kept mentioning its '*provenance*,' as if provenance was a big fancy new word he'd just learned and was trying it out to impress people. He said it should probably be in a museum. He had this air of—sort of desperation. Like he needed it to be valuable," Sarah continued.

Polly's interest was piqued. "Did you catch his name?"

"Hmm. No. Paid cash, as I recall. But I do remember he kept looking around like he was afraid someone might be stalking him."

Polly exchanged a glance with Rosalind. "Sarah, do you remember anything else about him?"

"Actually, when I was watching the show, I realized he was the owner of the clock Arley was valuing."

The words sent a ripple of—maybe suspicion—through Polly. "Can I ask another question? Did Arley Kingston ever come into the shop? Did you make a coffee for him?"

"I would have remembered that!" Sarah let out a short laugh, shaking her head. "The man had presence. That deep, smooth voice. And his smile—offset by that gorgeous, warm chestnut skin. Arley Kingston walking through my door? I'd have *definitely* noticed."

Pulling out her phone, Polly scrolled through her photos to the discarded coffee cup she'd found. She turned the screen toward Sarah. "This was near where Arley died," she said. "It's from Bound to Read. I just think it's a little curious since the production had a craft services truck on-site providing all the coffee anyone could want. Why would anyone go a mile or so out of the way to get coffee here? No offense. I'm sure it's the best in England."

"I'm not surprised," Sarah said. "I have a friend who works on movies in Hollywood, and she tells me the stuff their craft services offer is pretty revolting. Mass-brewed, watered-down, tastes like they've been reusing the same filter for a year. Yuck! We, on the other hand, take our coffee very seriously."

Rosalind lifted her cup. "That explains why this is about five hundred thousand times better than the tar they were serving on the set."

"Exactly. If someone wanted quality coffee, they'd come here," Sarah confidently replied.

Polly's fingers tapped lightly against the rim of her mug. *If Arley didn't come here in person, someone brought him that coffee. And I need to know who.*

14

It had been three days since Arley Kingston's sudden death, and a hush still engulfed Thistlethorne. The castle, indifferent to centuries of human drama, seemed to have absorbed the grief into its ancient stones. Afternoon sunlight spilled across the ivy-covered walls, golden and soft, but it couldn't quite warm the shadows pooling in the inner ward—where the tragedy had occurred.

As Polly knew well, grief doesn't follow a convenient timetable. It slips through the cracks of daily life like a draft through a window. Lurking in ordinary moments like a ghost that never truly disappears. It fades into the background, only to resurface in the melody or words of a favorite song, the scent of a sweet perfume, or the sight of an empty chair at the table.

Like everyone else, Polly had known her share of tragedy, endured heartbreak, and weathered losses. But she had never been one to allow sadness to anchor her in place for long. And she wasn't about to start now. She believed in the restorative power of activity and throwing herself into projects. It wasn't about ignoring the grief—it was about refusing to let the grief dictate the course of her life.

And in this moment, life—and death—was tugging at her sleeve. The coroner might be calling Arley's demise "natural causes," but Polly's instincts refused to be pacified by an easy answer. She'd been here before, unsettled by something that didn't sit right, feeling the itch of something unresolved.

So Polly did what she did best. She trudged forward.

It was finally Lush Hour—and one of those rare summer evenings in England when the air outside was a soft and balmy embrace. Beyond the French doors in the library, the flagstone patio was a quiet, secluded space, edged by fragrant lavender, potted geraniums, and climbing roses cascading over trellises. The residents and guest of Thistlethorne settled onto garden chairs. The bubbles in their champagne flutes fizzed lazily. And they all seemed to be inhaling the solitude. "Now this," Polly sighed contentedly, savoring the cool crispness of the champagne, "is exactly what we all needed. A few moments of peace, a glass—or three—of *boob-ly*, and a distraction from all our woes."

Tim cleared his throat. "Speaking of woe...sorry to bring it up, but Gray stopped by while you were out earlier. The Bristol Police are sticking to their initial 'natural causes' theory of Arley's death. No obvious foul play, they say. No further investigation is expected—just a few more toxicology tests pending."

"Just like that?" Polly scoffed. "Move along, there's nothing to see here? Arley dies in front of a live audience of millions, and we're all just supposed to shrug and accept it as rotten timing on his part?"

Rosalind swirled the champagne in her glass, watching the bubbles rise and burst. "It's easier for them that way. An end to uncomfortable questions for the network. No scandal. Just a sad, unfortunate incident. A clean story—with a hollow ending."

Maybe that really is the end of it, Polly thought. *An undiagnosed condition. No villains. Just the cruel indifference of life.* And yet that felt too tidy, like a door someone was trying to shut a little too quickly.

A beat passed before Rosalind added, almost apologetically, "I'm sorry—I know it sounds cold, but I just...I can't keep circling back to Arley all the time. The only way for me to stay upright is to let my mind land on something—anything—that isn't death."

She fell silent for a moment, her eyes fixed on a rose bush. "Sometimes, beauty feels like the only thing strong enough to hold the weight of sorrow." She gave a small, brittle laugh and gestured toward the garden. "It really is beautiful here, Polly. I rarely allow myself the luxury of stillness. Just being in a place that expects nothing of me—it helps." Her voice had softened, but Polly heard the shift for what it was—not a dismissal of Arley's death, but a quiet plea for reprieve.

"In London, even when I'm alone, I'm never *really* alone," Rosalind added. "There's always movement, noise, something demanding my attention. Here, I feel like the world has finally stopped spinning long enough for me to catch my breath."

"You're not saying you'd trade your glamorous TV career for puttering around in the garden, are you?" Tim tried to tease her out of her slump.

"Um...maybe...not quite," Rosalind said. "I'm hardly ready to take up knitting or baking biscuits for a village fête."

"I never thought I'd be feeding hedgehogs and debating the best way to grow runner beans," Tiara said, "but here I am...and loving it."

After another sip of champagne, Rosalind said, "Maybe I could get used to this. It might even do Ethan a world of good— if I could coax him away from his phone for five seconds and from that swarm of self-proclaimed 'entrepreneurs' he insists are 'visionaries.'" She gave a dry smile. "In my day, you needed an idea, a business, or at the very least a *job* before you started calling yourself a digital overlord. These days it seems all you need is a Wi-Fi signal."

Polly was reading something unspoken in her tone. Rosalind Fenwick, the woman who lived her life on television screens, was not used to stillness. But here, on this quiet evening, surrounded by nothing but the scent of flowers, the soft hum of bumblebees collecting the last nectar of the day, and the occasional visit from a blue tit or robin looking for crumbs, she seemed to be unwinding—if only a little.

Now a little more serious, Rosalind mused, "Being placed on 'administrative leave' isn't quite the glamorous getaway I had in mind. But frankly, it's not terrible. And I've been able to hang out with you. If Arley hadn't died, I'd probably be in a meeting right now discussing the next installment of the show. As it stands, who knows if I'll ever be brought back from this forced holiday. The network's probably still skittish."

"Oh, please," Polly scoffed, swirling her champagne. "The newsworthiness of Arley's death will have the shelf life of an overripe banana. Give it a minute. Remember that TV news analyst in America who was caught—how shall I put this delicately—polishing the family jewels during a Zoom business meeting? Thought his camera was off. Big uproar. Mass outrage then—poof! A few months later he was back on the air like nothing revolting had happened.

"Or take Roseanne Barr. Remember her? Tweeted something racist, got her sitcom canceled. But did that kill the show? Nope. They just rebranded it *The Conners*, axed her from the cast, and it ran for seven seasons. The public moves on. They always do. They love a scandal or any big news—until the next headline comes along."

Rosalind couldn't suppress a small smile. "You seem to have an unnerving amount of knowledge about immorality in television."

"Darling, when you've lived in Hollywood as long as I have, you see it all and learn that not even a high-profile disaster keeps a successful show, or star, off the air for long—as long as the network's making a buck. Sure, they panic for a split second. Pretend they're taking decisive action to shield the public and appease sponsors. Then, once the dust settles, it's forgotten. You and *Relic or Rubbish* will be back stronger and more popular than ever. I know these things. I'm a Hollywood realist."

Rosalind sighed. "I'd like to believe that. But right now, I feel like I'm floating away."

"Then start swimming, girl! Call someone up and find out what's going on with the show."

Rosalind gave a tight laugh at Polly's comment, but there was no amusement in it. "I can't appear to be interfering," she said, then paused, her voice dropping. "The truth is, I'm terrified if I poke too hard, I'll find out I've already been replaced. Or worse —that I was never really essential to the show to begin with. I like feeling indispensable."

"Oh, for heaven's sake. You don't have to ring up the executives—half the time, they don't know what's going on anyway," Polly scoffed. "You know who does know? Someone on the crew. They're on the ground, hearing whispers, seeing e-mails left open on someone's screen. If you really want to know what's happening behind the scenes, talk to someone who's not afraid to spill the tea."

Rosalind almost grinned. "You're probably right. Once, on a location shoot in Cornwall, the sound engineer found out we were being rebranded as a reality show *before* I did. An intern got cc'd an internal memo by mistake." She shook her head half appalled. "By lunchtime, the entire crew was calling it *Cash or Trash*." She took another sip of champagne. "Fine. I'll make a call or two. I have the cast and crew list on my phone..."

Polly's heart suddenly skipped a beat. In suggesting that

Rosalind call someone on the crew to find out the scheduling status of *Relic or Rubbish*, she'd just given herself a brilliant idea. Why hadn't she thought of it before? *The cast and crew list!* It wasn't just a list of names, it was a direct line to everyone who had been working on set all last week—who had been near Arley and might have seen or overheard something unusual. She kept her tone casual and relaxed as if she were merely indulging a passing thought. "Send me the list, and we'll go over it together. We can figure out who might be worth chatting up."

"Oh, darn," Rosalind said. "It's confidential—meant for production heads and on-air talent only." She exhaled, shifting in her seat. "Personal numbers, e-mails. You know how it is. If this fell into the wrong hands, it could be a disaster. Crew members don't have PR teams shielding them from online harassment or intrusive fans."

"It's a contact list, for crying out loud. Not nuclear codes," Polly persisted.

"You know how bad it can get," Rosalind said, her voice taut with a mix of frustration and concern. "I've seen assistant and junior provenance researchers harassed online over a single offhand on-air comment. I imagine Millie Travers will join that group given what she did to Howard Kettering. And don't even get me started on the appraisers—Ambrose once got threats because someone didn't like what he said about their so-called 'rare' family heirloom. This isn't just about privacy—it's about protecting people from the worst corners of the internet."

Utterly ridiculous! Polly thought but nodded as if conceding the argument. "I get it. I used to change my phone number monthly, just as a matter of course." She let the words hang there for a moment before adding, "Ninety percent of the people on that list probably have their contact info on LinkedIn anyway. Anyone can track them down with minimal digging."

Rosalind thought for a moment. "If anyone understands

discretion, it's you, Polly." With a small shake of her head, she tapped at her phone screen. "I never sent this."

Polly's phone buzzed. She casually took a sip of her champagne, ignoring the small jolt of victory that ran through her. "I don't recognize the number."

15

The evening meal was over, and Tiara was cleaning up in the kitchen. Tim was at the Fox & Hare for a pint with Gray. Rosalind had retired to her room to call her son. And Polly? She had slipped into the library. Seated at the partner's desk, she unlocked her phone and tapped on Rosalind's e-mail containing the cast and crew list. She scrolled through, locating the name and number she'd decided to reach out to first: Riley Laughlin—Lighting. She tapped the call icon.

The line rang twice before a voice answered, wary and alert. "Hello?"

"Riley? It's Polly Pepper. We met when you were at Thistlethorne Lodge taking down the *Relic or Rubbish* location set. Remember?" She softened her voice, adding just enough warmth to put the woman at ease. "I hope I'm not calling at an awful time. It is sort of late."

There was a shuffle on the other end, the distant sound of a television in the background. "No, it's fine. You all right? Everything okay?"

Polly cut straight to it. "I'm just still trying to wrap my head around what happened to poor Arley Kingston. I can't stop thinking about the day he died."

Riley exhaled loudly. "Yeah. Me too. It doesn't seem fair. He was too young."

"I remember you said you were in the makeshift studio tent all that day," Polly continued. "So you probably saw him before he went on camera. I just keep wondering—was there anything you heard or observed that stands out as odd or different from any other day? Even something small that didn't seem important or interesting at the time?"

There was a moment of silence on the other end before Riley muttered, "I mean...maybe?"

Polly didn't want to spook Riley—whatever "maybe" meant it sounded like something she hadn't planned to say out loud. "Can you tell me about it?"

"Well, it's just a little thing. But during Friday's lunch break, when most of the crew were in the craft services tent, I remember seeing Arley talking to Isla Morton, the lead provenance researcher. She's the one who goes rummaging into the history of the antiques the show features. Makes sure people aren't trying to pass off junk as treasure. A bit of a dragon lady sometimes, I think. But maybe she has to be.

"Anyway, she and Arley got into it. They were discussing an antique clock. Although 'discussing' might not be the right word. I wasn't eavesdropping on purpose, but I was working nearby, and they got pretty loud. They seemed to be disagreeing about something. Must have been the clock because it looked like she was trying to take it away from him. It got a bit tense. I didn't really catch a lot of what they were saying. Just a few words here and there."

Riley stopped, and Polly wasted no time trying to keep the conversation going. "What words?"

"I remember a few times he said something like 'you don't

have a clue.' Then she said words I've heard from her before like 'adjusting expectations' and 'reduced valuation.' I have no idea what that meant. And he countered with something like 'integrity and ethics.' Oh, and I clearly remember him saying, 'It's not your call. You don't have the authority.'"

Polly frowned, scrunching her face and drumming a pen on the desktop. "What did Isla say to that?"

"She said, 'No worries. It's already been handled. You don't need to think about it.' That's what stuck out to me because that seemed to make him really angry. And I remember thinking she sounded like she was talking down to him. Like she was more important or more in charge or was taking something out of his control."

"Any idea what she meant by 'It's already been handled'?" Polly pressed, hoping to get a little more info.

"Nope. And that's when Isla saw me and gave me sort of a mean look. So I beat it and went on my lunch break."

Polly let a thoughtful silence settle before she asked, "What did you mean before by 'Isla was a bit of a dragon lady'?"

"I just meant that I don't think she's easy to work with sometimes. Over the years, I've seen her clash with some of the other appraisers, even with directors. I don't think Isla cares who she pisses off. She's one of those people who always thinks she's way smarter than the rest of us. I think she has a couple of fancy university degrees, so I guess she knows her stuff. And it's an open secret that she has Simon's support for whatever she wants to do. He's sort of wrapped around her finger—if you know what I mean."

Polly recognized Isla's type. She'd encountered plenty like her over the years—sharp, ambitious, and maddeningly confident. The kind who wielded their tongue like a sword, cutting down opposition before it had a chance to fully form. Some people carried their knowledge with grace; others made sure you knew just how clever they were. And when someone like that had influence—especially in a field where reputation and precision mattered—that power could be intoxicating. Maybe even dangerous.

"Any examples of things she's clashed with others about?" Polly asked, leaning back in her desk chair, settling in for what she hoped was an informative conversation.

"Well, she's the lead provenance researcher, so the appraisers rely on her and her team in order to confidently assign value to an item," Riley explained. "I think that's how it works. I've heard she once tanked an item's value by casting doubt on its origin. Another time, so I've heard, she claimed to verify some fishy history of another antique, and boom—its value skyrocketed. Collectors with deep pockets take an interest in what she says."

Polly gripped her phone tighter. She wondered, was it possible Isla didn't just authenticate artifacts—but could perhaps shape their financial destiny? It sounded like she could send an item's value soaring or sink it into obscurity—based on her say-so. "Do you think Isla ever used her position for personal gain?" Polly asked.

Riley snorted. "I've heard. But good luck proving it. All I know is I've seen a few well-timed transactions—certain buyers who just happen to be in the right place at the right time, swooping in to buy something after an appraiser's low valuation. And sometimes, those buyers seemed pretty cozy with Isla."

Polly's mind raced. With that kind of influence, Isla might be able to control not just the value of items, but also who profited from them. And if someone like Arley—a man with a reputation for being meticulous and ethical—had realized what she was up to, maybe he'd confronted her about it.

"Do you think maybe Arley was being manipulated by her?" Polly asked carefully.

"Manipulated? Arley? I doubt it. I think he was a lot smarter than her. But I do know that he and Isla were not on the same page about that clock. That's why I remember what she said—it was so condescending. Like she was just brushing him off. 'It's already been handled. You don't need to think about it.'"

Polly felt uneasy. *Handled.* The word had weight. It suggested decisions already made. And if Arley had been questioning things, then maybe—just maybe—he'd been seen as a problem that needed to be *handled*, too.

Polly straightened in her chair. *Was there perhaps more going on between Arley and Isla than just a simple argument?* she wondered, drumming the pen on the desk again. "Riley, do you know if Isla was particularly interested in any specific items that came through the show this past week?"

There was a pause. "Maybe," Riley said cautiously. "She seemed to be spending a lot of time around that sea painting that Howard Kettering and Millie Travers clashed over. The one called *Tempest Rising*. And of course, that clock."

16

The breakfast room at Thistlethorne was alive with its usual morning symphony: the scrape of a knife over toast, the pop-hiss of a freshly cracked can of Red Bull, and Mr. Boots making a valiant attempt at persuading Tiara to part with a bite of her sausage. Tim, still wearing his jammies, lazily scrolled through his phone, alternating between frowning at the news and smirking at something on Instagram. While Polly sat, deep in thought, her fingers wrapped around her Bloody Mary, and staring into the middle distance between them.

Watching her closely, Tiara set her fork down with a little more force than necessary. "You're thinking too loudly, missy. What's up?"

Polly hesitated, looking around for potential eavesdropping house guests. "My gut tells me Arley Kingston didn't die...of *natural causes*," she whispered.

Tiara's eyes widened before she threw up her hands. "Oh, here we go again! You promised Terrence you'd stop playing Miss Marple. You're like an addict just out of rehab running to your dealer for a fix." She looked at Tim. "What's it been? A whole ninety days since her last murder investigation?"

Tim, still scrolling, didn't miss a beat. "Eighty-seven. But who's counting?"

"I am," Tiara shot back, folding her arms. "Because I distinctly remember a certain someone swearing up and down she was leaving all that *Murder, She Wrote* stuff to the pros. She was embracing a life of peace and quiet and—what was the phrase...fine wine and finer men.'"

Polly waved a hand. "That's still the plan. I just—"

"But here we are. Another dead body. Officially, a dead-from-*natural-causes* body. And you're about to launch your own investigation because you don't trust the police, the doctors, the coroner—basically everyone who's an expert on dead bodies." She stabbed her scrambled eggs. "You're starting to sound like one of those MAGA fools who think vaccines have tracking chips, chemtrails are government mind-control, and the moon landing was filmed behind a Walmart in Area 51."

When Polly didn't immediately respond, Tiara softened her voice and pleaded with her. "Please don't drag us into something that'll get us thrown out of England. I've learned to love it here, and I don't want to go back to all those guns, red caps, and measles!"

"Not to worry," Polly said. "Now that we've had a taste of life abroad, we'll never go back to a place where cheese comes in aerosol cans, and every February 2nd, an entire nation takes meteorological advice from a groundhog."

"And yet, you're about to investigate a murder again," Tiara said, pulling Polly back to the subject at hand. "And this time, according to the coroner, a *murder* didn't even happen."

"How many times do I have to repeat this?" Tim said, not bothering to hide his irritation. "Grayson said the Bristol Police don't find Arley's death suspicious."

Polly sighed, exasperated. "No offense to your darling Grayson and his esteemed confrères in Bristol blue, but think about it. The autopsy report? *Inconclusive.* They don't know—officially—why he died. They're just *assuming* it was 'natural' because nothing obvious jumped out at them. No blood. No broken bones. Not even a poison-tipped knitting needle jabbed in his neck."

Tiara frowned, rubbing her temples. "Pol, sometimes people do just drop dead. Freak heart conditions, aneurysms, whatever."

"And if Arley had been someone who lived on McDonald's and vodka, I wouldn't think twice. But he didn't. And yet, the official story is that his heart just stopped. And I'm saying that even trained professionals get it wrong sometimes. Just last week, I was there when one of the experts on *Relic or Rubbish* underestimated an item's worth because the provenance researcher suggested it might not be what the owner claimed. Then it was revealed to be valuable. Arley's death is the equivalent of an antique getting undervalued—it looks simple on the surface, but dig a little deeper, and suddenly, it's a whole different story."

"Okay, fine," Tim said, "let's say—for argument's sake—that you're right. That something's off. What's the next step? What exactly are you looking for?"

"Proof!" Polly's expression darkened with intent. "Any kind of evidence that suggests Arley didn't die for no good reason. That someone pushed him into the afterlife."

For a full quarter of a minute, a heavy silence fell over the room. It was Tiara who finally spoke again. "And what happens if you find something?"

Polly lifted her glass. "Then, my dear, we make sure that if someone had a reason to silence Arley, they start getting nervous." She tapped a manicured finger against the rim. "I started making calls last night. I've practically become a long-lost sister-from-another-mother to the lovely and talented lighting technician—Riley Someone. She told me Arley and the show's provenance researcher, Isla Morton, were having a not-so-friendly exchange before he died. He kept saying, 'You're wrong.' And Isla was saying, 'It's already been handled.'"

Tim took a final swig of his Red Bull. "Handled what? The fate of the free world?" He leaned back, stretching his legs under the table. "Because unless it was 'Don't worry, Arley, I've handled it and your soup has definitely *not* been laced with cyanide,' I'm struggling to see how this proves foul play. Or anything."

Polly gave him a look. "The point is, Isla was dismissing something Arley was clearly upset about. Brushing him off. And then, hours later, he's dead. Just hear me out. Maybe whatever Isla was 'handling' had something to do with why Arley is no longer among the living."

Tiara exhaled dramatically. "I knew this morning was starting out too quietly. What else did your Riley informant say?"

Polly shook her head. "Not a lot. But Isla Morton, as a provenance researcher, has the potential power to shape an antique's history. Her fact-finding helps determine authenticity before the appraisers assign value. Meaning she can influence an item's worth." She let that sink in before continuing. "If someone wanted to get their hands on a valuable antique at a bargain price, all they'd need is for Isla to cast a little doubt on its authenticity."

"You think Isla would deliberately raise questions about an antique's history—so someone could snap it up for a bargain price?" Tiara asked in disbelief but intrigued by the notion.

"Riley says she regularly sees someone who comes along just at the right time, and convinces antique owners to sell their item to them," Polly continued. "After the sale, who knows what happens? Perhaps there's a resale at a much higher price. *Boom.* If Arley suspected Isla was manipulating appraisals, that could be a problem for her."

Tim set his toast crust down. "And now Arley's perhaps *conveniently* dead."

Polly nodded grimly. "And the official story? *Natural causes.* No in-depth investigation. No second guesses. Just a tragic, untimely death."

"So what now?" Tiara asked.

Polly's expression hardened. "Now we investigate. Quietly. We're not telling Terrence or Grayson or anyone."

"You do realize Grayson is an actual police officer who might be able to help, right?" Tim said.

"And if I had any concrete evidence, I'd hand it to him straightaway and be done with it," Polly assured. "But all I have is a handful of questionable clues. The last thing I need is someone patting me on the head and telling me to be a good little snoop and leave it to the pros. At this point, we can't breathe a word to anyone. Not even Rosalind. That woman's a frustrated journalist with the ears of a Doberman."

Now the game was officially afoot.

17

———

A late afternoon breeze carried the scent of wildflowers through the garden. From the patio, Polly spotted Rosalind wandering by the small pond, hands tucked into her linen trouser pockets. Her usual poise subdued.

Polly watched for a moment, then made her way down the flagstone steps to join her. "What's got you stalking the grounds like Jane Eyre at Ferndean Manor? Contemplating the meaning of life?"

Rosalind sighed and stopped near one of the low stone walls overlooking a field of grazing sheep. "I'm thinking about Ethan. Among other things," she said.

"Ah, adult children," Polly hummed. "Our lifelong lesson in patience."

Rosalind tried to smile but instead shook her head and gazed into the distance. "I don't know what to do anymore, Polly. He's twenty-eight. Still living at home. No real job. No steady girlfriend. Maybe I *should* set him up with Tim. He has no real plans for his future. Just a new get-rich-quick scheme every few months. His latest idea? 'Personal brand management for influencers,' whatever the hell that means. I suspect it's code for scrolling through his Instagram all day and calling it work." She let out a humorless laugh. "He's convinced he's on the verge of something big. But he always is. And when I try to push him toward stability, he accuses me of not being supportive. Then I feel guilty."

"Guilt. The parental Achilles' heel. I get it," Polly said softly.

"You probably don't. Tim seems like someone who's always known who he is and has a well thought-out five-year plan."

"Oh, please!" Polly exploded in laughter. "I'd love to see that five-year plan. When does it start? Because unless I missed something, it's been auto-renewing like a forgotten streaming subscription. Tim's twenty-eight, too. And still living at home. I pay his 'deeply essential' accounts at Tom Ford, Palm Angels, and Rag & Bone. Don't get me wrong. He's got lots of talent. Maybe in too many areas. He's never been able to focus for long on just one. I assume he'll figure it out eventually. So will Ethan. Heck, I know plenty of people *our* age who still don't know what they want to do when they grow up."

Rosalind exhaled, rubbing her temple. "You spend years trying to protect them from the world—then realize you can't protect them from themselves. It's the hardest thing I've ever done."

Polly agreed. "Harder than working with Blake Lively. It's an exercise in tolerance and selective hearing. But if you let them think they're steering the ship while subtly moving the rudder, they maybe won't crash too often."

Rosalind took a long breath, watching the sheep in the field move in lazy patterns. "What if I'm steering him toward nothing? What if he never gets it?"

"Then he'll be exactly where he's meant to be. And you'll love him anyway," Polly assured her.

"I sometimes regret that I wasn't around more when Ethan was younger." Rosalind sighed. "I mean, I was there. But not *there*. Working, flying to different locations, filming at all hours. Maybe if I'd been more present, he'd have a real plan for his life."

"Who's to say that would have changed anything?" Polly said, stating the reality of it. "You could've been a stay-at-home mom, baking organic cookies, and attending every school or sports function. He still might have latched onto some absurd fantasy dream. That's how kids work. They terrify us no matter what. The bottom line is you'll always worry about him. That comes with the job."

She looked straight into Rosalind's eyes. "But let's not rewrite history. Your work gave Ethan opportunities other kids didn't have. You built a life that opened doors for him. Whether he walks through them or stands around waiting for someone to carry him over the threshold is entirely up to him."

"That sounds suspiciously like something his father would say," Rosalind groaned. "Damn him."

"There's one thing I've learned—you can want something for your kids, but you can't will them into ambition or responsibility or even adulthood. They have to figure it out themselves. At some point, you have to let them stumble—if that's what's going to happen."

Rosalind laughed at the shift in the conversation. "And here I thought I was just here for some fresh country air. Didn't know I'd get a full-on therapy session."

"Stick around. I'm full of unsolicited advice."

They stood in companionable silence for a moment, the distant hum of a tractor plowing a field drifting gently on the air.

Rosalind's next words were thoughtful, so quiet they were almost to herself. "I really thought Ethan was finding his footing last year when he was dating Isla Morton—the provenance researcher. I'm the idiot who encouraged them, thinking she'd be a good influence. Isla's smart and good at what she does. But I now see she's easily led by a man's smile and sparkling eyes."

Now that's interesting, Polly thought, her focus quickly back to her investigation plan. "What happened? Why aren't they together anymore?"

Rosalind scoffed. "Isla's more work-oriented than anything, which I hoped would rub off on Ethan. But Ethan's manipulative. Looking back, I think he saw dating Isla as a strategic move, not a romantic one. Don't get me wrong—she got a lot out of it too. Isla's no head-turner, and Ethan's—well, he's not exactly hard to look at. And she liked being seen with Rosalind Fenwick's photogenic kid. Great for her Instagram, too.

"Then, just like that, he dropped her. I used to think he was just immature. But now? I'm beginning to wonder if he's more calculating than I ever realized. And now, I've heard they're seeing each other again. If she's taking him back, maybe she's not as clever as I thought."

"Then she's probably not someone you'd be comfortable calling to ask when production on the show might resume," Polly said. "Have you reached out to anyone from the contact list like you said you would?"

"I meant to," Rosalind admitted, "but after talking to Ethan, I've been in...a *mood*."

Polly narrowed her eyes. "Sweetums, that sounds suspiciously like an excuse."

"It is. I just don't have the energy."

"Well, I'm way ahead of you. I got in touch with that lovely lighting tech person, Riley Somebody."

"Riley Laughlin?" Rosalind asked. "I've met her. Seems sharp. Been with the show for a couple of years. Did she say when we're returning to production?"

"No word on that. But she did mention seeing Arley and Isla in a rather heated exchange the afternoon before he died."

Rosalind let out a small hum of interest. "Knowing Isla, she probably induced enough anxiety to make him keel over. She's pretty good at that. Which is why she's not long for this world. The world of *Relic or Rubbish*, I mean. Confidentially, she's made waves over the past year."

"Ripples or tsunamis?"

"You didn't hear it from me, but Simon's not renewing her contract after this season. Some of the appraisers have lost trust in her. She's been wrong too many times. Their reputations are always on the line. If there's an issue with an item's provenance —if its history is murky or questionable—they can't make a confident assessment. They won't risk their credibility on something that might not be what it seems."

"What it *seems*?" Polly asked. "Would Isla ever—how shall I put this—adjust a valuation if it suited her interests?"

Rosalind gave a small shrug. "The antique world isn't some pure, untainted haven. Value can be subjective. If a museum suddenly takes an interest in a particular artist, their lesser works shoot up in value overnight. Prices plummet if a collector dies and their estate floods the market with their collections. Isla understands those shifts better than most."

"That sounds like it would give someone in her position room for exploitation," Polly said as she was thinking, *tell me more.*

Rosalind smirked. "It's called strategy."

"Strategy? Or manipulation. Has it ever been suggested that Isla could use that *strategy* for her own gain?"

Rosalind hesitated. "Not officially."

"Unofficially?"

"Last season, there were *murmurings*...there was a painting she cast doubt on. Claimed its provenance was shaky. It was later proven to be highly valuable—but only after it had been sold by the owner for next to nothing. When it changed hands again, it went for hundreds of thousands of times that amount."

"And the appraisers have to trust her research."

"Look, they're the faces of the show, and their opinions carry weight. But provenance is king," Rosalind said. "That said, there's a certain...fluidity to the whole process. Appraisal isn't always as rigid as people think. An antique's value isn't solely based on its history or craftsmanship—it also depends on what someone is willing to believe its worth and pay for it. If a collector, museum, or investor suddenly *must* have a piece, the value can skyrocket. Sometimes, it's less about what something *is* worth and more about what someone *wants* it to be worth."

"So, hypothetically, Isla has the ability to change an item's perceived value?" Polly said.

"It's possible. There have been *incidents*. Ambrose, for instance, strongly disagreed with Isla's research on a nineteenth-century oil painting. It turned out, he was right."

Polly's brain was like a runaway train at this point, headed straight to the investigation. "Has there ever been talk of...let's say, certain items being conveniently undervalued, only to be re-valued later and sold for a lot more than originally valued?" Polly asked.

Rosalind let out a dry laugh. "There's always speculation. Especially when a rare item quietly changes hands for far less than it's later worth. Ever watch *Antiques Road Trip* on the BBC? Those experts stroll into antique shops, talk down a price, get a 'bargain,' then send the same piece to auction where it miraculously triples in value. Perfectly legal, perfectly acceptable—because that's just 'the market.'"

Polly tilted her head. "So when someone on *Relic or Rubbish* undervalues an item...it could be the same principle?"

Rosalind offered a noncommittal shrug. "One might argue

it's a keen understanding of the market. And maybe, just maybe, a little nudge in the right direction."

Polly studied her, then asked, "And what about Arley? How did he get on with Isla?"

Rosalind took a breath, her gaze flicking toward the distant hills before settling back on Polly. "They had their moments. Arley was a straight shooter. If he thought something was off, he wouldn't let it slide. But as far as I know, he and Isla worked fairly well together. She can be abrasive, but Arley wasn't one to back down if he disagreed about something."

"But did they ever clash?"

"Isla clashes with plenty of people. She doesn't suffer fools, and she's not afraid to assert herself. She sometimes acts as if *she's* in charge—not Simon Belmore, the producer. But Arley..." She trailed off. "Arley was different. He had an unusual amount of integrity. He cared about getting things right. He wouldn't let Isla—or anyone—pressure him into going along with a valuation he didn't believe was correct."

Polly's memory of what Riley had said and what Rosalind was now confirming smashed through her thoughts. They both suggested Isla Morton was in a position to control the historical narrative of an antique before the appraisers even touched it. If Isla wanted to manipulate the value of an item—drive the price down so another buyer could snap it up and then later reveal its true worth—she could do it. And if Isla had tried to engineer something shady, and Arley wasn't playing along...

A silence stretched between them, punctuated only by the distant bleating of sheep. Rosalind finally let out a slow breath, arms still folded tightly across her chest. "Okay. This conversation reminds me of how much I miss working, and I'm eager to get back to it. You've motivated me to make a couple of calls about the future of the show. I think I'll start with my favorite cameraman, Pete. Built like a human tripod. Those broad shoulders, his cargo pockets stuffed with enough gear to rebuild half the set if he needed to. That square jaw and no-nonsense eyes. He's another reason I miss being on set. And on the road in anonymous hotel rooms. Ha-ha!"

Polly joined in her laugh. "Oh, the still waters of Rosalind Fenwick run deep! Who knew? At Lush Hour, I'll quiz you on all things Pete the cameraman. Be prepared to dish!"

With that exchange, they parted, Rosalind to the sanctuary of her bedroom. Polly to the kitchen to find Tiara.

18

———

Polly eased the kitchen door open with the caution of a cat burglar. She slipped inside and flattened herself against the wall like Lucy Ricardo in a community theater production of *Dial M for Murder*. "Psst!" she stage-whispered to Tiara, then jerked her head toward the door to the larder.

Tiara, elbow-deep in kneading dough, barely glanced up. "No."

"What? I haven't asked you anything yet!"

Tiara dusted her hands off, shaking her head. "You don't have to. I know that tone. It means you're dragging me into something."

Polly scoffed but didn't deny the accusation. She cocked her head toward the larder again, eyes urging.

"Oh, for heaven's sake!" Tiara sighed, as she untied her apron and followed Polly, grumbling under her breath.

The larder was a cool, stone-walled room, originally built to store perishable foods long before the invention of modern refrigeration. Its naturally low temperature helped preserve meats, game birds, dairy, and vegetables.

A heavy wooden door separated the larder from the kitchen, and Polly eased it shut behind her with a quiet *snick*, sealing them inside. She rubbed her hands briskly over her arms, suppressing a shiver as the cold air settled around her. "Minimal risk of eavesdroppers," she declared.

Tiara gave her a long, skeptical look.

"What I'm about to say requires absolute secrecy. Rosalind told me there's been quiet speculation that Isla Morton, the provenance researcher on *Relic or Rubbish,* may have manipulated antique valuations. She maybe undervalues items that later sell for small fortunes. What if someone was on to her scheme and was about to expose her?"

"Arley Kingston?"

"That's what I'm thinking. That would make him a problem for her. A problem that—" she rubbed her cold arms for warmth, "—had to be removed."

Tiara gave her a long, skeptical look. "Polly, that's sort of a huge leap. Is there any real evidence? Or are you filling in the blanks with guesswork?"

"It doesn't sound completely wild," Polly said, meeting her gaze. And what if it's not just Isla? What if others are in on a scheme like that—profiting from undervalued sales?"

Tiara hesitated. "You'd better have more than a hunch, my friend. Because right now, you smell smoke where there's maybe no fire."

At that moment, the larder door suddenly creaked open. They whirled instinctively. Tim stood in the doorway, arms crossed. "What is this, Thistlethorne's secret interrogation chamber? You know we have a dungeon for that."

"Timmy. Sweetums," Polly motioned for him to join them. "Just in time. You need to hear this too."

"I probably don't," Tim groaned, quietly closing the door.

"For the record, Rosalind had her ear pressed to the door, so I figured you were in here. She darted off the moment she saw me clock her."

Polly pressed her lips together, something like vindication flickering in her eyes. "I was right to be cautious." She repeated to Tim the intel she'd gathered from Rosalind.

"That's pretty farfetched," Tim said. "Isla maybe undervalues items on *Relic or Rubbish*. Claims they're worthless or inauthentic, or the provenance is too shaky to verify. The owner, trusting her expertise, sells their item to a buyer for next to nothing?"

"A well-placed buyer," Polly said. "Someone in the know. A corrupt dealer or a private collector. Then, like magic, the item is suddenly authenticated. And once it's true value is established...?"

"If this is true," Tiara sighed, "she's not just stealing an antique's value, she's laundering its history, turning heirlooms into bargain-bin castoffs, and lining her—or someone's—pockets in the process."

"*Relic or Rubbish* has to have checks and balances," Tim supposed.

"In theory," Polly agreed. "Every item is supposed to be vetted by provenance records. But that's assuming everyone plays by the rules. If Isla was the one assembling the provenance files—and no one was double-checking *her* research—she could easily fudge details. A small omission here, a misplaced document there."

"And if those files never made it to the expert appraisers or were quietly replaced later, who would know?" Tiara said. "Especially if the item was dismissed as a reproduction and quietly resold later by someone on the inside. Maybe Arley suspected that—or wouldn't go along with her valuation of something. That clock, for instance."

"And if he were standing in her way," Polly mused, "then tell me, what do criminals do when they don't get what they want, or someone threatens to expose them? I think I have a plan to find out more. But it's going to take a teensy-weensy bit of help from you. "We're going to Bound to Read," she said, gathering her bag. "I need caffeine, clarity, and a location where Rosalind's guaranteed to not be eavesdropping from behind closed doors."

The trio had strategically positioned themselves near the fireplace in a corner of the coffee shop away from prying eyes. The last thing they wanted was for anyone to overhear them discussing plans to investigate possible unethical practices at *Relic or Rubbish*. The place was just busy enough to provide cover. The hum of voices and the occasional clink of spoons against stoneware mugs drowned out their hushed discussion.

Tiara absently stirred her cappuccino, casting a wary glance around the room. "I still think it's insane that we had to leave our own house to talk privately. There are dozens of rooms at Thistlethorne. Rosalind would never hear us."

"We know she tends to listen at doors. I needed neutral ground—somewhere we could talk without her popping in. And I can't be one hundred percent certain if she catches wind of what we're doing, she might—even inadvertently—say something to the wrong person—or tip Isla off."

"So we skulk about like Cold War spies in a Paul Vidich novel?" Tim said. "You know, Mother, as much as I adore watching you scheme, I'd love it if, just once, you tackled an investigation the old-fashioned way. It's called letting the actual professional authorities do their jobs."

Polly bit back a laugh, waving away his argument with a flick of her wrist, patting his hand as if he were a particularly naïve child. "Oh, my sweet summer lamb. You're adorable when you're acting all gullible. But really, where's the fun in letting pros do all the work when we're quite capable ourselves?" She set down her cup and leaned in, eyes glinting with mischief. "Besides, the police wouldn't investigate Isla or *Relic or Rubbish* over some shadowy antique appraisal scheme. Heck, they don't even suspect foul play in Arley's death. Which brings us to my perfect, foolproof plan."

"Foolproof," Tiara muttered under her breath and added a roll of her eyes. "Accent on the first syllable."

Then Polly dropped her bombshell. She was sending Tim to infiltrate the tight-knit world of the professional appraisers on *Relic or Rubbish*.

Tim froze mid-sip of his coffee. For a fleeting moment, he wondered if he had misheard her—if perhaps his mother had merely suggested something mildly absurd rather than categorically insane.

But no.

Tim set his mug down, folded his arms, and tilted his head. "Do explain, *Mommy Dearest*, why I've been selected for this mission and not, say, literally anyone else?"

"It's obvious. First of all—look at you." She gestured with both hands as if presenting a particularly fine sculpture. "You're sophisticated, well-dressed, and you look like the kind of young man who would own valuable antiques. You're what the Brits call 'posh.'"

"I'm not posh. *I'm affected.*"

"Secondly, thanks to your father's and my genes, you're extremely good-looking. And trust me, that will be an advantage with Ambrose Carouthers."

"I fail to see how my cheekbones factor into an antique appraisal."

Polly's grin widened. "Oh, darling, you underestimate

Ambrose. He has a keen eye for more than just fine porcelain. And if anyone in the world can charm his way into getting information from him—it's you."

"So I'm to be the real object of interest?" Tim asked, wishing he were unsure where this was heading.

"You are rather decorative," Tiara smirked behind her cappuccino.

"Thirdly, you're good at schmoozing," Polly added. "And no one can do that as well as you."

Tim agreed this was actually true. He was a natural and recalled charming his way into a private viewing room at Sotheby's, convincing an executive that he was the estranged grandson of a deposed European monarch. A title, he claimed, that came with a tragic exile, a crumbling estate in the Alps, and—most importantly—an inherited curiosity about fine antiquities. It had worked spectacularly. Tim smiled at the memory. Yes. He could schmooze. He was an expert.

"And fourthly, the appraisers on the show all know me, so I can't approach them myself."

Tim paused. That, unfortunately, was true too. Over the past week, Polly had become chummy with most of the show's team. If she started poking around with pointed questions now, it would surely raise questions—or worse, tip someone off. But Tim? Tim was more or less a blank slate. A charming, well-dressed slate with aristocratic cheekbones and a disarming smile.

Polly sat back, looking immensely pleased with herself. "See? It's perfect."

Tim rubbed his temples, inhaled deeply, and released a long sigh of resignation. "If I'm forced into the clutches of some middle-aged antiques expert with an enthusiastic appreciation for my aesthetic appeal, I fully expect hazard pay. You owe me."

Polly waved a dismissive hand, already moving on to the

finer points of the assignment. "Step one," she said, ticking with her fingers, "contact Ambrose Carouthers. I have his e-mail.

"Step two: Spin the perfect story. You're the owner of a possibly priceless vase—a family heirloom shrouded in mystery. Tell Ambrose that Arley Kingston took an interest in it, believing it could be of significant historical value. But before he could formally appraise it, Isla Morton intervened and said it was a tacky knockoff."

"And why, pray tell, did she do that?" Tim asked.

"Exactly. That's the question you'll plant. Isla dismissed it outright. Said it wasn't worth considering for the show, but implied she knew someone who might be interested in buying it anyway. For a modest sum, of course."

"Suspicious," Tim said, finding himself getting into this crazy scheme.

"Step three: Raise the stakes. You'll claim to have uncovered new provenance—irrefutable documentation—linking the vase to the court of Louis the Fifteenth or some such decadent monarch. You'll say, Isla conveniently overlooked that. It'll get him thinking."

Tim nodded slowly, considering the plan. "But what about the vase itself? We've got that one in the entryway, but Rosalind's already pointed out it's early twentieth-century. And I probably shouldn't travel with such a delicate piece anyway."

"You're right. Too risky," Polly agreed. "We'll take photos. Surely, Gray has a proper forensic camera at the police station. Far better than anything we'd manage with our phones. Then he can photoshop a few hallmarks onto the base."

The mission was set. It was time to see just how much Ambrose Carouthers knew about Isla's possible behind-the-scenes maneuvering.

Resistance was futile. It always was with Polly. She smiled sweetly, and the next thing you knew, you were infiltrating antiques circles like a Regency-era confidence man. Tim would meet with Ambrose. He would perform. He would lie beauti-fully—because apparently, that was an inherited genetic trait.

Taking a last sip from her mug, Tiara muttered, "Next stop, prison. But at least we got to live in a castle for a while."

19

Ambrose Carouthers didn't ordinarily reply to unsolicited e-mails—especially from viewers of *Relic or Rubbish* who were convinced they owned an antique treasure and wanted his professional appraisal. Over the years, his inbox had been stuffed with messages begging him to bend his policy of never examining items except through proper channels: the show's velvet-draped tables or reputable antique dealers.

It wasn't mere snobbery (well, it sorta was). He knew the floodgates would open to anyone with a dusty heirloom if he made an exception. He had learned long ago it was best to keep the line firmly drawn. Anything else was an invitation for trouble.

And yet...

This morning's e-mail and attached picture gave him pause. The item was interesting—and so was its owner. Ambrose had an appreciative eye for aesthetics—whether in the delicate craftsmanship of an eighteenth-century vase or the allure of a well-curated physique. After all, he was a man of taste. And the subject of this photograph—Thèo Poivre (according to the signature line)—was, by any measure, a fine specimen. *Perhaps just this once,* Ambrose thought about bending his rule.

The photo of the vase wasn't a hastily snapped shot. It was carefully composed—crafted rather than captured. Grayson had posed Tim holding the vase, with his shirt unbuttoned just enough to hint at the warmth of his skin. The lighting was soft and strategic, designed to flatter and entice, casting subtle shadows that sculpted Tim's cheekbones, defined jaw, and traced the curve of his lips—lips that didn't quite smile but hinted at ... *fill in the lascivious blank.* And then there were the eyes. Direct. Penetrating. A gaze that reached through the camera lens.

Ambrose studied the image in silence. Then, with the ease of a man who had seen many fine things in his life, he exhaled a soft hum. "Quite an exquisite piece." With the smallest smile, he added, "And the vase is rather lovely, too." He reread the e-mail with more interest:

Dear Mr. Carouthers,
I hope this message finds you well. I have a vase that, at
first glance, might seem like any other example of
eighteenth-century French craftsmanship. However, it
may not be so ordinary. I have provenance that
suggests it was in the court of Louis XV. I am looking
for an educated perspective from someone who under-
stands the value of such things. I believe you may find
the vase—and the story behind it—intriguing. Please
let me know if this interests you.
Best regards,
Thèo Poivre

Ambrose clicked Reply.

Dear Mr. Poivre,

I do find your possession intriguing. A vase of that period, particularly with provenance, could be quite a discovery—if the details hold true.

I believe an in-person conversation is in order. I will be in Bristol at Henshaw's Antiques & Fine Curiosities all this week. I hope the setting will be agreeable with you. Please advise. Best wishes,

Ambrose Carouthers

Ambrose clicked Send, then leaned back. He examined the picture again as a small smile played on his face. This was shaping up to be a most interesting day, indeed.

Tim arrived at Henshaw's Antiques & Fine Curiosities, and an assistant ushered him through the main gallery to the back-room office, where Ambrose Carouthers sat behind an ornate Renaissance Revival desk. The dim lighting lent the space an air of secrecy—or exclusivity, depending on whom you asked. They shook hands, and Tim settled into a wingback chair opposite. He reached into his messenger shoulder bag and retrieved a sleek black folio and placed it before his host.

"Where's your lovely vase?" Ambrose asked.

"Call me cautious, but I thought the train to Bristol might not be the safest mode of transport for a fragile eighteenth-century treasure," Tim said. "These are high-res images." He flipped open the folio, revealing a series of enlarged photographs mounted neatly on cream-colored backing.

The first image showed the vase in its full splendor—the deep blue surface, a rich, velvety backdrop for the intricate gilded scrollwork that framed it. The gold, obviously applied with masterful precision, shimmered under soft light, accentuating the elegance of its contours. The other photos revealed close-ups—a hand-painted pastoral scene, delicate as a dream, its brushstrokes so exquisitely fine they seemed to have been whispered onto the porcelain rather than painted. Rolling meadows, dappled sunlight, and figures frozen in time told a story of idyllic serenity, rendered with the touch of an eighteenth-century master.

Then came the detail shots. One captured the underside of the vase, where delicate hallmarks and inscriptions offered clues to its history. Another focused on the graceful curve of the gilded swan-neck handles—a testament to the artisan's craftsmanship.

And then—the flaws. In the spirit of full disclosure, photos had been magnified to reveal several chips and hairline cracks.

Ambrose's fingers hovered over the photographs, his expression shifting slightly. *Do I recognize this vase?* he wondered as his memory unspooled. He vaguely recalled the first day at Thistlethorne Lodge for the *Relic or Rubbish* production meeting. Had he perhaps spotted the vase there? His eyes flicked up at Tim. "Fascinating. How did this lovely thing come into your possession?"

Tim didn't hesitate, his story rehearsed on the train. "Oh, you know how it is. Things get inherited, tucked away, forgotten until someone with a sharp eye stumbles across them." He lifted a shoulder, deliberate in his nonchalance. "I imagine you see it all the time in your professional work. People discover they've been living among pretty things, completely unaware of their value."

Ambrose's lips twitched. "Indeed," he murmured, drawing out the word. His gaze lingered on Tim just long enough to suggest he wasn't considering only the vase. "The things people overlook. The treasures that go unnoticed—sometimes sitting right in front of them."

Tim knew what was happening. It was a familiar dance. He let the silence stretch, then simply smiled. *Message received.* He knew Ambrose was toying with him.

Ambrose leaned forward slightly, resting his forearms on the desk. His voice, still casual, explained, "It's just...have I seen this vase before?" He gave a thoughtful tilt of his head as if piecing together a puzzle. "In a dealer's catalogue? An auction?"

Tim's pulse quickened but his expression didn't falter. Internally, he was adjusting and recalculating. "Perhaps at the *Relic or Rubbish* live broadcast in Abbots Clover? I tried to have it appraised there."

Ambrose gave a languid shrug. "Perhaps. One sees so many objects of similar design, doesn't one?" He took his time studying Tim. "So tell me, why does a man with your—charms —come all this way to enquire about an antique vase?"

"Just before his sudden death, your colleague—I think his name was Arley Kingston—took a keen interest in it. Then someone else—from provenance research, I think—dismissed it. 'Not worth our time,' she said, right in front of me. They had a heated discussion about it. I'd just like to know who was right."

Ambrose glanced at the photograph again. "Sounds like Isla Morton. If she dismissed this as valueless, why was Arley so interested?"

"That's the question."

Ambrose reached for a crystal water decanter and poured three fingers into a Waterford glass. He let out a small sigh. "Isla has been known to err. We all do, from time to time."

A beat of silence stretched between them. Tim studied Ambrose's expression, then he leaned in slightly. "I've heard... rumors...about the provenance staff."

Ambrose tilted his glass slightly, watching the light refract through the water. Then, without looking up, said, "My wise mother—bless her soul—always warned, 'Be careful about repeating rumors. There's a fine line between speculation and accusation.'" His voice was light, but there was weight to it. Then, changing the subject, he picked up another of the photographs, holding it under the desk lamp. "You're certain Arley Kingston was interested in this?"

Tim nodded. "Quite. He said he thought it might be significant. Look here." He pointed out the stamp photoshopped onto the bottom. "Interlaced L's. Arley said it was Louis the Fifteenth's monogram. But then, after a brief phone call with someone else —the producer, I think—he came back and said he was told to take direction from Isla and not bother with it. He seemed livid that the show wasn't interested. I thought it odd being dismissed so capriciously, and he seemed genuinely sorry, too. Curiously, I could have sold it on the spot to a gentleman who said he didn't care that it was of little value—he admired it anyway and wanted to buy it."

Ambrose was silent for a short stretch, then continued as if revealing a confidence. "Not long ago, Diedre Paige—the show's gemstone expert—appraised a lovely lavallière necklace as a common and unremarkable nineteenth-century reproduction, unlikely to fetch anything significant at auction. The owner was, of course, disappointed. But wouldn't you know, another party was standing by, eager to buy it."

Tim's heart was beating fast. "Did the owner sell it?"

"Wisely, no. Later, purely on a whim, she had it appraised in London. Turns out, it was quite rare and valuable."

"How unlucky for Diedre."

Ambrose chuckled softly. "And for Isla, who should have known better." He leaned forward slightly. "According to tittle-tattle, there have been other *incidents*. I don't doubt Isla's expertise, but I do find it curious that certain items seem to slip through her net only to resurface later in very fortunate hands."

Tim kept his face neutral, but inside he was thrilled with this information and the direction their conversation had taken. "Fortunate hands?" he echoed.

Ambrose continued, choosing his words carefully. "Last season, there was a situation with Isla over a vase from the Ming dynasty. Not ostentatious, but—how to put it—the kind of item that would send a proper collector into raptures. The owner had no idea what he had, of course. Thought it was just something his great-aunt had picked up on a trip to East Asia."

Tim arched an eyebrow. "And Isla didn't see it that way?"

"Categorically not. She told the owner it was a late nineteenth-century reproduction—probably made for the export market. Said it had no real value beyond decorative appeal. Even pointed out supposed flaws in the glaze and foot rim. The owner, trusting her, let it go to a buyer Isla suggested. Then, not six months later..." he paused, his jaw tightening, "...the same vase turned up at a major auction house. Verified. Seven-figure sale."

Tim let out a low whistle. "Isla's explanation?"

"'Honest mistake.' She said her initial examination was rushed. She added the customary 'nobody's perfect' defense."

"Do you think Arley suspected she was doing something shady?"

"Shady? Items misjudged, overlooked, deemed worthless... only to find new owners who later discover their true value? I'm not one to judge. I like having a job."

Tim gave him a look. "So, Arley Kingston could have observed a *scheme*?"

Ambrose's amusement vanished. He looked at Tim—not as just a charming, well-dressed young man with an interesting vase, but as someone who was here for more than professional appraisal services. "Arley was many things," he finally said, "but *fool* wasn't one of them. If he did observe something untoward—well, fortunately for someone, he's not around to look into it anymore, is he?"

Silence stretched just long enough to feel uncomfortable.

"Arley was inquisitive. I wouldn't be surprised if he was mindful of...something," Ambrose murmured, fingers tapping idly on his desk. "He liked asking questions. The inconvenient kind."

Tim could feel an undercurrent. Was Ambrose intentionally revealing something? Baiting? Hinting that Isla had deliberately dismissed valuable items, allowing someone else to buy them dirt cheap, only to have them miraculously authenticated later? And Arley suspecting this?

"Arley was an exceptionally clever man," Ambrose continued. "Unlike some in this field, he had no tolerance for deception. That made him unpopular in certain corners—not just with Isla. What most viewers don't realize is that the expert appraisers on the show aren't the ones deciding which items get airtime or how they're presented. Producers, sponsors, even network executives can influence what's highlighted, what's appraised, and—crucially—how it's framed. If you can steer the narrative, you can shape perceived value. That kind of behind-the-scenes power opens the door to all sorts of potential manipulation. Our producer, Simone Belmore, for instance, firmly believes antiques are entertainment first, accuracy second. Arley didn't agree. They clashed more than once."

Ambrose was still for a moment as a memory played in his head. Then, as if having considered the consequences of his words he said, "Arley had a particular talent for seeing what others overlooked. It was one of his more admirable attributes. And one of his more perilous ones."

Perilous. The word curled around Tim like a tendril of smoke, elusive yet impossible to ignore. "Perilous how?" he asked, keeping his tone casual though his pulse quickened.

"Let's just say no one likes the class snitch."

Tim's fingers lightly gripped the armrest of his chair. "That probably depends on who is being snitched on."

Ambrose's lips morphed into a half smile. "Yes," he murmured, eyes sharp. "Perhaps more importantly, *what* they're snitching about."

Tim held his gaze, waiting. He could sense a closed door cracking open just enough to glimpse what lay beyond. "Anything more?" he said, voice smooth but edged with interest. "I do love a good whistleblower story."

"Some people in this business prefer observations to be kept to oneself. Arley maybe should have learned that, after the writing-desk debacle. A seemingly simple item: Oak. Late seventeenth century. Didn't look like much. Fabian Dupont, the furniture appraiser, was ready to go on camera and tell the owner it was a reproduction. But Arley—Arley spotted something in the inlay, the dovetailing. He had a feeling about it. Turns out it was an early William and Mary piece. Very rare. And very valuable."

Tim's pulse quickened but he remained quiet, allowing Ambrose to reveal as much as he wanted to without coaxing.

"Rather than have Fabian appraise it and then have Arley rebut the assessment, Simon Belmore shut it down altogether," Ambrose continued. "Arley was furious. He was angry because he'd already caught other valuable pieces dismissed by *Relic or Rubbish*, only for them to end up in the hands of others who knew exactly what they were. He called it what it was—theft in broad daylight."

Ambrose tapped a finger against his glass. "Simon Belmore, you see, likes to keep *Relic or Rubbish* running smoothly. No complications. No unnecessary scrutiny. And Arley, dear boy... was becoming a complication."

Tim's fingers curled slightly against his chair's armrest. "Do you think Belmore could have had anything to do with..."

Ambrose cut him off with a languid wave of his hand. "Oh, I wouldn't dream of making accusations. Remember what my mother said?" He gave Tim a knowing look. "But in our world of antique appraisals, sometimes omissions are their own kind of confession."

There it was. A flicker of confirmation buried in ambiguity. Tim could almost hear Polly whispering *Bingo!* in his ear. Ambrose had practically gift-wrapped his suspicions. Not only did he apparently criticize Isla for provenance research errors with a genuine lavallière, Ming dynasty vase, and William and Mary desk, but he seemed to be hinting at something deeper. Something deliberately kept quiet. Something inside the *Relic or Rubbish* family.

Tim held his gaze, letting the silence stretch just long enough.

"Are you enjoying this? Our little tête-à-tête? This interrogation?" Ambrose finally asked, his voice edged with something between amusement and unease.

"Interrogation?" Tim managed to say.

Ambrose gave him a measured look, fingers still idly toying with a photograph. "Your questions have nothing to do with your antique porcelain."

Tim quickly considered his next words. A full denial would insult Ambrose's intelligence. Instead, he offered just enough to satisfy without fully conceding. "Well," he said, offering a half-smile, "I suppose it's fair to say my curiosity extends beyond just the craftsmanship of a vase."

Ambrose's expression didn't shift, but his eyes showed an unmistakable gleam of amusement. "And here I was, thinking you'd come all this way to bask in the glory of my professional expertise."

Tim shrugged. "If anything, I find our conversation more valuable than I expected." His tone was light, but the implication was clear.

There was a pause. Ambrose chuckled under his breath, shaking his head. "Be careful not to step on the wrong toes, my friend. Some dance partners don't take kindly to missteps." Then—so casually it might have seemed like idle conversation —he asked, "How's your dear mother?"

Tim's spine stiffened. His smile didn't falter, but Ambrose saw the reaction. It was barely a hesitation—a fraction of a second. But it was there. Then Ambrose said, "I've been in this business for a long time, Mr. Poivre—which I've known since your e-mail is the French word for 'pepper.' And I know when I'm being used. Subterfuge is so unattractive, don't you agree? Even on someone endowed with more than their fair share of... attractions."

"Subterfuge?" Tim was now aware of how carefully Ambrose had been controlling their conversation. Conceivably he was intentionally offering hints about behind-the-scenes double-dealing at *Relic or Rubbish*, as if he wanted the information revealed but didn't want to be viewed as the blabbermouth hall monitor of the antiques trade.

Ambrose cocked his head. "You know...I can't decide if you're being incredibly bold or just painfully naïve."

"I've been accused of both."

"Then let me offer you a piece of *bold* advice. Tread carefully, dear boy. The world of antiques is a small one. Reputations are fragile—like the treasures we deal in. A single misstep can crack careers beyond repair. Let's conclude this meeting with me saying that some collectors and dealers value their secrets as much as their acquisitions."

Leaning back, he studied Tim with an appraising gaze. "A misattributed provenance, the wrong whisper in the wrong ear —these things have consequences. Some people play fair. Others..." He let the sentence dangle, then added, "Well, let's just say they don't take kindly to intruders meddling in their affairs."

"That sounds ominous. A warning?" Tim said.

"A kindness."

20

The summer evening was warm, and the day's heat still clung to the flagstones on the patio at Thistlethorne. Bumblebees drifted lazily among the potted lavender, their fuzzy bodies dusted with pollen as they burrowed deep into the fragrant blossoms. High above, a kestrel was nearly motionless in the sky, wings spread wide, its sharp gaze fixed on the field below, watching for the slightest movement—a vole, a field mouse, the next unsuspecting prey. From the music system inside the house, the air carried the honeyed voice of Nancy LaMott.

Polly lounged on a cushioned wicker chaise, effortlessly regal, one hand lazily trailing over Mr. Boots's velvet fur. In her other hand was a half-filled flute of champagne. Tiara, a pink linen blouse draped over her frame, perched at the wrought-iron table. She twirled the stem of her champagne flute between her fingers, and a slender gold bangle on her wrist caught a glint of the fading sunlight.

And then—a presence at the edge of the patio shifted the atmosphere. Tim strode forward, shrugging off his long train journey with a look of exhaustion.

Polly looked up. "Well, well, if it isn't the weary knight returned from his quest. Did you slay the dragon? Charm the beast into giving up his secrets?"

"Depends on how you look at it," Tim said, as he slid the strap of his messenger bag off his shoulder and set the bag on the table. He barely had time for a sigh of fatigue before Polly pounced.

"All day I've been pacing like a caged animal, imagining every possible moment of your little confab with Ambrose. For all I knew, he was peeling you like a hard-boiled egg."

"That's one way to scramble a metaphor," Tiara said.

A low groan escaped Tim's throat as he sank into a chair. "Oh, the things I endure in support of your extracurricular activities, Mother." He took a long sip of the champagne Tiara handed him. "Ambrose was actually rather helpful. If you consider riddles and veiled warnings a form of help. But here's my big takeaway: He suggested Arley Kingston wasn't just a problem for Isla and her provenance research team. Ambrose thinks he was becoming a thorn in the backside of the show's other appraisers and maybe producer Simon Belmore, too."

Tim swirled his champagne, continuing to recall the events of the day. "According to Ambrose, Simon runs a tight ship and doesn't take well to undisciplined subordinates. He's the boss. He micromanages. He's involved with every aspect of *Relic or Rubbish*. Meaning, nothing about the show gets past him. If Arley was aware that something wasn't right, then it's possible Simon wasn't just ignoring it. He might have been part of it."

Polly's grip tightened around the stem of her glass. "So we already suspect Isla has a history—whether through incompetence or intent—of dismissing valuable items, conveniently allowing them to end up in the hands of fortunate buyers. And now Ambrose suggests Simon, as Mr. Boss Man, would be aware? So, could this be about more than the occasional misjudgement or sloppy appraisal? Maybe something—orchestrated?"

Tim set his glass down. "I thought about that all the way home. I'm sort of wondering how deep this maybe could go at *Relic or Rubbish*."

"And Arley—poor, meticulous, uncompromising Arley—may have been the one person on the show who bucked Simon's order of things," Polly said, swirling the golden liquid in her glass.

"According to Ambrose, Simon and Arley had a serious dust-up over an appraisal last season. Some writing desk—a William and Mary. Simon, Isla, and the furniture expert, Fabian Dupont, declared it a reproduction. But before Arley could prove otherwise, someone swooped in and bought it from the owner for next to nothing. A few months later, it turned up at a major auction house with verified provenance. Ambrose suggested Arley was becoming a disruption on the show—and Simon can't handle disruptions when it comes to his *Relic or Rubbish* baby."

"Very curious," Polly said, her voice trailing as something caught the corner of her eye—a faint blur shifting in the glass panes of the French doors. It was gone almost instantly. She blinked, uncertain.

A beat later, Rosalind stepped onto the patio from inside the house, her tone breezy. "Sorry I'm late for Lush Hour," she said, reaching for the champagne bottle. "I was trying to ring Ethan, but I think he's ghosting me. And I couldn't help overhearing that bit about Simon Belmore. I must say, I'd be very surprised if he'd do anything improper on his own show."

Pouring herself a glass, she turned to her friends with a smile. "I've known Simon for years—he's an exacting producer, yes, but he's not the sort to engage in anything underhanded. He loves the show too much."

"Then how do you explain last year's William and Mary desk incident?" Tim asked. "Ambrose Carouthers told me about it."

"Sounds like *Mr. I'm Not One to Gossip*. The desk thing? It wasn't some grand conspiracy, I'm sure. Just an unfortunate error. Simon relies on his instincts and the provenance team. And in that case, they all got it wrong. Plus, the desk wasn't telegenic enough for him to put on camera in the first place. It was too plain."

She took another sip and added, "*Relic or Rubbish* is a television show first and foremost. Simon's not as concerned with the precise value of every item as he is with pacing, drama, and keeping the audience engaged. Items get dismissed if they don't translate well on camera. That's just how the program works."

Polly exchanged a glance with Tiara, then looked to Rosalind. "You're saying Simon only rejected that desk for entertainment value?"

"I'm saying decisions get made quickly, sometimes for aesthetic reasons. But that doesn't mean there was anything untoward going on."

"Yet someone snapped up that desk for a fraction of its value," Tim said. "Pretty convenient, wouldn't you say?"

Rosalind hesitated. Then she let out a soft laugh, a beat too late to sound completely natural. "Antique dealers are always keeping their eyes peeled. If something inadvertently slips through the cracks, you can bet someone will be waiting to take advantage. That's the nature of the business."

For the briefest moment, a shadow crossed Rosalind's face —the careful restraint of someone who knew more than they were comfortable revealing. "Simon can be ruthless about ratings, yes—but not reckless. He'd never do anything to jeopardize *Relic or Rubbish*. That show is his legacy. He might overlook a questionable appraisal if it kept the audience entertained or boosted viewing figures. But actively sabotaging an item?

Nah. That's a different kind of ruthless. He'd never cross that line."

"So you'd say he had no reason to want Arley gone from the show?" Tim persisted.

Rosalind hesitated for just a fraction of a second. "I can't see why he would. Arley was a rising star. They were offering him a permanent spot on the show. Simon would have been involved in the network discussions." But something in her expression had changed. A flicker of uncertainty, the briefest furrow of her brow.

Polly caught it immediately. "You've just thought of something, haven't you?"

"Oh, it's nothing—just a passing thought."

"Indulge us."

"It's just...if we're talking about people who had conflicts with Arley and wished he weren't part of the *Relic or Rubbish* family, I suppose you'd have to look at Diedre Paige."

Polly frowned. "The gemstone expert?"

"She and Arley... Frankly, I think she started out fancying him—but that grew into loathing. Probably because of that business with the lavallière."

Having heard Ambrose's version of the story, Tim prodded. "I've heard bits and pieces about that. What's your take?"

Rosalind looked as if she regretted mentioning it at all. "Okay. Last season, Diedre dismissed an antique lavallière. Said she could tell from a mile away it was nothing special. A pretty little trinket, late nineteenth century at best, and barely worth a second glance. She told the owner it was a common reproduction, the kind you'd find gathering dust in a pawn-shop, and not worth the show's time. But here's the thing— Diedre's no fool. She knows her gemstones as well as anyone in the business. Although she dismissed that lavallière, it couldn't have been because she didn't recognize its quality.

Either she was too stubborn to admit she'd misjudged it—and I think Diedre would rather eat her shoe than be wrong—or..."

Polly filled in the gap. "Or someone *wanted* that lavallière to be ignored and valued at less than its worth. And then Arley came along and spoiled that."

"As often happened, Arley wasn't even assigned to the piece," Rosalind continued. "But, of course, he couldn't help butting in. Said the craftsmanship was far too refined to be a reproduction. The gold work was impossibly delicate, each filigree curl so precise it could only have been done by hand. He conceded the clasp wasn't original, but that was probably to accommodate a more contemporary chain."

Her eyes flickered with memory. "The engraving...that was what Arley later told me had stopped him cold. He recognized the hallmark instantly—*Pierre-Étienne Norvins*, one of the most sought-after Parisian jewelers of the late eighteenth century. A master of rococo design, Norvins was known for his aristocratic clientele, including the House of Montvoisin."

Rosalind set down her glass, her expression scoffing. "Turns out, Diedre had dismissed a masterpiece. One owned by none other than the Duchesse de Montvoisin. The pendant was adorned with mine-cut diamonds—each painstakingly set by hand—and a deep blue sapphire."

"And let me guess—she wasn't just any duchess?" Polly surmised.

Rosalind snickered in agreement and then filled in the back-story. "The Duchesse de Montvoisin was one of the most infamous women at court. She was rumored to be a confidante of Marie Antoinette's, though some say she was more than that—a fixer, a schemer, someone who knew where the bodies were buried—sometimes quite literally. And when the Revolution came? The Montvoisins were among the first families to flee

Paris, vanishing overnight, their vast collection of jewels and art supposedly lost in the chaos."

"So this lavallière was part of that lost fortune?" Tiara asked.

"Some believed the duchess smuggled a portion of her wealth out of France before she was arrested," Rosalind nodded. "Officially, she was executed during the Reign of Terror—but unofficially? There were rumors she made a deal. She traded something—or someone—to secure passage out of Paris. And that lavallière? If authenticated, it would have been the first known piece of the Montvoisin collection to resurface in over two hundred years."

Polly was momentarily confused. "How could Diedre have dismissed it? She's an expert for crying out loud."

Rosalind shrugged. "Maybe she was advised to?"

"Which means someone walked away with a missing piece of history—for a fraction of its value," Polly said. "And the person who realized its authenticity? Arley Kingston. Surely, Diedre was embarrassed."

"She was seething. Arley just got lucky, she said. Personally, I don't think luck had anything to do with it. Arley just saw what Diedre didn't—or wouldn't. After that, Diedre wanted his head."

Rosalind looked at her watch and set her champagne glass down. "Can we pick this up later? I need to try calling Ethan again. It's unlike him to not call me back right away. The silence either means he's avoiding me, or he's in trouble. And frankly, I'm not sure which worries me more."

She excused herself, and a hush settled over the patio. But the weight of the conversation lingered. Talk wasn't necessary, but Tiara saw Polly gazing across the lawn to the ever-present flock of sheep in the field beyond. After a long moment, she whispered, "You've got that look."

Tim agreed. "That 'I'm-about-to-do-something-wildly-reckless' look."

A beat later, Polly returned to the moment. "I haven't decided whether it's reckless."

"But she has decided on her next move," Tim added, as if Polly weren't present.

Polly looked around to make sure Rosalind was nowhere in sight and motioned for Tiara to close the patio doors. Once she was certain they were alone, she leaned in and lowered her voice.

"Who has the most to lose if shady appraisals are happening on *Relic or Rubbish*? Simon Belmore? Isla and Diedre might get fired or blacklisted, but Simon..." She let the thought linger. "Simon would take the fall for the entire production. Twenty-five years of the show being a beloved tradition? Gone. Because if it's more than just a questionable valuation, *Relic or Rubbish* wouldn't just look sloppy. It would look like a con."

She paused. "And if Arley had proof of that? If he was about to go public...." Polly let that question hang in the air. "Well... that would be a very inconvenient truth—for someone."

"Don't you think *Diedre* had a good reason to eliminate Arley, too?" Tim reminded her. "He publicly humiliated her over that lavallière. That's not exactly something most people would let slide."

Polly considered his argument. "She may have despised him. Perhaps even fantasized about stuffing a diamond choker down his throat. But...murder?" She shook her head.

"So, Deidre's off the hook?" Tim asked.

"Far from it," Polly hastily said. "But if we're talking about who had the most to lose, in my book that's Simon. That's who I need to visit next."

Tiara looked intrigued but unconvinced. "What about Isla? I'm becoming totally suspicious of her."

"Oh, I'll definitely get to her. If Isla's doing anything under-handed, and Arley suspected that, she has a motive to eliminate him," Polly agreed. "It's one thing to be publicly embarrassed—Deidra could claw her way back from that. But Isla? If Arley exposed her for deliberately undervaluing antiques to benefit certain buyers, she wouldn't just lose her job—she'd probably face criminal charges. Fraud. Breach of trust. You name it. That kind of stain never wears off.

"But here's what bothers me," Polly continued. "Simon's the one with real power. If he knew what Isla was doing and let it slide—maybe even protected her—he wouldn't just be disgraced. You'd have to ask Grayson for details, but Simon would probably face conspiracy charges. Or at the very least, aiding and abetting fraud. It would all come down on him. Twenty-five years of reputation, gone in a flash."

Tiara gave her a thoughtful look. "So, if I know you well enough—and I do—you'll waltz into Simon's office and demand answers?"

"Of course you know me," Polly said, plucking a sprig of lavender from the planter and sniffing it. "And *I* know that men in television thrive on attention. They want to feel brilliant. Indispensable. Maybe even feared. So I'll flatter, I'll fawn, I'll quote his best ratings week like scripture. And just when he's basking in the glow of his own magnificence..." She leaned in, eyes glinting, "I'll turn his whole world upside down."

21

Producer Simon Belmore's office reeked of chaos. His large oval desk was cluttered with papers, documents, folders, and office supplies. A laptop was partially buried under the mess. The overall impression was of a busy, overwhelmed professional working in a high-paced environment with little time for tidying up.

On the walls, a collection of framed accolades and memories reinforced Simon's stature in the television business. A signed black-and-white glossy photo of Fiona Bruce, from *Antiques Roadshow* fame—inscribed, "With enduring admiration"—hung beside a *TV Times* magazine cover featuring *Relic or Rubbish*. A newspaper clipping from *the Financial Times* declared the show, "A National Treasure," while a production still photo showed Simon mid-discussion with an appraiser, captured in a perfectly staged moment. Awards gleamed on a polished bookcase: a BAFTA Television Award for Best Factual Series, a National Television Award, and a Royal Television Society Award, each a testament to the show's long-running success.

Polly had taken the train with Tiara from Abbots Clover to London under the guise of pitching Polly as a possible new presenter of *Relic or Rubbish*. But Polly's true objective was far more calculated. Simon Belmore was the gatekeeper of everything that happened behind the scenes. If secret appraisals were happening, he should know about them—or ensuring they stayed secret. And if Simon had any deeper knowledge about the circumstances surrounding Arley Kingston's death, Polly intended to tease that out.

While Tiara indulged in a leisurely afternoon shopping at Harrods, Polly strode into Simon's office with the confidence of a woman who had once commanded prime-time television in America and had no intention of being anything less than the star of this particular performance.

"Simon Belmore, you darling man!" Polly declared, sweeping into his office and shaking his hand before settling into the visitor's chair on the other side of his desk. "I love, love, love your *Relic or Rubbish*. Honestly, it's one of my top ten or twenty favorite ways to spend a boring evening—watching genteel pensioners have seizures when they're told their grandmother's ghastly vase is actually worth a million. Or better yet, when someone brings in something they're *convinced* is priceless, only to be told it's worth more as a doorstop. Delicious!" She laughed. "But sweetums, the program does need sprucing up. I'm here to help."

Simon looked perplexed. "Ms. Pepper, my show has been on the air for twenty-five years. It doesn't need 'sprucing up.' It's a well-oiled machine. A British institution."

Polly waved a dismissive hand. "Darling man, everything needs to hit *refresh* now and again. The sallow lighting you use. Must every guest look like they've just clawed their way out of a crypt with whatever antique treasure they're holding? A touch of warmth, a strategic spotlight—it's television, Simon. Not a post-mortem examination room."

She leaned forward, eyes gleaming. "And let's discuss the

reveals. The way it's set up now, your experts rattle off a valuation, the guest gasps, and we all pretend it's riveting. *Dull!* Where's the drama? I propose a countdown. Ten...nine...eight... *Suspense*, Simon! *Anticipation!* Maybe even—" she paused for effect "—*fireworks*. Or better yet, a *trapdoor* under the guest's chair—if their item turns out to be worthless, *buh-bye!* Give the people *theater*, Simon!" She took a sip of cappuccino an assistant had set before her. "I know you're dying to hear more. I've got a million of 'em."

They'd only just begun, and Simon's patience was already thinning. "According to your phone call yesterday, you believe you're the ideal person to provide 'Hollywood magic' to my show?" His posture stiffened ever so slightly. "Ms. Pepper, I created *Relic or Rubbish*. I know what's best for the broadcast. We're a heritage program. A cornerstone of British television. Not some superficial puff piece."

Polly placed a hand over her heart in mock sincerity. "Darling, sweetums. I would never suggest that your beloved *Rubbish* is anything less than a national treasure." She took another sip of the cappuccino. "But even the king's crown needs a spit shine now and then. Twenty-five years, Simon. That's how long Rosalind Fenwick has been on your show. The public gets bored."

Simon frowned. "Rosalind Fenwick is melded with the show's core identity. The viewers love her. Trust her. She's built relationships with collectors, experts, and institutions. She's not just a presenter—she's the primary face of *Relic or Rubbish*."

"Yes, yes, and a lovely face it is. But she's almost an antique herself. Well-preserved, of course. But audiences crave a bit of a shake-up now and then. I starred for almost fifteen years on *The Polly Pepper Playhouse* in America. And while my audiences never deserted me, I wisely left before they had the chance to start saying I was resting on musty laurels. Timing is everything in our business."

Simon was on the verge of annoyance. "You're comparing your old TV variety show to a British legacy program?" He stabbed his fingers on the desk. "The network trusts Rosalind Fenwick. And the audience—"

"Audiences would trust a fresh, charismatic, utterly captivating *new* host," Polly cut in, letting a silence stretch just long enough to make Simon uncomfortable. Then, with the precision of a well-aimed dagger, she struck. "Remind me, sweetums, who stepped in at the last minute when poor Rosalind fell ill during the live broadcast at Thistlethorne Lodge?"

"You did," Simon offered a reluctant sigh.

"I *did!*" Polly agreed. "And I was marvelous. No need to gush. But we can't ignore the facts: There was an emergency. I took over. I daresay the audience adored me. Fresh energy. Quick wit. Just the right touch of glamour. I handled a live death with flawless composure. No screaming. No fainting. No hysterics. And I kept the audience engaged while poor Arley Kingston skipped off, mid-broadcast, into his next life. Simon, if I can glide through that without so much as a hair out of place, surely I can manage a few chatty pensioners with questionable heirloom brooches."

Simon appraised her with narrowed eyes. "You're enjoying this, aren't you?"

Polly's smile was all innocence. "I'm merely pointing out what you already know, darling. *Relic or Rubbish* needs me. Besides, you've benched Rosalind. You've put her on ice. Just keep her there. Indefinitely."

Her voice lowering just a fraction, she offered another counterpoint. "I happen to know Rosalind's not taking your treatment of her very well. She's disappointed in you, Simon. Feels like she's being punished for something beyond her control. She thinks she deserves better from her *family*. Can you blame her? One minute, she's representing *Relic or Rubbish*—the next, she's placed on leave while the network gets its act together investigating Arley Kingston's sudden on-air death. Any news on that, by the way?"

Simon exhaled sharply, shifting in his chair. "The network isn't investigating Arley's death, Ms. Pepper. That's a job for the police. We're just doing our due diligence. Standard protocol when something like this happens. Not that anything like this has ever happened before. But we don't want a media circus. We need to be certain there's nothing... untoward associated with *Relic or Rubbish*."

Polly tilted her head, studying him. "Untoward?" she echoed. "That's an interesting choice of words."

"I mean, the less scrutiny, the better. If you're such a great friend to Rosalind Fenwick, why are you trying to steal her job?" His voice carried a note of dry amusement.

Polly let out a soft, unruffled laugh. "Simon, darling, this is television. We both know loyalty only gets you so far. Opportunity, on the other hand, gets you everywhere. Besides, Rosalind and I are very different women. If she's wise, she'll use this time to enjoy some well-earned rest. And if you decide she's not coming back, well...the show must go on."

Simon studied her, clearly weighing her words. "It seems to me you're *creating* the opportunity."

"I prefer to think of it as filling a void," she said, as she traced the rim of her cappuccino cup with a manicured finger, then lifted her gaze to meet his directly. "You know what I think, Simon? I think you've got an employee problem on your hands. Not just a sidelined presenter, but a staff member who feels betrayed. Someone who devoted years to you and your show and suddenly finds herself discarded."

Polly now made her voice soft and deliberate. "That kind of

disillusionment changes people, Simon. Maybe she's no longer grateful to you for her career. Maybe she's started wondering if she owes you anything at all. And once someone stops feeling indebted—once they stop playing the good soldier—well, that's when they start being disloyal." She let that hang, watching the way his jaw tensed.

"I imagine you'd hate to think she was out there...talking," Polly said, her tone smooth as silk. "Talking to people about what it's like behind the scenes at *Relic or Rubbish*. The sort of people who make a living turning over stones looking for worms. Reporters, bloggers, podcasters—anyone with a taste for a juicy scandal." She tilted her head, a mock expression of concern on her face. "Once someone stops feeling valued—once they start to believe they've been pushed out..." She paused, letting the silence press down. "Well, then, you're not just dealing with a former employee, Simon. You're dealing with someone who knows where the bodies are buried. A wild card with nothing to lose."

She let the words settle, then lifted her cappuccino with deliberate nonchalance. "Of course, I could be wrong," she mused, taking a slow sip. "Maybe Rosalind's at home, reading a novel, quietly waiting to hear from you, loyal as ever. But then again...she *has* been rather chatty with Terrence Marks over at the *Abbots Clover Overview*. Our humble village paper. Apparently she made a few comments about how 'certain people' don't value her decades of experience. It sounded less like a complaint, more like a...warning shot." Polly shrugged, as if merely passing along idle gossip. "Still, it's probably nothing."

Then, with a breezy shift, Polly flashed a dazzling smile. "Now, picture this—a bold, stylish, lively new host. Someone with wit and charisma, who already owns a couture wardrobe." She placed a hand on her chest. "Someone like, oh, I don't know...*moi*."

Simon pinched the bridge of his nose, appraising her with exasperation. "What do you even know about antiques, Ms. Pepper? Can you discuss styles of furniture, paintings, silver, or collectibles with any authority? Do you know the difference between Regency and rococo? Would you say a Ming vase was 'darling?' I shudder to think what you'd say on television about a Louis the Sixteenth commode. You can't just flash a dazzling smile and expect viewers to take you seriously."

"Why not? Who says I need to be an expert? Isn't that what the appraisers are for? The audience doesn't want a presenter who drones on about wood grain and silver hallmarks—they want someone who makes it entertaining. Someone who can ask the questions they'd ask. React the way they would. And keep them hooked for the hour-long broadcast."

She gestured broadly as if painting a vision of her own brilliance in the air. "Some of your appraisers sound like they're reciting tax code. That's where I come in. I make things fun. Give the show some sparkle! If I can carry an entire TV variety series, I can certainly do wonders here."

Polly leaned forward, dropping her voice to a conspiratorial murmur. "And to be honest, darling, I've watched Rosalind drone on about provenance and thought, *Oh, for God's sake, woman! I know you're British but inject some life into this!* Face it, Simon, you need a performer. A showman. But to your concerns about my lack of an antiques background, I'm a quick learner. I already know the process involves historians, researchers, fact-checkers, legal consultants. Fill me in on the rest."

Simon exhaled wearily as he regarded Polly with irritation. "It's true—no one watching the show has any idea how much work goes into every appraisal on *Relic or Rubbish*. We don't just have some antique nerd glancing at a stamp collection and tossing out a valuation figure. There's a whole process. Layers of expertise. And a dozen moving parts before any item ever makes it to air."

Polly took a fake sip of her now-tepid cappuccino, careful to mask her satisfaction with the direction the conversation was now taking. Simon seemed about to give her a peek behind the curtain. *Stay charming. Stay curious. Let him keep talking,* she thought as she swirled the dregs of her drink. "Enlighten me, darling."

"Our production assistants do the first pass," Simon said. "They weed out the junk from anything potentially valuable."

"And when something makes the cut?" Polly asked.

"It goes to a specialist—furniture, jewelry, military, you name it. Then provenance gets involved to check its history and verify the story behind it."

"And if it's a dud?"

"We let the owner down gently. No need to crush dreams on camera."

"Even if their 'priceless Ming dynasty vase' came from the China Pavilion at Walt Disney World?"

"Especially then. We say things like, 'It's a charming piece with sentimental value,' or 'It reflects the style of the period beautifully,' which usually means it's not worth a penny. We've elevated gentle disappointment into a kind of performance art."

Polly nodded. "All right, so let's say someone brings in a potentially valuable piece. What happens then?"

"If it's legitimately interesting, meaning it's not only valuable, but has an intriguing backstory, or just makes for great TV, one of my segment producers steps in. Together, we decide what gets filmed. Not every appraisal makes the cut."

"So even if someone brings in a masterpiece, if it's not telegenic enough—?"

"Precisely," Simon confirmed. "If an object is visually dull or the owner is as lively as an unplugged lamp, we might pass. A rare 17th-century manuscript? Fascinating for scholars but a disaster on television. An exquisitely carved Georgian snuffbox? Lovely craftsmanship, but try keeping an audience awake while someone drones endlessly about tobacco products in the eighteen-hundreds." He waved a dismissive hand. "But if it's something dramatic—like a lost royal artifact, a piece of silverware from the Titanic, or a medieval sword with a bloodstain—then we definitely move forward."

"And after that...?"

"We prep for filming. We coach the guests a little—nothing scripted, just making sure they react naturally and don't turn to marble the moment the camera appears. The appraiser redoes the examination for the cameras, building suspense leading up to the valuation. And when they finally reveal the potential price? We hope for a gasp, tears, or—ideally—a stroke. I can dream."

Polly smiled, but inside, her pulse quickened. She had maneuvered Simon in the direction where she wanted him—talking freely, explaining things in a way he probably didn't even realize was illuminating. Every detail he offered was another chance to figure out exactly how deep the potential *Relic or Rubbish* rabbit hole went. "And I can dream of winning an Oscar," she said lightly, carefully masking her eagerness behind another fake sip of cappuccino.

"It's all about the theatrics," Simon agreed. "That's why we fact-check everything before it airs. Every valuation gets reviewed by our research team. If something turns out to be misidentified or overvalued, we fix it before it makes it to air. Of course, we couldn't do that with the live broadcast from Thistlethorne."

Polly's heart gave a little leap. There it was. The opening she wanted. She leaned in slightly. "And if a serious mistake occurs?"

Simon's expression darkened slightly. "We handle it."

"You correct it? Or pretend it never happened?"

Simon harrumphed. "We do what needs to be done."

Polly nodded slowly as if weighing his words. "Hmm. I imagine even the best experts get things wrong now and then." She gave an airy wave of her hand. "But it must be terribly embarrassing when, say, an appraiser dismisses something as being worthless, only for it to show up at auction fetching a heart-stopping sum."

Simon's jaw clenched. "That's rare."

"Of course," Polly agreed, her tone light. "But I hear it has happened. When someone on your team gets it spectacularly wrong—well, I imagine that's a bit of a headache for you." She took a thoughtful sip of her now completely cold cappuccino. "Take Isla Morton, for example. I've heard..."

A flicker of nervousness flashed across Simon's face, but he masked it. "Isla Morton is a respected researcher. And as I've already said, mistakes happen. No one is infallible."

Polly continued breezily as if she were merely making small talk. "And Diedre Paige, too—stellar reputations, both. But they've had a few...shall we say, 'wobbles'?"

Simon's gaze darkened. "Every appraiser on this show is vetted for their knowledge and expertise."

"Of course, sweetums, of course. No one would question their aptitude. I've botched my share of lines. But the trick," she said, with a tone in her voice that was far from innocent, "is selling it so well no one notices." She cocked her head, eyes narrowing ever so slightly. "I imagine that's second nature to someone in your position."

She let the moment stretch, then added, almost offhandedly, "Still, one can't help but notice when something is appraised for a pittance...and somehow reemerges, sparkling with provenance and fetching a king's ransom."

"Look, mistakes happen," Simon reiterated. "These aren't

automated calculations—we rely on human judgment. An item comes in looking unremarkable, the provenance isn't clear, maybe it's in poor condition, or the owner gives misleading information. If the right paperwork isn't there, or a key historical connection isn't known at the time, well..." He gave a small, dismissive shrug. "It's easy to make a mistake when you're working under the constraints of television."

"The tyranny of the shooting schedule?"

Simon's nostrils flared slightly. "I'm only saying that sometimes information comes to light after an appraisal has aired. Sometimes, it's a matter of research catching up. Other times, a previously unknown factor suddenly makes something valuable. It happens in the antique world all the time—context changes everything."

Polly's gaze remained steady. "And yet, with all the checks and balances you so thoroughly outlined earlier, those 'mistakes' still made it to air?"

"We agreed—no one is perfect."

Polly murmured with the faintest of smiles, "But when certain experts—reputable, experienced, trusted professionals—make those mistakes, well... someone might think that looks a bit less like stupid human error and more like—something else?"

"What 'something else'? What are you implying?"

Keeping her voice light, as though she were merely musing aloud, Polly dug in, getting specific. "Take Diedre Paige, for example. Such a sharp eye and a distinguished career in gemmology. And yet, she mistook an exquisite lavallière for costume jewelry, didn't she? Told the poor dear who owned it that it was charming but essentially worthless. What was the phrase I heard she used?" Polly tapped a finger against her chin in mock thought. "Ah, yes. 'A sweet little trinket, but more sentimental than significant.'"

Simon's lips pressed into a hard line. "Where are you getting your information?"

Polly ignored the question and continued, "And yet, three months later, the piece shows up at auction—authenticated, all scrubbed up and gleaming under Sotheby's brightest lights— and selling for a sum that would make a Saudi prince weep. A couple of mistakes are understandable. Even the best of us falter. But then there's Isla."

Simon was becoming exasperated. "Isla's been our head of provenance research for several years. She has an extremely challenging job. If she tells me an item isn't worth our time to value or put on the air, I trust her judgment."

"But it's still puzzling that Isla also grossly undervalued an Art Nouveau silver tea set. Told the chap who owned it that it was a mass-market reproduction when, in fact, it turned out to be an original Froment-Meurice. Quite a coup for the buyer who snapped it up right after the wrong valuation, don't you think?"

"That was an outlier," Simon exhaled sharply.

"Was it? Because then there was the matter of a William and Mary desk." Polly feigned an apologetic wince. "Oh, wait. Sorry. That one never even made it to on-air appraisal, did it? There was a difference of expert opinions."

"It was a reproduction," Simon said, indignant. "We can't afford to waste our time on inauthenticity."

"And yet," Polly sighed, "the private collector who acquired it somehow saw things very differently. In fact, he had it verified as a genuine late 17th-century piece, and as I understand it, it fetched quite a hefty price when he sold it at auction."

Simon's eyes flashed, but he forced a thin smile. "As I said, sometimes the value of an item changes with new information."

Polly let the words settle, then leaned in just a fraction more towards him. "Or sometimes, an item is never given the opportunity to be properly valued in the first place."

Simon tensed and his polished veneer cracked. "That's absurd," he snapped, his voice sharper now, laced with the controlled frustration of a man who had spent years navigating difficult conversations but was suddenly finding himself on the back foot with this one. "Every item brought to *Relic or Rubbish* is given due consideration. We don't dismiss objects on a whim. We have standards," Simon said flatly. "If an item doesn't meet the criteria for a segment—if it lacks provenance or is simply not compelling television—then we make editorial decisions."

"Editorial decisions," Polly echoed as if tasting the words. "Fascinating. And would you say that those decisions are always made purely for the integrity of the show?"

Simon's patience finally splintered. "I don't know what you're trying to say, Ms. Pepper, but *Relic or Rubbish* has been a respected program for a quarter of a century. We don't deal in conspiracy theories or baseless accusations."

Unfazed by Simon's outburst, Polly sat back. "I'm just trying to understand the intricacies of working on this show—if I'm to be part of it. I'm completely interested in your fascinating world. Though I do wonder—who gets to decide which treasures are allowed to shine and which ones are dismissed? That's you, isn't it?"

Simon's expression was now cold and guarded. "That's enough," he said, his tone brooking no further discussion.

Polly sensed she was getting closer to information Simon was afraid he might accidentally reveal. "Just think of the lavallière, the silver set, the William and Mary desk, and how many others? It's almost as if valuable pieces keep slipping through the cracks. Odd, don't you think?"

"Ms. Pepper, if you're suggesting there's some grand palace intrigue going on at *Relic or Rubbish*, I assure you—"

"Oh, sweetums, every workplace has its intrigue. One of the biggies at my old television show was, who kept stealing my parking space? But I find it curious that certain objects—valuable, significant—seem to be misidentified, overlooked, or dismissed entirely. I wish I could be one of those lucky buyers who hit the antiques jackpot."

Simon let out a short, humourless laugh. "You sound just like Arley Kingston..."

Polly's heart gave a sharp, unexpected jolt. "That wasn't necessarily a good thing?"

"Questions, questions, questions. Arley was always digging into appraisals and challenging valuations. Even on items he wasn't assigned or had no expertise in." Simon's gaze met Polly's—sharp, deliberate. "He challenged authority. And now...he's dead."

Polly kept her expression neutral, though her mind jolted into motion. Was Simon suggesting that Arley's curiosity had gone too far? The implication hung in the air like the final note of a warning bell. She let the weight of it settle. "You make it sound like curiosity's a workplace hazard on *Relic or Rubbish*."

Simon shook his head. "Not at all. I valued Arley. I really did. He brought heart to the show—something real. But others thought of him as threatening. The night before he died, I called him. I'd had a long talk with Isla earlier that day. She was unusually upset. Said Arley kept pressuring her—and others. Digging into provenance files that were already closed. Questioning her and her team's work."

He paused, visibly uneasy. "She didn't say it outright, but the implication was clear: It was my job to rein Arley in. So I told him—politely of course—to back off. To stop contradicting Isla and the other expert appraisers—especially on air. I said—quote— 'If you keep this up, someone's going to make damn sure you stop.' I just meant he'd get stonewalled. Sidelined. But now—I wonder if someone actually took it as far as Isla suggested."

Polly felt her stomach turn. *As far as Isla suggested?* Had Simon really just said that? What had Isla suggested, exactly? Or had that been merely a sarcastic quip? A careless remark in the heat of frustration? Had she genuinely warned Simon that Arley might suffer consequences for his relentless excavations? The more Polly turned the phrase over in her mind, the more it sounded like Isla had floated the possibility of shutting Arley down—and someone, somewhere, had taken that a step further.

Simon tried to regroup. "Arley just got so caught up in his work, he didn't realize when he was rocking the boat. He didn't chase camera time like the others or try to outshine anyone—he was just good at what he did. And that made things complicated."

"Complicated?" Polly asked, determined to keep him talking.

"There are people who've been with *Relic or Rubbish* for years. They've earned their stripes. Then, in walks this new guy, young, ridiculously knowledgeable, and telegenic as hell—and suddenly, he's getting a lot of the interesting pieces to value on camera. Not because I gave them to him, mind you—he was just the right expert for the piece. And some saw that as him muscling into their spotlight.

"So I called him to give him a heads-up. To tell him to let things breathe—especially during the upcoming *live* broadcast. I told him to listen more and speak less and not to jump in and contradict anyone—especially Isla. That not everyone wanted an eager young expert stirring the pot and publicly correcting them."

"And how did he take that?" Polly asked. "Was he offended? Upset?"

"The opposite," Simon let out a sigh. "He apologized. That's the thing. Arley wasn't some cocky upstart. He genuinely didn't want to bother anyone. He just...loved this work too much to pretend he didn't know when something was wrong or being misidentified."

"Do you think he took your message to heart?"

"I do. That was his nature."

The pause that followed felt different—no longer contemplative, but curt. Simon shifted in his chair and straightened a few papers on his desk. Polly recognized the move. She'd done it herself a thousand times when a conversation had played itself out.

"Look, Miss Pepper," Simon said, a tight smile forming as he glanced toward the office door, "I've been generous with my time..."

"You have!" Polly said, standing. "And please do give some consideration to what we discussed about my presenting *Relic or Rubbish*. Or perhaps a spin-off show? *Trash Talk, Estate Sale Smackdown, Antiques Road Rage*. I've got a million ideas, and you'll have another hit! It would be marvey to work with you!"

Simon rose with her. "We'll be in touch." Then, with a brief pause and a flicker of something unreadable in his tone, he added, "If only Arley had been a little more...clever. But I suppose by the time we spoke that night, it was too late. The damage was done." He offered a pleasant smile, already moving toward the door.

Polly stepped into the hallway, the door shutting with a click behind her. She took a breath—slow and steady—then squared her shoulders and started walking.

By the time we spoke that night, it was too late. The damage was done. What the heck? Polly wondered.

22

———

Polly stepped out of the London Broadcasting House offices and into the warm summer afternoon. The stately Georgian façades of Portland Place stretched to the left and right. She took a steadying breath, trying to shake off Simon's parting words, then slipped a hand into her clutch to retrieve her phone. She thumbed quickly through her contacts and pressed Tiara's number. "I'm ready," she said, her voice light despite the storm surging inside her head. "We have time to hit the Vesper Bar before our train. Momma needs something stiff —and I don't mean a Brit's upper lip."

The Vesper Bar at the Dorchester Hotel radiated with Art Deco elegance. Plush velvet banquettes in deep emerald and sapphire curved around small tables. A hand-painted mural of literary and cultural icons from the 1920s and '30s cast a watchful eye over the room. Polly and Tiara sat in a prime corner with their coupe glasses of champagne resting on a gleaming lacquered table. As Polly recounted her meeting with Simon, she swirled the pale gold liquid in her glass, watching the light from the chandelier refract through the drink.

Polly repeated Simon's ominous words, "'If only Arley had

been a little more...clever. But I suppose by the time we spoke that night, it was too late. The damage was done.'" Around them, the room carried on—laughter, clinking glasses, small talk—but something felt off-kilter.

Tiara's stomach twisted. "People don't say things like that unless part of them believes it. So maybe we're not the only ones thinking Arley's death was a little too tidy. But why be coy—unless he's scared? Or hiding something?" She glanced at Polly, voice dropping. "Let's say someone *did* want Arley out of the way. Maybe Diedre Paige, the gemmologist? They had history."

Polly nodded. "I thought about that. Diedre built her career on being an expert, and suddenly, this newcomer made her look careless. Or worse—incompetent."

"Or corrupt," Tiara added darkly. "If Arley suspected—or knew—she was involved with something illicit, she'd have every reason to see he didn't go public."

Polly sipped her drink. "Then there's Fabian Dupont..."

Tiara's mouth twisted. "Fabian? Please. He's about as exciting as plywood."

"I know, but he's been part of *Relic or Rubbish* for years. He's a fixture—respected, authoritative. If Arley was being brought in as a permanent appraiser, that meant someone else's airtime was about to shrink. Or worse—disappear altogether."

"Maybe even being replaced," Tiara finished, eyes widening. She set her glass down. "Maybe Fabian saw Arley as a threat to his livelihood?"

"What if all the appraisers did?" Polly mused, swirling the last of her champagne. "Think about it. The show has been running for years with the same experts—familiar faces and predictable segments. TV doesn't work like that forever. It evolves and thrives on novelty. *Relic or Rubbish* may have a loyal audience, but it's starting to feel like *The Lawrence Welk Show* just before it was axed for being out of step with the times.

Relic or Rubbish is practically glacial. Those poor guests sit down and are treated to a slow, reverent monologue about their biscuit tin, as though it's the Dead Sea Scrolls. Lovely for a nap, less so for ratings. People want authenticity these days, not a tranquilizer in tweed. That's why Arley was being brought in. He was young, brilliant, and, most importantly for television—watchable."

Tiara's brows lifted. "And maybe he was just the beginning of big changes for the show."

"Exactly," Polly said. "If the network were planning to shake things up—phase out the old guard and bring in a new generation of bright, camera-ready experts—Arley would've been just the beginning. And there'd be more like him waiting in the wings. That kind of change would probably make some people nervous."

"Imagine you've spent years cultivating your position as an appraiser on one of Britain's most beloved television programs," Tiara agreed. "You've built a reputation. A career. And suddenly, some shiny new thing swoops in and starts stealing the focus. We both know change isn't kind to older people."

"And if the producers were already talking about bringing in new blood, then all the appraisers would be feeling the pressure. Maybe they were even panicking. Panicked people do desperate things."

Tiara exhaled and stared into her drink. "So we've got professional jealousy, bruised egos, maybe even a fraud cover-up woven into the fabric of *Relic or Rubbish*. Toss in a bit of cast-thinning to chase a younger audience—and suddenly it's quite the cocktail."

Polly raised her glass. "Let's take a sip, darling, and find out who mixed it."

23

The two-hour late-afternoon rail journey from London to Abbots Clover was a strategy session for subtly interrogating Rosalind about her professional colleagues. To be effective, Polly knew she needed to be shrewd. She planned to play the role of curious bystander, letting casual conversation tease out the truth. And when she and Tiara arrived at Thistlethorne, they conveniently found Rosalind seated at the wrought-iron table on the patio, a novel open before her—though her gaze was locked somewhere in the distance.

"We're home," Polly announced the obvious while kicking off her shoes. "London was chaotic, as always. But it makes me appreciate the serenity of the countryside."

Rosalind blinked as if just noticing her. "Mm," she murmured, closing the book but not marking her place. "Fun trip?"

"A riot," Polly wisecracked, while reaching for the champagne glass Tiara had just filled. "I ran into your charming producer, Simon Belmore. Crazy coincidence," she lied. "We had a lovely chat."

That earned Rosalind's full attention. "Simon? Did he say anything about me? Or when I'd be released from limbo? When we're going back to work?"

"*Nada*," Polly said, swirling her champagne. "We mainly talked about Arley. I had no idea there was so much resentment toward him from some of the other appraisers."

"It's a particularly competitive industry," Rosalind said.

"I get it. But still, it was sort of eye-opening. You must have seen the conflicts firsthand."

Rosalind hesitated. "Polly, you, of all people, know show business is cutthroat. Did I witness the others' discontent with Arley? Sure. Was there a degree of envy and resentment? I'd say so. Did I hear talk about how much easier things would be without him? Sometimes."

"Did Arley know how the others felt?"

"Must have," Rosalind admitted. "But I don't think he realized how vexed they really were. He just kept doing his work—brilliantly—and assumed that, eventually, his sincerity and dedication would win people over—or at least make them understand him."

"Irritating others is one thing," Polly replied. "Making enemies is another."

Rosalind gave a slow nod. "*Relic or Rubbish* may seem genteel on the surface, but it's a machine—layered, political, and not always kind. Arley stepped into it with fresh ideas and a spotlight already chasing him. Not everyone appreciated that. Especially those who'd spent years carving out their territory and weren't keen to see it trampled by a rising star."

"So tell me, just how deep did those disgruntlements run?" Polly asked, raising her glass to Rosalind.

"You want me to air the show's dirty laundry?"

Tiara interjected with a slight cackle. "If you haven't figured it out by now, missy *lives* for dirty laundry. The stinkier, the better!"

Polly smiled in fiendish agreement. "So *Relic or Rubbish* isn't quite the refined little lovefest it pretends to be. Big egos, fragile reputations. The experts play nice for the cameras, but it's open season once the red light's off. Arley Kingston...the rising star... Simon said he 'stepped on toes.'"

"Not intentionally," Rosalind confirmed. "He just...didn't play the others' games. Fabian, Diedre, Ambrose, Clara—they've been on the show long enough to balance showmanship with their expertise. Arley didn't care about showmanship. He cared about authenticity. And sometimes that made certain people look rather bad."

"Meaning?"

"No one takes kindly to having their credibility questioned."

"And what about Simon? Was he encouraging Arley? Or trying to restrain him?" Polly asked.

"Simon—" Rosalind paused to gather her thoughts. "Let's just say Arley made for compelling television, and that's what Simon valued most. But others complained that he was...too unpredictable. He habitually went off script, following his instincts. That rattled a few."

"People like Clara Montague? Diedre Paige? Ambrose Carouthers? Fabian Dupont?"

"No one wants to be upstaged." Rosalind said.

"And did any of them ever say, in so many words, that they had it in for him," Polly asked.

"You're wondering if one of our expert appraisers might have had a hand in eliminating Arley from the show? They each complained at one time or another."

Polly drained her flute in one smooth motion, setting it down for Tiara to refill. "Darling, I rely on my instincts. Always have. I'm not psychic, but I am intuitive. I've spent my entire career reading between the lines of script dialogue and characters' interior dynamics. Knowing when someone's hiding something. Sensing when the air shifts just so. And right now? The air is thick with intrigue."

Rosalind studied her for a long moment. "That could be a dangerous way to think, Polly."

"Dangerous thinking is how people get ahead in showbiz, darling. We both know that. I've made a career out of knowing when someone's *acting*."

Then, almost reluctantly, Rosalind asked, "What does your 'dangerous thinking' tell you about Fabian Dupont? I know he doesn't seem like much. He's sort of a geezer. A long-time fixture on *Relic or Rubbish*. Maybe that is exactly why you *should* think of him."

Tiara nodded. "People who blend into the background are often the ones you need to watch the most. Maybe he thought his position on the show was secure—until Arley came along."

Rosalind nodded. "And let me enlighten you further. I overheard a conversation—one I wasn't meant to hear. It was after Arley had politely called Fabian out—again—on the historical facts surrounding a piece he'd appraised. He wasn't doing it to be difficult, but you've seen how Fabian overreacts. He was furious. He ranted to Clara Montague that Arley was a big problem for everyone. He was making all the professionals look like the old codgers they actually were. Out of step with the 21st century. Then he said something I found rather curious." Rosalind hesitated, as if weighing the potential consequences of revealing what she'd heard. "He said, 'If no one else is willing to put him out of *our* misery, maybe I will.'"

The air on the patio didn't just go taut—it snapped, charged with something dark and electric. Polly's mind reeled. A million thoughts rushed through her brain and suddenly, the summer evening didn't feel quite so warm. Fabian Dupont—the furniture appraiser, hadn't just seen Arley as competition. He had seen him as more than just a nuisance. A problem that needed solving. And he'd spoken of potentially eliminating that source of trouble.

"That sounds a lot like a threat *and* a possible motive," Tiara said. "Me-thinks you'll want to pay a wee visit to *Monsieur* Dupont to see how he fares when *he's* the one being appraised."

"Fabian isn't easy to corner," Rosalind murmured. "He's somewhat reclusive. If you want the best chance to locate him, don't look at his London studio. He spends as much time away from the city as possible. He has a cottage in Dorset. Disappears there on weekends and whenever the show isn't filming. But he's pretty introverted. Maybe even slightly agoraphobic. Doesn't like to leave home and isn't known for offering invitations."

"I don't wait for invitations," Polly said. "I show up with an excuse. An invitation means they're prepared for you. An excuse? That means you slip in under the radar—right when their guard's down."

Rosalind gave a soft laugh. "I know you have a reputation for getting what you want, Polly. But even you might have trouble if you don't know where to find him. He's tucked away down a narrow one-track lane in some speck of a village."

"I know you'll be a darling with the GPS coordinates."

Rosalind hesitated, then reached for her phone. "Fine. But you didn't get this from me." She tapped the screen a few times and slid it across the table. "It's somewhere around Shaftesbury. Secluded. Quiet. No prying eyes. The poor man's probably hiding from the press." Rosalind gave her a long look, then gathered her things. "Well, I need to make a few calls. Let me know if you find anything interesting."

Once she was gone, Tiara leaned in with a smirk. "And let me guess—you already have the perfect plan to lure Fabian into your web."

"A little admiration. A well-timed question about a Louis the Fifteenth writing desk. And the irresistible charm of our dear, handsome Tim."

"Of course you're using Tim as bait," Tiara said, not even pretending to be surprised.

"*Bait* is such an unsophisticated word. I prefer to think of Tim as an *asset*. I saw the way Fabian was eyeing him when *Relic or Rubbish* was here. Our Mr. Dupont appreciates fine craftsmanship—whether it be furniture or men.

Tiara laughed, shaking her head. "You are diabolical."

"I'm simply giving Fabian what he wants—a charming guest who happens to be interested in antiques. And if, in the process, he lets something slip about Arley Kingston, well...what a delightful bonus."

Tiara raised her glass, eyes gleaming. "To Fabian Dupont—who's about to be thoroughly examined for provenance, patina, and hidden flaws."

24

———

The drive to Broadwindsor, which was tucked into Dorset's rolling hills, was postcard pretty. Tim, however, was too busy white-knuckling the steering wheel to notice. He piloted the car with all the focus of a man performing brain surgery while riding a roller coaster, muttering under his breath about "driving on the wrong side of the road."

Polly, naturally ensconced in the backseat like visiting royalty, had assumed the role of navigator with her usual authority—and zero aptitude. "We're definitely close," she announced, peering at Google Maps on her phone. "Turn left at the next junction—or maybe it's right. It's hard to tell with these high hedgerows."

A quiet apprehension settled over the car as they followed the GPS instructions and turned down a narrow lane, the overgrown and unruly hedgerows on either side clawing at the car. The cottage at the end of the road was settled behind low, lichen-covered stone walls. The house was absurdly charming— a rambling rose climbing one side of a mullioned window, and a blue front door with a brass lion's head knocker. The gravel drive crunched beneath their tires as they pulled in.

"This makes sense," Tim muttered, eyeing the tidy window boxes and the lavender neatly trimmed along the walk. "He struck me as a country mouse sort of guy. Perfectly content with his jam jars and geraniums. Until someone from the big bad world—like us—turns up at his door."

Polly stepped out of the car, smoothing her slacks. "I've met enough country mice to know they can bite when cornered."

Tiara adjusted her oversized sunglasses and surveyed the property. "I still say we should've brought a Bundt cake. It's the only way to make a surprise visit seem wholesome."

The trio approached the front door along a flagstone path. Polly rang the bell, and after a long pause, it creaked open just wide enough to reveal Fabian Dupont. Dressed in pressed linen trousers and a pale blue shirt with his sleeves rolled neatly to the elbow, he squinted at the group on his doorstep. "You're not dressed well enough to be Jehovah's Witnesses," he muttered, before his eyes settled more clearly on Polly. "Oh, it's you!"

"The one and only," Polly beamed.

"And young master Tim," he added, his covetous eyes drifting appreciatively over Tim. "This is a...surprise."

"We were in the area, and I'd heard you lived around here in an oh-so-charming cottage," Polly said. "The Anglophile in me just had to see it for herself! Plus, I missed the opportunity to get to know you better during the short week you and *Relic or Rubbish* were at Thistlethorne. We'll keep it brief. Just a quickie social visit, and we'll tootle on."

Fabian's gaze flicked back to Tim, who offered a perfectly timed smile and ran a hand through his artfully mussed hair. The top two buttons of Tim's shirt—already undone when they'd left home—had somehow become three, expressly for Fabian. "Excuse my manners," Fabian said. "Since you've come all this way...I'll serve tea."

Polly smiled. *Operation Fabian* was officially underway.

The interior of Fabian's cottage was as refined and picturesque as its postcard-perfect exterior. Though modest in size, it exuded timeless charm, as if a cover photo from *Country Living* magazine had come to life. The small sitting room boasted an inglenook fireplace flanked by narrow bookshelves, their contents neatly arranged. A Louis the Fifteenth settee upholstered in faded rose damask sat beneath the window, and the air carried the faint scent of lavender and old paper.

As they walked through, Fabian narrated a tour—pointing out a Georgian *escritoire* he'd restored himself, a rare pair of Empire bronze candlesticks, and a Regency breakfast table that gleamed in the late morning light. The kitchen, though small, featured gleaming copper pans and a farmhouse sink deep enough to bathe a spaniel.

The back garden, accessed through a Dutch door, was nothing short of a manicured jewel box. The grass was verdant green, bordered by beds of peonies, foxglove, and geraniums. Bumblebees danced lazily between the blooms. A wrought-iron table and chairs sat center stage on the patio. Fabian paused there, letting the moment breathe, his pride in the place unmistakable.

Polly took it all in with a serene expression. "If antiques ever stop paying the bills, you could open a botanical retreat," she said.

"I may have to," he agreed. "This old place might end up doing more for me than my pension." He glanced around with affection in his eyes. "But for now, this is my sanctuary. When the television cameras and city noise become too much, this is where I remind myself that not everything valuable needs appraising."

It was obvious to the threesome that Fabian wasn't thrilled about playing host. He lived for order and for solitude. His days were arranged for self-indulgence. Unexpected guests, no matter who they were, unsettled the symmetry. But social protocols prevailed, so he offered them Earl Grey, in bone china cups, and a slice of almond-and-lemon drizzle cake (which he'd planned to enjoy all to himself. Darn it all!).

Polly let her fingertips graze the rim of a delicately painted saucer as she admired the tea service Fabian had laid out—Wedgewood with gilt trim. "This is all quite divine, Fabian," she said, tilting her head as she surveyed the garden blooms. "I must say, you live in pure serenity."

Fabian smiled thinly as he poured the tea. "Serenity must be curated like anything else. Carefully. Intentionally. Especially when your professional life is full of...noise."

"Noise. That's a tactful way to put it," Polly said, nodding." She sipped her tea, staying silent for a moment, hoping that calm might help Fabian engage. "And speaking of noise," she tried to sound affable, "there was certainly a lot of it when *Relic or Rubbish* visited us at the castle last week! I've always been fascinated with the inner workings of live TV shows. I remember my own experience and how audiences only see polished results. But the backstage is far more fun and colorful. Don't you agree?"

"I suppose," Fabian said, starting to warm slightly to his guests. "But it's probably similar in any workplace. Clashing egos. Frantic deadlines. Everyone secretly plotting—or wishing for another's downfall."

"Tensions run high when putting on a show," Polly agreed. "Especially when new faces pop in. I had a new guest star every week on *The Polly Pepper Playhouse*—my hit TV show in America, in case you didn't know. Donny Osmond, Jerry Hall, and even Petula Clark. Every one of them came in trying to make an impression, stir the pot, or steal a little more screen time."

She set her cup down. "Arley Kingston—bless him—must have been like a guest star on your show. But I heard he was about to trade guest status for a permanent member of the troupe. That would have been marvelous for him."

Fabian hesitated, just long enough for that to register. "Permanent. Yes, that would have been lovely for him," he said distantly, sipping his tea. "You know, people assume we appraisers earn lots of money for appearing on *Relic or Rubbish*. But the truth is, we're paid a pittance. Just enough to cover travel expenses and keep one's dignity intact. The real currency is visibility. Reputation. A clip that goes viral. A lecture booking or two after an especially clever on-air remark. All the experts rotate on the program throughout the year...in different cities and at different events. They stagger us, depending on availability and specialty."

He glanced across the table, his tone turning slightly brittle. "That's why we all wanted a regular spot on the program. *Permanent* would mean much more airtime, more influence—and bigger paydays. But that position was non-existent. Rosalind Fenwick was the only full-time regular. Then along comes Arley Kingston. Young. Handsome. Media-ready. And he was offered what the rest of us had been auditioning years for."

Fabian, who was more than willing to engage at this point, continued, "No, he didn't ruffle feathers, dear. He uprooted the entire pecking order."

Polly's brain seized on Fabian's apparent resentment about Arley's advancement on the show. "I get it," she said innocently. "Nobody likes a maverick. They disrupt the rhythm. Or shine light where some would rather keep the curtains drawn."

"But good for Arley—if that's what the network wanted." Fabian tried to sound supportive. "I mean, it *would have been good* for him. "He was a lovely young man. Very talented. Very enthusiastic. Such a pity."

"Pity's one word for it," Polly replied, with an empathetic smile she hoped would help Fabian relate to her. "Your producer, Simon Belmore, suggested he was undermining established roles. Apparently, Arley had a habit of correcting his colleagues' appraisals. On camera. That must have bothered some of you."

"That was Arley's nature. I didn't take it personally. I don't think any of us did. He couldn't help himself. He just wanted everyone to do the best job they could. That's what we all want. I was probably the same way when I started out a quarter century ago. Audiences love youthful exuberance. And now...well, I'm old. My experience and vast knowledge mean nothing. And the time will soon come...Anyway, I don't know how the others dealt with Arley's meteoric rise. I'm not really close with any of them. And I don't involve myself in idle gossip or administrative decisions. That's above my pay grade. I do my job. I go home. I have a life."

Lulled by the warm sun on her face, Polly was momentarily silent, but the feeling that something was off nagged at her. Why was Fabian feigning indifference about Arley and his future on *Relic or Rubbish*? He was obviously bothered. She smiled at him, serene and bright. "Of course," she said smoothly, "I understand the need to keep one's head down at work. I spent decades in Hollywood and saw how quickly the landscape shifts when someone younger, shinier, and just naïve enough not to know better suddenly starts getting all the attention." Her gaze drifted toward the garden, then returned to Fabian. "It must have come as a shock when Arley suddenly died. He was way too young."

Fabian nodded. "None of us knows when our hour will come. Life has a way of—rearranging the cast so to speak." He gave a small, humorless smile as though that explained everything.

Polly was watching him carefully. "Though sometimes, it feels less like fate."

"People underestimate how punishing the job is," Fabian

said. "The pressure to be brilliant, camera-ready, authoritative—all at once. It grinds you down. Perhaps especially for someone like Arley. He wanted perfection. He took everything so—seriously."

"But not all stress ends with a death certificate," Polly said, letting the words breathe, her gaze unblinking. "Unless, of course, something—or someone—adds to it." There it was again—that subtle shift in Polly's tone, the one that moved from curiosity about Arley's character to the circumstances of his death.

Why, Polly wondered, *does Fabian seem so uncomfortable with this conversation?* With her eyes never leaving him, she stayed on track. "Do you remember the evening Arley died?" she asked. "Of course you do. I should too, but everything happened so quickly. I really have almost zero recall of the event. All the commotion. The sirens."

Fabian didn't respond verbally, just adjusted the angle of the cake plate slightly, as if it required perfect symmetry.

Polly continued, "I remember the director, Chad, yelling for someone to call medical. But otherwise..." She gave a soft, helpless shrug. "It's all foggy. Can you recall exactly what happened?" Her tone had just enough innocence to keep the question from sounding loaded. Just enough pause to make it feel like a question from someone lost in the haze of a traumatic moment.

"I was seated at another appraisal table at the far end of the marquee," Fabian said. "I was reviewing the next item on the docket. I only *heard* the commotion. I didn't *see* anything."

Polly's brow creased, a trace of mock confusion playing at the corners of her mouth. "Arley's French clock was supposed to be the final segment of the evening. Why were you prepping another valuation?"

"Isla said there was a last-minute submission. A Victorian

mahogany side table. She told me Simon was going to pull Arley's segment."

Fabian's words were circling in Polly's head. She let the silence linger—just long enough to become noticeable—then, her tone airy, as if they were merely chatting about a film they'd half-enjoyed, "Does Simon often involve himself in the assignment of valuations?"

"Of course. Simon's the ringmaster," Fabian said. "He runs the whole circus. Producer, showrunner, crisis manager, PR wrangler. He stitches every thread of *Relic or Rubbish*. Casting, scheduling, valuations—we're all just pieces on his game board. He chooses who gets air-time. He approves the items. He knows who's handling what and when. And if something goes wrong— if an object is misattributed..." Fabian faltered, catching himself mid-flow. "Well, he's the head honcho."

Polly narrowed her eyes. "If Simon's the captain steering the ship, then he gets the credit when things go well—and should take the blame when they don't." She paused for a short moment. "Like that fiasco with Diedre's lavallière. Misidentified on national television? That wasn't just a slip—it was a full-on crash. And if Simon's in charge, well...the fallout lands in his lap. But did it?"

"You're referring to the necklace she dismissed as costume jewelry," Fabian said, rising from his chair. "Yeah, not her most brilliant moment. We all make mistakes from time to time." He strolled to a potted begonia, studying the bright petals with forced interest, as though hoping the flowers might absorb some of Polly's scrutiny.

"What about the Art Nouveau silver tea set?" Polly pressed. "Isla had said it was a reproduction. And that William and Mary desk? It never even made it to camera. Both were deemed inauthentic but turned out to be valuable originals."

"Those were anomalies. A tiny fraction of the valuations we

make each season. Simon understood that which is why he protected—I mean defended—the experts."

"But those errors weren't just embarrassing—they were costly. Arley never made mistakes like that, did he? Tell me, when those errors happened, did you think they were merely carelessness? What did the network suits say? How about the provenance research team? Could anyone have benefited from those slips?"

"Nobody benefits from mistakes," Fabian snapped, returning to his chair at the table.

"Except when a piece is dismissed as worthless—and then quietly goes to auction by someone lucky enough to have bought it for a song."

"When something is incorrectly appraised, that's regrettable —but it's never deliberate," Fabian said. "We live by a professional code. Valuations are given in good faith, with the information we have at the time. We don't have crystal balls."

"But you have provenance databases," Polly reminded him. "And networks of collectors. And friends in the auction world who know how to spot an undervalued gem. How could there ever be such big mistakes?"

Fabian's eyes narrowed. "I hope you're not suggesting one of us would intentionally misidentify a piece for personal gain."

"Darling, I'm not suggesting anything unscrupulous. Of course not. Just wondering aloud. Might someone be tempted to undervalue a piece, then quietly flip it at auction? Or perhaps Simon simply misassigned items, giving the wrong expert the wrong object and letting the chips fall where they may?" Her eyes met his, steady and bright. "That William and Mary desk you were supposed to value on air, for example..."

"That desk wasn't suitable for the show," Fabian almost barked. Trying to cover his tone, he sat back, took a breath, and calmly explained, "That desk was an aberration. We don't get weeks to study each piece before we appraise them on camera. It's television, not a courtroom." He reached for more tea to further settle his nerves but changed his mind. "As for flipping pieces at auction—do you honestly think any of us would risk our reputations for a payout that barely covers a weekend in the Cotswolds? We're professionals, not opportunists." He offered a tight smile, but the flush creeping up his face told a different story.

Not one to fold, Polly persisted, "But that desk turned out to be genuine. Arley was prepared to go to bat for it."

Instead of answering, Fabian shot back, "So what if we disagreed about its value? Or about everything else?" Fabian tried to catch his temper from flaring, but it was too late.

Polly dug deeper. "So you and Arley *were* at odds with each other?"

"Not at all!" Fabian spat. "But he embarrassed some people —including me—with his knowledge. And yes, he made a few of us look foolish. That William and Mary piece I was set to appraise—I wasn't convinced it was genuine. He was."

Polly watched closely. The veneer was cracking. His voice had gone tight, clipped around the edges. "And he was right," she said. "Even though furniture appraisal wasn't his strongest area of expertise. But it was yours."

"Yes! All right! I was wrong!" Fabian spat. "Are you happy?"

Tim shifted in his seat, his posture alert, no longer just playing the part of charming tagalong. He casually asked, "Where were you *really* when Arley died?"

"Where was I—*really*?" Fabian exploded. "I told you! Preparing another appraisal. What are you insinuating? That I —or someone—had something to do with Arley's death?" He gave a brittle laugh, more air than sound. "The experts on our show are many things—petty, irritable, occasionally unkind. But no one among us could harm that young man if we tried. We mentored him. I argued with him, yes, like everyone else. But he had real talent. All of us would have happily taken credit for nurturing him, not...disposing of him."

Polly's tone was pure velvet. "Fabian, I have no doubt you were proud of Arley. It's satisfying to watch someone with genuine talent rise in their area of expertise. But sometimes with rising stars come shifting shadows. The more Simon used Arley on the show, the less time there was for you and the others. Fewer segments. Fewer appearances. Less income.

"That kind of meteoric success can unsettle those who've been in the spotlight a long time and see their starlight dimming." Her voice was still soft, but her words were forceful. "I know several of the experts were embarrassed when Arley found fault with their valuations. And I think he was very close to revealing something more...something someone didn't want revealed."

Fabian's face drained of color. He drew in a breath, steadying himself. "You sit here, tossing out suspicion like bait, hoping I bite—insinuating that I, or one of my colleagues, could've done something vile. Arley was respected. Admired. If he ruffled feathers, it's because he was damn good at his job." He pushed back his chair and stood. "I think you've overstayed your welcome."

Tiara blinked. Tim gave a quick glance toward Polly, then fiddled with the cuff of his sleeve—but Polly remained serene. She stood slowly, brushing imaginary cake crumbs from her skirt. "Thank you for the tea, Fabian. You've been very gracious... and illuminating."

Stiff and silent, Fabian ushered them back through the cottage to the front door. When the trio stepped outside, Polly turned once more to say goodbye, but the door had already closed.

"Well, that was awkward," Tiara said when they reached the car.

The drive home unfolded in a hush. Afternoon light stretched long across the hedgerows, and the fields rolled by in shades of green and yellow. Tim eased up on the accelerator for a blind curve, his hands steady on the wheel. "You think Fabian had something to do with Arley's death, don't you," he said, not quite a question, not quite an accusation.

"I think Fabian knows something about Arley's death. But he strikes me as more of an accomplice type—if anything."

Tim grinned despite himself. "You do love your supporting-character suspects."

Polly gave a faint smile. "The villain is rarely center stage, darling. They usually keep a low profile—watching from the wings. Waiting."

The car finally turned onto the familiar road leading into Abbots Clover, the spire of St. Clematis just visible through the trees. Beyond that, Thistlethorne rose like a dream, but Polly's mind was elsewhere. "I think I need to talk to Isla next. If someone was deliberately skewing the appraisals, she'd either be complicit—or she'd have seen the signs. I'm told she's a clever girl."

25

The late afternoon sun was beginning to soften into evening when they drove through the main gate archway at Thistlethorne Lodge—only to be met by the unexpected sight of a cherry-red Range Rover in the car park. A vehicle none of them recognized.

As the troupe stepped out of the car, Mr. Boots emerged from the shrubbery and trotted over with an indignant "meow," then paused dramatically to glare at the unfamiliar vehicle. The cat turned his back on it entirely. His message clear: *Not approved!*

"Who's the pretty kitty? You are! You are!" Polly cooed to Mr. Boots, reaching down to scratch behind his ears. "And who belongs to the Rover, hmm?"

Mr. Boots gave her a flat, unimpressed blink, followed by an exaggerated lick of his paw and a leisurely grooming session. *No idea, lady. But he looks like one of those Gen Z-ers: all teeth, tan, and tragically, little substance.*

As Polly and her posse entered the house, a quiet murmur of conversation drifted in from the direction of the patio—low, relaxed, and punctuated by Rosalind's familiar, melodic voice. They followed the sounds through to the garden, where the air carried the scent of thyme and roses.

Rosalind sat on a cushioned wicker chair, her legs elegantly crossed, holding a glass of white wine. But the man beside her drew the eye—young, tall, and distractingly handsome, with the kind of golden tan that suggested both leisure and confidence. His obviously custom-tailored pale-blue linen shirt clung sheath-like to imply a well-sculpted torso beneath—one gym mirrors likely admired as much as he did.

Everything about him, from the ease of his posture to his long-*ish* hairstyle and the amused gleam in his eye, suggested someone used to being looked at. He exuded that effortless magnetism that turned heads without trying. He had the self-assurance of someone born with charm—and bored by how easily it worked on others.

Tim came to a full-body halt mid-stride. "Oh-my," he breathed. Then, forgetting his usual languid composure, he surged forward so quickly that he clipped the side of the French door with his hip. "Hi! Hello!" He offered his hand with too much enthusiasm and a slightly dazed grin. "I'm Tim. I live here. Well, with Polly and Tiara. My mother. Our maid. Oh, it's not what it sounds like...I'm quite capable of..."

The visitor stood, smiling like someone who knew exactly what his smile did to people. "Ethan Grant," he said, taking Tim's hand. "Rosalind's son."

Tim blinked. "Ethan. Of course. I've seen pictures online. Not that I've been looking...I mean, I wasn't stalking you or anything..." he stammered, as Polly and Tiara exchanged barely suppressed smirks.

Rosalind stood, smoothing the hem of her blouse. "Polly, I'd like to introduce my son, Ethan. He popped down from London for a surprise visit. Isn't that...lovely."

The pause was almost imperceptible. But Polly caught it. There was something guarded in Rosalind's posture, something about the way she angled herself ever so slightly away from her son, as though still deciding how welcome the surprise really was.

Ethan extended a hand to Polly. "I've heard a lot about you, Ms. Pepper. Even saw some of your television work on YouTube. Brilliant!"

"I'm all ears for flattery, dear," she said before glancing at Rosalind—who smiled dutifully. Still, something in her eyes didn't match the occasion. It wasn't exactly unease, but it wasn't joy or pride either. Polly knew that even pleasant surprises sometimes arrive with heavy baggage.

Ethan turned his attention to Tim, who was hovering just a little too close and pretending to look entirely casual about it. "I've seen on Instagram that you're a party planner in Beverly Hills. That must be amazing. You must know lots of rich people. Anyone really famous?" he said, with a bewitching kind of eye contact.

"I—yeah. Guilty. That's me." Tim ran a hand through his hair and gave a little laugh. "I'm Polly's handy-dandy live-in wardrobe consultant and emotional support pet, too. You know how it is...whatever's needed. Probably not that much different than you and your mum."

Tiara watched the exchange with a wary eye and the faintest twitch of concern. She knew that look on Tim's face: starstruck with a side of possibility. Under different circumstances, it might've been cute—except Tim was involved with police constable Grayson Jenkins. And Tiara had plans for them. Capital-*P* plans. The kind you don't leave up to fate—or handsome distractions in fitted linen shirts.

"Tiara is just about to start thinking about dinner, aren't

you?" Polly said smoothly, slipping into hostess mode with practiced grace. "Ethan must join us."

"I'd love to. If it's no trouble," Ethan said, settling back into his chair. "I booked a table at the Fox & Hare—where I'm staying—but I'd much rather spend time with my mother. And her interesting friends, of course."

"Dinner will be far more entertaining here," Polly predicted, ending the matter with a casual wave. "Besides, the Fox & Hare overcooks everything and under-seasons what's left." She caught a brief flicker in Rosalind's expression—something between surprise and reluctance—before the mask of maternal fondness returned. Rosalind might have said it was lovely to see her son, but she perhaps hadn't entirely wanted his company.

Tiara, watching the subtle play of faces, took a small step closer to Tim and gave him a smile that looked sweet but meant business. "Ask Gray to join us," she said lightly, as if it had just occurred to her. "That would make an even five: boy, girl, boy, girl." She paused, then added with a pointed little twinkle, "Well —nearly even."

Tim blushed, the tips of his ears giving him away before the rest of his face caught up. He gave Tiara a glance—half grateful, half caught. He knew exactly what she was doing.

And she was right.

By the time the sun had dipped low over the castle walls and the wine on the patio table had begun to breathe, the sound of a car on the gravel forecourt signaled Gray's arrival. He knocked at the front entrance at exactly 7:00, wearing what he called his "civvies"—dressy jeans and a white Oxford-cloth shirt with the sleeves rolled up to his wrists—holding a bottle of wine and wearing a sparkle in his eyes. Tim answered, and there was just enough time for him to give Gray a quick rundown on the guests before they stepped onto the patio. Ethan stood as they approached, an easy grin spreading across his face. Gray leaned into Tim and whispered, "You weren't joking," as he sized Ethan up.

"You must be Gray. I'm Ethan—Rosalind Fenwick's son," he said, offering a hand and his self-assured, movie-star smile.

"Grayson Jenkins. Tim's boyfriend." The words weren't boastful—territorial perhaps—but unmistakably clear. Gray's tone carried the quiet confidence of someone not interested in playing anyone's games.

There was a pause, just long enough for the subtext to settle. Then Ethan gave a small nod and flashed a wider grin, this time directed at Tim, as Gray turned to greet the others with a polite nod of his own.

Twilight deepened by slow degrees, and the festoon lights over the patio flickered on automatically, casting a golden haze that softened the outlines of Thistlethorne's ancient stone walls. The scent of honeysuckle soon mingled with Tiara's grilled lemon-and-rosemary chicken, and conversation rose and fell in gentle waves. Plates were filled, chicken bones nudged to the edges, and roasted vegetables ignored. The wine had been topped up more than once. Everyone, it seemed, had found their conversational lane. It was the kind of evening that invited stories—half-true, half-remembered, all enhanced by vino.

Tiara, one arm draped loosely over the back of her chair, was telling a tale that had the unmistakable shape of a setup for a punch line. "...and that," she declared, eyes sparkling, "is how Polly Pepper ended up dangling from a chandelier in full Marie Antoinette drag on national television."

The table erupted in laughter. Grayson nearly spat out his

wine, and Ethan clapped louder than necessary and said, "Oh, I need to see that footage! You could do something with it! Make some money!"

"It was a special effects malfunction," Polly explained. "The chandelier was meant to just shimmer, not swing. And the wig was only supposed to catch fire." With a glint in her eye, she added, "My ratings went through the roof. And it earned me my seventh Emmy."

Laughter and admiration circled the table, warm and wine-loose, as Polly wore the satisfied smile of someone who knew she had an audience in the palm of her hand.

Ethan, meanwhile, had passed from charming to performative. His wineglass seemed to refill itself, whether by his own hand or through gravitational pull. And his shirt had slipped another button south. He gave another soft laugh at the story. But when the attention drifted back to Polly, he shifted in his seat, visibly restless. He found it unbearable to orbit someone with more magnetism than him—unless he could outshine them with volume.

"I'm telling you, you could monetize that on TikTok or YouTube," he declared, a little more insistent than necessary. He pointed a casual finger at Polly as if bestowing a marketing tip. "I could produce the segments. Seriously. You don't even need talent—it's all timing. You post the right content at the right moment, with the right hashtags—boom. Ten thousand views. Maybe a hundred thousand. Sponsorships. Travel perks. Brand deals. You name it."

Ethan, blissfully unaware that he'd just dismissed Polly's genuine talent and lived experience, topped off his glass and sat back, clearly pleased with himself. He had no idea who Polly Pepper was—not really. Or worse, he did and couldn't imagine anyone over forty being relevant without algorithmic assistance and a trending video.

The silence that followed wasn't long, but it was heavy—with awkwardness. Ethan's comment hadn't just missed the mark; it had insulted the very thing Polly was celebrated for: comedy. Around the table, the others shifted in their seats, unsure whether to challenge him or simply pretend he hadn't spoken.

Tiara said nothing, choosing instead to take a slow sip of wine, her eyes fixed somewhere over the rim of her glass.

Grayson glanced at Polly briefly, subtly as though checking to see if she needed him to jump in and set things right.

She didn't.

Polly's smile didn't waver. She waited, studying her plate like it might offer her the right seasoning for what she was about to verbally serve. "Well," she said at last to Ethan, her voice sounding amused and almost sweet, "it's always lovely when someone believes in the magic of reinvention. Especially when they're still working on their own first act."

The air shifted—just slightly. A fork paused in mid-air. Tiara glanced sideways with a small, but admiring, smile, like someone watching a seasoned actress land a monologue with a dagger tucked into the punch line. Rosalind said nothing. And Ethan? He beamed, missing the point entirely. "Exactly!" he said, raising his glass in triumph. "We'd make a great team."

Tim and Gray exchanged knowing looks, and Polly, serene as ever, sipped her wine as if nothing had happened.

Rosalind gave a tight smile, but the tension in her posture gave her away. Not quite shame—more the weary discomfort of a mother accustomed to smoothing over the edges of her son's obliviousness.

Ethan, still blissfully unaware, had already slipped his phone into his lap and begun scrolling.

There was a small pause—just long enough to register—

before Rosalind leaned in slightly toward Polly, her voice a touch too casual. "So...you stopped by Fabian Dupont's today. How'd it go? He can be rather...florid."

"Mm. That he can." Polly gratefully accepted this new topic of conversation. "He wasn't too pleased to see us at first. But he warmed up—before he went completely sub-zero. We actually had quite an enlightening visit," Polly continued, her tone light and almost conversational. "Naturally, we spoke about Arley." She paused just long enough to draw attention without seeming theatrical. "Fabian called him brilliant, of course—but also a bit disruptive. Apparently, Arley had a habit of challenging the experts. And while that kind of spark makes for good television, it doesn't always make for popularity among colleagues."

She let the words linger a moment, then added, "It does make you wonder, doesn't it? If someone felt their position was threatened as Arley's star continued to rise."

Rosalind's expression flickered—briefly—and Polly was watching. "It was the way Fabian talked about him," Polly continued. "Almost as if the fact that Arley's unerringness in his valuations was somehow a flaw."

"Well, no one enjoys being outshone, do they," Rosalind said. "I think the others felt Arley was rising too fast. He was getting a permanent spot on the program, and someone else was probably soon to be shown the door."

Ethan, half-listening now, leaned forward. "Are we talking about the dead dude?"

"He had a name," Rosalind said with an edge to her voice. "Arley Kingston. He was a colleague. And a friend. Please try to be respectful." *For once.*

"Right," Ethan said, unfazed. "Bit of a mess, that one."

Rosalind opened her mouth to speak, but Ethan—on his way to intoxication and flushed with self-importance—cut in before she could. "Honestly, I don't see what the big deal was with the guy. I heard nobody really liked him. Isla said he poked his nose into things that weren't any of his business. Wanted to cross-check records, ask questions, dig into old paperwork—all the boring stuff no one cares about. Some people just don't know when to shut up and stay in their lane."

Rosalind looked as though she might chastise him. But instead, she reached for her water glass. She didn't speak—just took a sip, as if willing the tension to dissolve before it could unravel the mood entirely.

"Maybe Arley was just being diligent to better inform his appraisal decision-making," Tim suggested.

Ethan snorted, rolling his eyes. "Oh, please. He wasn't working for the bloody Heirloom Enforcement Agency or anything. He just liked making people squirm. Isla said he had this whole, 'I'm on to you' vibe." Ethan shrugged. "Who knows? Maybe he thought someone was passing off fakes, or something equally pointless—insider stuff. She said he was stirring things up. Working on some big deal...or whatever. Then he croaks, so—guess that's the end of that. Problem solved, right?"

The table went still. No clink of cutlery. Just the distant sound of birdsong.

"Did Isla really say that?" Polly asked. "That Arley's death was 'a problem solved'?"

"Well—I mean, maybe she didn't say it exactly like that, but —yeah, something was brewing," Ethan said, stumbling as he tried to pull back what he had let slip. "Isla said he was maybe putting something together. Like maybe a sort of—proof of concept."

"Fascinating," Polly murmured. "And Isla told you all this when? I thought you weren't seeing each other anymore."

"Sure," Ethan said, waving a hand. "I still see her sometimes. When she gets lucky. Ha-ha! We work together on stuff. She's weirdly stressed for someone who basically works in a filing room."

"Isla works in the provenance office," Rosalind said stiffly, "where she's responsible for verifying the historical legitimacy of every item that passes through the show. But I imagine that kind of detail work might seem stress-free and invisible to some."

Ethan grinned, missing the jab entirely.

Now Rosalind looked at her son with something between pity and disappointment. "Funny how the most interesting things are often said by people who aren't even trying."

Ethan *had* said too much. But more importantly—he hadn't realized it.

In her own investigative world, Polly was silently ruminating on what Ethan had said about Arley's possible covert endeavors: *Someone passing off fakes, maybe. Or something equally pointless—insider stuff.*

As for his phrase *proof of concept*, she'd only ever heard that when someone was pitching a TV pilot or product endorsement —a preliminary demonstration of how a show or advert would be presented: *"We're putting together a sizzle reel as a* proof of concept—*just enough to show the network how the format would work and that we've got something fresh."*

She sat very still. Ethan's words had struck a chord. He'd tossed them out as if he were pitching a social media stunt. But the more Polly turned it over in her mind, the more he made some sort of sense. It was tech-speak. Media jargon. But it potentially revealed something more important.

The late evening air had turned cool, and the festoon lights glowed softly against the inky sky. The patio, previously alive with laughter and clinking glasses, had fallen quiet. The faint hoot of a barn owl marked the late hour. Polly set her napkin on the table and announced, "Well, what a fascinating dinner this turned out to be. Thank you all for coming—and contributing to the fun. We'll have to do it again soon. I simply love what some people say...when they think no one's paying attention."

She rose smoothly to her feet—gracious and composed, but inside, her thoughts were racing. She'd just found another thread—one she hadn't known she was looking for.

26

Morning arrived and the breakfast room was subdued. Blueberry muffin crumbs were scattered on plates. Polly's Bloody Mary was drained, the celery stalk slumped to one side. Tim sipped his Red Bull, eyes half on his phone. Tiara played with a grape. Sunlight glinted off a silver toast rack. No one said a word—but it wasn't awkward. Just the easy, unhurried silence of people who didn't need to fill the air with words.

Then Rosalind appeared in the doorway. "Morning," she said weakly, heading straight for the chair she'd unofficially laid claim to. She sat, reached for the teapot, and sighed. "I need to say something about last night. Ethan wasn't exactly at his best. I'm sorry on his behalf. He won't remember it or think he did anything wrong. He's always been like his father—convinced his good looks and charm are a free pass to act as he pleases. Rules don't apply if you can smile your way past them."

Tiara offered a shrug. "He's young. *Ish.* We've all had our moments."

"Ethan's not the first man to confuse attention with admiration," Polly said, expanding on Tiara's comment about misguided youth. "You and I perform on television. Some have to settle for the dinner table."

"Thank you," Rosalind said. "And thank you for not setting fire to him last night. Although he deserved to be singed."

As Tim cracked open another Red Bull, he thought, *how did I almost fall for that guy*? Last night, he'd seen it all plainly: Ethan's narcissism, the slick charm, the way everything about him was a performance. And yet, somehow, Tim had been momentarily dazzled by cheekbones and eye winks. He groaned inwardly. *I've lived in Hollywood most of my life, for crying out loud. I should have antibodies against that stuff!*

Rosalind stirred her tea, as she offered more insight. "He didn't come down from London because he missed me or anything sentimental like that," she said. "He came to pitch another of his grand schemes. He wants backing. He's convinced he's launching a game-changing platform for online antique sourcing—pop-up valuations, influencer tie-ins. That sort of thing. Said he's calling it AntiqueX. Does every start-up now need an X?"

Polly suppressed a laugh. "AntiqueX sounds like a dating app for emotionally unavailable furniture."

"Swipe right on a Regency commode," Tim joked.

"He says it's a 'marketplace-slash-content-platform-slash-*curated* experience,'" Rosalind explained. "I don't think he even knows what any of that means. He wants to offer exclusive access for collectors before items go to auction. Says it'll 'revolutionize the antique *ecosystem*.' His words, not mine."

"Exclusive access to what? *The Mona Lisa*?" Polly asked.

"He said he's found a way to '*monetize provenance*.' He couldn't explain what that meant, but he threw out phrases like '*return on investment*,' '*search engine optimization*,' and '*hyper-personalization*.' Honestly, it's a whole other language. I didn't understand half of it. He's fluent in what I call '*Tech-*

splaining.' Not a word of it means anything. It's gibberish he's picked up from his loser friends. He's got no *real* plan. Just a *vague* promise of a website and list of potential collectors he scraped from *my* phone. I said *no* to investing. Politely. But firmly."

"Let me guess...he sulked," Polly said.

"Said I never support him. I guess the Range Rover he drives to impress doesn't count. Nor the monthly allowance. Said he didn't really need my help anyway. He was just giving me '*an opportunity to get in early.*' Lucky me."

"Are these 'other sources' coming from *Relic or Rubbish*? Maybe from Isla, for example?" Polly asked. "She can identify which pieces are quality. Maybe she could alert Ethan, who would then connect with private collectors before the appraisers even have a look. Maybe it's not actually a start-up. At least not from scratch. Just rearranging other people's furniture and calling it a new idea."

Tiara chimed in and advanced that theory. "To attract investors, he could drop names—like yours, Rosalind—and say something vague like 'advised by industry insiders.' Something to get the ball rolling."

"In theory, yes," Rosalind agreed. "Isla could give him insight into what provenance excites collectors, and Ethan's clever enough to know how to manipulate that information. But I do hope he isn't skirting ethical lines. It would be...awkward, to say the least, if someone thought he had inside access because of me."

"He could even be poaching private leads," Tim added. "People who submitted things to the show and got turned away. He gets their names and tells them he sees something others didn't."

"That's entirely possible," Rosalind added. "Isla has access to items that haven't even been properly evaluated yet. She'd be the ideal source if someone wanted a head start on acquiring something valuable."

"So if Ethan needed an insider, someone who could quietly tip him off about overlooked pieces...Isla would be perfect," Polly thought out loud. She looked at Rosalind, hoping to catch her thoughts.

Rosalind let out a slow breath, as if she were exhausted by her son. "Isla's been with the show for several years. I like her well enough. Bright. Quiet. One of those people who can tell you why a Welsh dresser from 1810 is worth a fortune if it's missing a knob—but practically worthless if it still has all four—because it means no one's ever used it, no history, no character, just a pristine museum piece pretending to be an antique. She's tireless, though probably under-acknowledged by the expert appraisers—who think they know it all. Ethan always did know how to make people feel flattered while he was using them. If he's pulling her strings, Isla may not even realize she's helping him."

"She's essential to the show, right?" Polly double-checked.

"Unquestionably," Rosalind said. "If something rare or valuable comes through, she'd know. Likely before anyone else." She hesitated, a flicker of discomfort crossing her expression. "That's actually how Isla met Ethan. He was supposed to be shadowing the production team for some kind of video blog he was starting. Something vague, self-promotional of course, and entirely forgettable. He wandered into Isla's workspace, pretending to be fascinated by provenance research." Rosalind gave a dry smile. "Which let's be honest, hardly anyone finds riveting.

"They dated for a while. Off and on. He'd vanish for weeks, reappear with a new scheme and a fresh smile. I think Isla was intrigued by him. She told me he was the first man who made her feel attractive. That he really listened to her. Frankly, I think he listens like a thief listens to tumblers in a lock, catching the faintest signals that someone's ready to share what they usually keep hidden."

Rosalind continued, "When I heard they were seeing each other again, I told myself it was harmless. They're just friends. But Isla's been different lately. Distant. Skittish. If someone wanted to exploit her, they wouldn't have to do much. And all she would have to do is flag the right submission or make sure it's quietly dropped from public valuation before filming. Or tip someone off before the owner knew what they had. A whisper here. A detail there. That might be all it takes. I don't want to believe she'd do something like that, but where Ethan may be involved..." She sighed and looked away, afraid to let the half-formed images coming to mind crystallize into something real.

27

If someone had told the young Isla Morton that the adult Isla Morton would one day be the provenance researcher for *Relic or Rubbish*, she would have agreed. No false modesty. No trace of surprise. It was never a question of *if*, but *when*.

Back then, Isla hadn't known what a provenance researcher was. Not exactly. But she understood the intrigue of backstory, of unearthing truths that no one else had thought to look for. While other little girls played dress-up in their bedrooms or pretended to be pop music stars, Isla was in the attic with a flashlight and a notebook, cataloguing old toys, holiday decorations, and vintage clothing, and saying things like, "Possibly Edwardian, though the filigree suggests a revival piece."

By the time she was ten, Isla had long since traded Saturday morning cartoons for old episodes of *Relic or Rubbish* on YouTube. She watched them the way other children inhaled fairy tales. She practiced the ballet of an appraiser's hand: the pinkie hovering above a hairline crack in a porcelain figurine, pointing out an imperfection. She mimicked their subtle pause before a valuation was revealed.

When she applied to university, the decision had already crystallized: she would work for *Relic or Rubbish*. Not as one of those on-air experts, dispensing opinions like party favors. She knew she didn't have the right look to play that part. No—her place was meant to be behind the scenes. Hidden, but essential. She wanted to be the one who sifted fact from fiction.

Isla earned an art history degree from Oxford and a master's in library science from the University of Sheffield. She had a browser history littered with digitized estate sales and shipping manifests. When *Relic or Rubbish* finally hired her, it didn't feel like an opportunity. It felt inevitable.

Isla Morton had the type of face that people, if they remembered her at all, would politely call "nice enough" before forgetting it altogether. Her thin brown hair was always pulled back with neat precision. Her clothes were in shades of oatmeal and bone. She never wore lipstick or mascara. She wasn't unattractive. Just unremarkable. A footnote at the bottom of a page. Being unnoticed had never felt like a failing to her. If anything, it gave her a bit of freedom—an invisibility that let her move through the world unobserved and unburdened.

The producer of *Relic or Rubbish*, Simon Belmore, referred to Isla as "our in-house oracle." Rosalind Fenwick, too, respected Isla but from a distance. Their history was further complicated, since Isla had once dated Ethan. Their working relationship had been polite, but entirely professional. And Isla could never quite forget that Rosalind had been hired for her polish rather than her provenance skills. Isla doubted Rosalind could tell a forged hallmark from a coffee stain without someone like her behind the scenes, proving which was which.

So when Rosalind rang Isla to say Polly Pepper wanted a meeting with her, Isla agreed. Not even out of politeness. More like professional courtesy. And curiosity.

What could the American funny-lady-turned-castle-heiress

possibly want? Isla had heard the stories, of course—Polly Pepper had a reputation for digging into the circumstances surrounding dead people and how they got that way. And now, since Arley Kingston's death, she was sniffing around *Relic or Rubbish.*

As the program was on hiatus, Isla had time on her hands. She was filling her days running around the Southwest of England playing tourist. She just happened to have scheduled a visit to a nearby country house, Pendlehurst Hall. *A Guide to Britain's Lesser Historic Houses* described Pendlehurst as "A charmingly unrestored manor with an idiosyncratic collection of *objets d'art* and family memorabilia." That was all Isla needed to be enticed to book a day at the estate and gardens. She agreed to meet Polly there.

Isla loved places like Pendlehurst Hall, and had spent a full hour in the blue drawing room, examining a badly framed painting of a fox hunt. Badly framed not just in the literal sense (though the gilded frame was chipped and peeling), but compositionally disastrous as well. Still, as an avid art lover, Isla was curious about the painting. The canvas had been signed in the lower right-hand corner—M. Crenshaw, 1824—a minor name she remembered from school. Crenshaw had made what living he could, painting the dogs on crumbling estates—loyal creatures captured with a depth of feeling he never seemed to find for the people who owned them.

Now, seated in the old stables-turned-tea room-slash-gift shop, and halfway through an Earl Grey tea and a slice of carrot cake, Isla waited. Polly was due at noon. And when she appeared, she was exactly as Isla had imagined she would be: confident, composed, impossible to miss. Tim and Tiara trailed behind, like satellites caught in her gravitational pull.

They hadn't been formally introduced during the *Relic or Rubbish* shoot at Thistlethorne, but Isla had been there, of course—hovering just out of frame, ensuring the provenance reports were accurate and the right files landed in the right appraiser's hands.

"Ms. Morton?" Polly said warmly, extending her hand before sliding onto the seat opposite her. "It's nice to finally meet you properly."

"Of course," Isla said. "It's my pleasure. I saw you from a distance during the week at Thistlethorne. You were practically welded to Rosalind Fenwick's side the entire time."

Tim sat beside her and unleashed his signature, tilt-the-room smile. "Tim Pepper. And this is Tiara—Mother's right hand and best friend. Wherever Polly goes..."

"We've actually met," Tiara said, smiling. "Briefly. You were up to your elbows in a folder marked *Napoleonic Curiosities*."

"That does sound like me," Isla laughed with a small, proud smile.

"What brings you to our neck of the woods?" Polly asked, eyeing the last bite of cake on Isla's plate and suddenly craving something sweet.

Isla motioned toward the manor house beyond the tea room windows. "I've been playing tourist. The show's been on hiatus since Arley Kingston died, and it occurred to me—I've lived in England my whole life and barely seen any of it. Ridiculous. Centuries of history at my doorstep, and I've spent most of my adult life shut up in windowless archives and damp basements. So I made a list. Ten places I ought to visit. Pendlehurst Hall is number six."

Polly smiled. "Worth the train fare from London?"

"Maybe. There's an interesting mourning locket in an open velvet box in the nursery. Barely displayed, practically hidden. Inside is a curl of baby hair and a note that says, 'James. Ten days. Taken too soon.' Most visitors probably breeze right past. But I wonder about things like that. Like, who wore the locket?

And how long did they wear it before it was tucked away forever?" She paused. "I can't stop thinking about...Baby James."

Polly blinked, her attention drifting. "You see what others don't," she said, as if trying to move the conversation along.

"It's not necessarily all about *seeing*," Isla clarified. "It's about awareness. Some details don't shout for attention. They wait to be noticed." She reached for her tea, hesitated, then set it down untouched. "This time off from the show..." Her voice trailed momentarily. "It's been a little disorienting. I thought I'd welcome the break. But I sort of miss work. The rhythm of it—the research, the chaos, the feeling of chasing something important." A small smile flickered and disappeared. "I even miss the appraisers," she added. "Well—maybe not *all* of them. Ambrose can be a bit much." Her glance at Polly carried a devilish smile.

"And what about Arley Kingston?" Polly asked. "Will he be missed?"

"Will Arley Kingston be missed?" Isla echoed, almost incredulous. "Of course. At least in theory. Death has a way of editing someone's best attributes into a highlights reel, doesn't it? I wouldn't want to say anything judgmental. He's dead. That sort of silences the room, no matter what you thought of him."

Her comment settled over the table like a draft of frigid air. Polly didn't press the issue but waited quietly, sensing more information coming.

And Isla didn't disappoint. "Arley wasn't like the other experts. He was more—demanding. About the work. About getting everything just right. I am, too. We had that in common —to a degree." She hesitated, choosing her words. "He once spent two weeks tracing the provenance of a monogrammed Victorian hip flask. We weren't even airing a segment on that silly piece. I thought it was a waste of time. But it mattered to him."

Polly leaned in slightly. "So you respected him?"

"Sure. I mean, definitely. But..." Isla's eyes dropped to her hands. "Sometimes he made me feel—less-than, if you know what I mean. It wasn't deliberate, I'm sure. He wasn't condescending or anything. He just had this way of doing his work—so thoroughly it made everyone else feel like they were cutting corners by comparison." She glanced up. "It wasn't arrogance. Maybe conviction? Like he honestly couldn't imagine doing the job any other way."

Polly studied her. "Did that bother you?"

Isla gave a small, dry laugh. "No. I pride myself on being thorough, too—on getting things exactly right. But with Arley, there were moments where I felt...unfairly scrutinized. Like he was double-checking my work not because it was flawed, but because he assumed no one else could possibly do it as well as he did." She paused. "And after you spend hours tracing an item's provenance through water-damaged shipping manifests from 1911, that kind of assumption can get under your skin."

"So you didn't resent Arley," Polly said softly, not wanting Isla to feel defensive at what she planned to say next. "He just cast a shadow over what you brought to the table. Because his way of working made it harder for anyone to notice you."

For a moment, Isla said nothing, Polly's words hung like dust motes in the light. She hadn't thought of it that way. And yet, Polly's analysis seemed to fit with a kind of brutal simplicity. She looked up slowly. "Maybe. I hadn't put it together like that. But maybe you're right." A brief, wry smile ghosted across her lips. "You're very good at this. A little unsettling, maybe."

"Did Arley have any enemies?" Tim asked.

Isla's eyes flicked to him. "I wouldn't say *enemies* per se. But sure, he rubbed certain people wrong. Some of the more senior appraisers especially—Ambrose Carouthers, Clara Montague, Diedre Paige, Fabian Dupont, all the usual suspects. I know they weren't thrilled about a relative newcomer contradicting or undermining them. Sometimes while on camera."

"Even if he was right?" Tiara asked.

"*Especially* if he was right," Isla said.

Polly didn't react immediately, but her eyes remained on Isla's face.

Isla studied Polly, too. "You're asking a lot of questions about Arley—although I thought you might." She tilted her head, more curious than accusatory. "Is there a reason? I mean I know his death was sudden, but I—" She broke off, then added, more cautiously, "Are you thinking there was more than just professional friction between him and the others?"

"And Simon?" Polly continued, ignoring Isla's question. "How did he and Arley get on?"

"Simon liked a lot of what Arley brought to *Relic or Rubbish*. His academic credentials, his insights, his good looks, and he was attracting a younger audience. Let's face it—he was practically designed to appeal to the girls and the gays."

Tim sighed. "That ever-convenient demographic lump."

Isla blinked, unsure whether he was teasing or calling her out. "The network especially loved him," she continued, "which is why they were pushing to bring him on full-time."

"Wasn't that Simon's idea?" Polly asked.

"Hell no. Simon likes to act like he runs the whole show, but this came from above—from the suits. They want younger viewers, and Arley ticked that box. I think the other appraisers were huffy because he didn't come up through the usual ivory towers. No Sotheby's internship. No Christie's pedigree. Just a museum job in Yorkshire and a background in archaeology."

"Would Fabian Dupont qualify as a case in point? Someone who wasn't thrilled that Arley's *Relic or Rubbish* star was rising?" Tim asked.

"A perfect example," Isla confirmed. "Plus, Fabian loathes

being told he's wrong about anything—especially by someone younger by more than half his age, and who doesn't at least have an auction house pedigree, and with the gall to make his case in front of a camera. Even though Arley was never rude about it. That was maybe the worst part. He was right *and* polite, which made Fabian especially look even worse. Nothing wounds a man like him more than being outclassed *gracefully*."

"I know there was a William and Mary writing desk problem," Polly slipped in. "Fabian was ready to go on the record and say it was a reproduction. Arley disputed that. "And Diedre? Didn't she appraise a valuable lavallière as costume jewelry only to have Arley prove it was an important piece?"

Isla gave a faint smile and reached for her tea. "Diedre's sharp. Sharp enough to avoid blame, anyway. Arley caught several inconsistencies and couldn't understand how she missed them. He was professional about it, but you could practically see steam coming out of her ears. I don't think she's ever let go of the indignation. Not really. She blamed me. Said I should've flagged it before it got to her. Easier to fault the researcher than admit she'd botched it."

"What about Ambrose?" Polly prompted, her voice calm but pointed. "What was his relationship like with Arley?"

Isla's expression became cooler, more serious. "Underneath Ambrose's perceived affection for Arley, I know he was concerned about his own place on the show. Ironically, it was because of Ambrose that we got our first introduction to Arley Kingston. Ambrose had to back out from one episode last season, and Arley was called in to substitute. He walked away with the whole damn show. It was a full-on 'a star is born' thing. Arley was an instant hit. After that, every time Ambrose or anyone else was unavailable, Simon called him. Ambrose then lived in fear of being permanently replaced by him."

The words brought a faint sense of satisfaction to Polly, and she decided it was time to find out what cracks might be hiding behind Isla's own polished veneer. She went for it, her voice light but purposeful. "And what about you, Isla? You've mentioned others' errors—Ambrose, Diedre, Fabian—but you're supposed to provide sound research. What happened with the lavallière? The William and Mary desk? That silver tea service you said was a reproduction but turned out to be original?"

"Yes, well. My bad," Isla said, readjusting things near her on the table. She decided it was better to explain than evade. "The desk valuation was rushed. The owner claimed it had been in the family since the eighteenth century. But I didn't trust the story—which is generally a good idea in my line of work."

"And the tea service?" Polly said.

Isla shrugged, dismissing it as a one-off. "I was distracted, and, if I'm honest, the owner didn't look like someone who'd own such a piece. I know that's 'classist.' I made assumptions based on someone's appearance. It was a prejudicial snap judgment. I probably learned that from some of the arrogant appraisers I work with."

"But we heard there were other items you misidentified," Tim said, hedging his suspicions that these instances were merely the tip of an iceberg.

Isla kept her expression flat, suggesting there was something she didn't want to say—or was afraid something she might say could incriminate her. Then, decision made, she looked straight at Polly. "We had a nice, happy little family on *Relic or Rubbish*— until Arley Kingston came along. I just mean he upset the balance of things. He wasn't like the rest of us."

Polly's thoughts were racing as usual. "Usually, when someone disrupts the status quo, it's because they're either very good...or very bad...or very dangerous. Which was Arley?"

When Isla didn't comment, Polly tried again. "Did you notice anything—unusual around the time Arley died? Or during the week? Anything that seemed out of place?"

Isla hesitated, the muscles in her jaw tightening. "Like what?"

"The French automaton clock, maybe? It was supposed to be the crown jewel of the final *live* broadcast. A showstopper. But then—someone wanted it pulled from the lineup."

"Right," Isla said. "I was told the inner mechanism might not match the period. Too clean. Too modern. All wrong for a 1780s French clock. Simon wanted a further review, just to be safe."

"What did Arley say about that?" Tim asked.

Isla let out a breath, the memory sour in her mouth. "He was not happy. He believed the clock was genuine, and if he was right, the valuation could've been astronomical. But there were...concerns. Things were moving fast that day and Simon had a lot on his plate in London and couldn't be on location. The decision to pull the segment was left to me, but Arley wouldn't listen and went ahead with it anyway. Chad would have stopped him if he'd been given a direct order by Simon. He wouldn't listen to me."

"You did the research. Was the clock authentic?" Polly pushed.

"Can't say a hundred percent. The workmanship was exquisite. And the mechanism didn't look modern to me. It felt old. But when the provenance disappeared—"

"Disappeared?" It was obvious to Polly that Isla had perhaps stumbled and said something she instantly regretted.

"The digital file. The physical paperwork too. Gone," Isla gave in, her voice trailing off. "Arley accused someone of deliberately scrubbing it."

Polly steeled herself before asking the next question, her eyes never leaving Isla's face. "Do you believe that? Would someone want to sabotage the segment or undermine Arley?"

Isla didn't answer. She stared down at her cold tea, pressing her lips together until the color drained from them.

Polly's tone was casual, but her eyes were sharp. "You and Ethan Grant are close, right?"

"So?" Isla asked, wary of this shift in topic. She was tempted to just end this meeting which had been turning into an interrogation for awhile. But her curiosity had let it continue.

"I know Ethan's launching some flashy antiques sales platform," Polly said.

The color drained from Isla's face, something she could not control. There was a long pause. Isla set her cup down with care. "You seem to know everything already. So why are you asking me questions?"

"Because I don't know enough," Polly said.

A light summer rain had let up by the time Tim maneuvered the car down the narrow road heading toward Thistlethorne Lodge. "So...the provenance file for the clock disappears—hard copy and digital. That's quite a coincidence," he said to Polly, seated in the back with Tiara.

"That's design, dear," Polly said. "Obviously, someone didn't want that clock authenticated. No provenance means no story. No story means no spotlight. It drops off the radar. Quietly. Then —boom—I smell a private sale."

"Or maybe the provenance disappearance wasn't about the clock," Tim said. "Maybe it was about *Arley*. To make him look unprofessional or incompetent. It could've been someone trying to knock him down a peg to damage his career."

"What if it's worse than just a mistake?" Tiara said. "What if that file had something dangerous in it—like a forged provenance, or proof the clock was stolen? Maybe deleting it was a way to erase the risk. No file, no liability."

"But Arley still wanted to appraise it," Polly said. "Maybe he'd already seen something in the file before it disappeared—something that convinced him the clock was important. And if he didn't go ahead, the whole thing could disappear. No segment, no paperwork, no record it ever existed. By doing it live, he guaranteed it couldn't be buried. Once it aired, the clock was out in the world—the TV audience saw it. Experts saw it. You can't hide something once it's been on national television."

"Maybe it was his way of blowing the whistle," Tiara said. "If you suspect a cover-up, visibility is your best protection. Broadcast it, and it's too late to hide."

"Or maybe the opposite," Polly said thoughtfully. "Maybe someone deleted the file to make it look like it was lost. That way, Arley could 'stumble' across the clock live on air. Make it feel spontaneous. That's catnip for a show like this."

"But Simon's the producer," Tiara said. "He told Isla to pull the clock."

"Unless..." Polly's eyes narrowed. "Unless he *expected* Arley to defy him. Arley was a maverick. If the valuation went badly, Simon could deny everything. But if it went well? Ratings gold."

She paused. "Either way, Simon wins. Unless Arley found something he wasn't supposed to—and refused to play along."

Tim looked over. "You think Simon would really do that? Set Arley up?"

Polly hesitated. "He's a producer. A ratings whore. All producers are manipulative. Maybe he wanted Arley to go rogue." She turned toward Tim, her eyes sharp again. "Step on it, sweetums. Mamma needs a confab with her Highness, Rosalind Fenwick."

28

"Educate me," Polly said to Rosalind as they sipped the evening's first champagne with Tim and Tiara. "Why might someone want to secretly remove a provenance file from *Relic or Rubbish*? What might that achieve?"

Rosalind took a breath. "I can think of a few reasons. Provenance files can cause all kinds of headaches. They might show that an item was stolen, or passed through shady hands, or even belongs to someone else. That kind of history makes valuable things harder to sell."

Tim frowned. "So if the file disappears..."

"Then the problem disappears with it," Rosalind said. "No messy backstory, no one asking awkward questions. It's just a pretty object with no strings attached."

"Like wiping the slate clean," Polly said. "No proof, no trouble."

Tim nodded. "And the seller can say, 'Oh, I had no idea.'"

"Exactly," Rosalind said. "No trail, no questions. You can't be accused of ignoring red flags if the flags are gone."

"Brilliant," Polly said dryly. "Chapter one in the *Official Guide to Moral Flexibility*: What You Don't Know Can't Indict You."

"And then there's ego, too" Rosalind continued. "Suppose an appraiser thinks they've made a major find—but the provenance tells a duller or messier story. Delete the file and *snap*—the story's theirs to invent. No inconvenient facts to trip over."

"So maybe it's not just about hiding the truth. It's about rewriting it," Tim mused.

"In television," Rosalind added, "the best story wins. Not necessarily the truest one. Authenticity doesn't trend. Shock does. Just ask your country's very own truth assassin and orange oracle of alternative facts. A neat provenance? That's just home-work. But a 'nobody heirloom' that turns out to be a royal relic or stolen masterpiece? That's a headline. That's clickbait."

Polly leaned in, hoping to catch all reactions to her next words. "And if someone didn't want a scandal—but still wanted the object itself? Then they erase the paperwork. No record. The past disappears. And if that's what happened with the automaton clock..."

"If that's what happened, someone knew the value of the clock and how hard they could push to get it," Rosalind confirmed, and set her glass down.

Polly let that statement settle. But behind her stillness, her thoughts raced. If Arley chose to appraise the clock on-air—after the provenance file vanished and after being told not to do the valuation—he wasn't just being obstinate. He was being—Arley: driven to do whatever he thought was right and ethical. And then he died."

Polly's eyes narrowed—the way they did when suspicion began to crystallize. "Now I sort of understand the possi-ble *why* of the missing file. But I need to understand the *who*. Who made the clock's provenance disappear?" She turned to Rosalind. "Simon makes all the big decisions on the show. And the director would have followed his orders. So why didn't Chad pull the clock when told by Isla that Simon had given that directive? Maybe because he and Simon never spoke. Isla just passed the edict from Simon on to Chad. And maybe Chad wasn't taking direction from anyone but the boss himself."

Tiara spoke up, playing devil's advocate. "It's been suggested before that maybe this had nothing to do with the clock itself. What if someone only wanted Arley to *look* incompetent? They had it in for him. And, if he went on air talking about some grand provenance for the piece—and then that provenance didn't exist—he'd look inept. I imagine Fabian would love for that to happen. And Diedre, too. And how many others? So maybe the only foul play would be one of embarrassing Arley in public. Just as he'd done to them."

"Bruised egos," Polly agreed, grateful for Tiara's insight. "There's another theory that been rolling around in my head." She turned to Rosalind again. "Ethan wants to launch a platform to sell antiques—unvetted, off-market. He's sniffing around for overlooked treasures." Her tone softened. "Rosalind, I need to ask something I don't want to ask. And I'm sorry in advance."

"Which means you're going to ask it anyway. And I think I know what it is."

Polly gave a small, apologetic smile. "Ethan came to you for financial backing. Isla didn't deny he approached her about his venture. Did he ever ask you specifically about the clock?"

"Not directly," Rosalind said flatly. "But he did float what he called a *hypothetical*. Asked me how someone might deliberately undervalue a high-ticket item on the show."

Polly's brows lifted.

"I was vague. I said, in theory, you might misattribute the piece, make it look like it's from a lesser maker, maybe assign it to the wrong expert...or lose the provenance. If no one asks the right questions, it's buried in plain sight." Rosalind was quiet for a long moment before adding, "Ethan has a way of making conversations transactional. You don't realize it until it's too late."

"Do you think he could've convinced someone—Isla or anyone else—to delete the file?" Polly asked.

Rosalind met her eyes. "I think Ethan is capable of far more than I've allowed myself to believe."

29

———

Polly hadn't bothered asking Rosalind for the automaton clock owner's contact information. Rosalind had no reason to have that information. But who would have it? A production assistant? Maybe. Or perhaps a segment producer—they assign appraisers to antiques and manage the shooting schedule. Maybe the head of security?

Polly retrieved the cast and crew contact list from her phone and scanned it until her eyes locked on Event Coordinator. "Ding! Ding! Ding!" she whispered. From her own television days, she knew event coordinators were the keepers of preregistration forms, emergency contacts, and assorted paperwork no one else wanted to manage.

It only took a quick, polite phone call—and the explanation that she was "sending a personal note of sympathy to the gentleman whose antique had been involved in the on-air tragedy"—for the coordinator, to hand over the information without a second thought.

This was how Polly found herself holding Gilbert Farringdon's name, address, and phone number.

The following morning, Polly, Tim, and Tiara were standing

before Farringdon's cottage—a slouching stone house half-swallowed by ivy, its roof sagging at the edges as if burdened by its years. The narrow road that led to it seemed less a lane than a suggestion, barely wide enough for a car and probably more accustomed to the slow, indifferent traffic of sheep.

Polly stepped up to the weathered door, the fox-head knocker cold and weighty in her hand. She gave it a couple of strong raps. From behind a filmy lace curtain, a flicker of movement betrayed that someone inside had spotted them.

Tiara muttered, "If we were hawking *Watchtower* magazines, we couldn't look more like a traveling conversion team."

Polly allowed a small, understanding grin. Years of well-meaning Jehovah's Witnesses and Mormons had trained half the world to perfect the art of pretending they weren't home.

The door creaked open a few cautious inches, and a pair of wary eyes appeared. After a round of polite and convincing introductions, they were ushered into a sitting room. Tea was produced, and Polly accepted her cup with the radiant gratitude of someone presented with a rare vintage.

Once they'd all settled, she leaned forward, her voice dropping into a velvet tone of heartfelt sympathy. "Mr. Farringdon," she smiled demurely, a study in tender concern, "I know it's been a dreadful week for you—and for everyone touched by the tragedy at *Relic or Rubbish*." She paused, letting the phrase "touched by tragedy" delicately hang in the air. "I simply had to come by and personally extend my deepest sympathies. I mean —imagine! Standing there, sort of minding your own business, and the poor man dies at your feet, right there in front of half the country." Polly let out a soft shudder, lowering her tea with a slight tremble she didn't bother to hide.

Farringdon nodded, looking faintly stricken—as Polly conjured the whole awful event again right into the room.

"I remember you telling Arley that evening a little bit about the history of your beautiful clock. It was bequeathed to your grandfather by a prominent antiques dealer, then stolen. Earlier this year you rediscovered it at an auction while on holiday in France. What an amazing story and a lucky break! Exactly the sort of anecdote that *Relic or Rubbish* thrives on!" Polly waited a beat, then added, "I also remember you said something about a curse. Can you tell us about that?"

Farringdon shifted uncomfortably in his chair, his gaze darting for a split second toward the fireplace mantel. Polly caught the glance and tucked it away.

He cleared his throat. "Well—yes. I suppose I did mention a curse. I'm actually skeptical about those things. Or—I was. Yes, the clock did go missing the day my grandfather died. We thought it was gone forever. Then last year, I was on holiday in France, browsing a village auction—and there it was. Same markings. Same automaton features. No doubt in my mind. So I bought it. Felt like—fate, really."

Polly gave a small nod, grounding him again. "Back to the curse?"

At that moment, an old wiry terrier padded into the room and nudged Farrington's leg. He absently stroked the dog's head as he spoke, his fingers brushing its ears with absent-minded fondness. "It's just a legend, of course. But my grandfather was warned—the clock brings bad luck to anyone outside the original owner's bloodline who tries to claim it. Nonsense, I thought. Until things started happening."

His voice dropped nearly a whisper. "My grandfather's friend —the antique dealer who owned it first—died suddenly, weeks after telling him about the curse. Then my grandfather passed under odd circumstances. No illness. No warning. Just gone. He was ninety-one, but even so—"

He shifted in his chair and looked toward the window, as though weighing the wisdom of continuing. "When I brought the clock home, there was a kitchen fire—flared up out of nowhere. Ruined half the floorboards. Then I got into a car accident barely a mile from the house. They said I was lucky to walk away. And then—at the *Relic or Rubbish* broadcast, when Mr. Kingston suddenly died. Well, you can imagine how I felt. Another death!"

Polly deliberately looked at the empty space on the mantel. "Where's the clock now?"

"Sold it." He hurried on as if defending his actions. "A man contacted me that night. Said he'd seen it on the *Relic or Rubbish* broadcast. He somehow knew the show's provenance team couldn't find Arley Kingston's initial appraisal notes. Said its value would be greatly reduced if it were to go to auction. Offered cash. A good sum, really. And after what happened that day, I couldn't bear the thought of it in the house any longer. It felt—tainted."

Polly smiled gently. "Mind if I ask the name of the buyer?"

He shrugged. "It was a cash transaction. I didn't ask questions. I just—wanted it gone. I lived without it for twenty years; I won't miss it now."

Although Polly could understand Farringdon's reasons for selling the clock, she couldn't hide disappointment. She'd lost her best lead for tracing the clock's whereabouts and its buyer. Now it had slipped into the shadows again.

"You know how it is," Farringdon explained further. "Those sorts of exchanges don't come with receipts. They said it was for a private collector who didn't want the fuss of auctions or agents. Seemed very keen to take it off my hands. The more I thought about it, the more I thought maybe it was looted art. You hear about that sometimes, don't you? Things taken during the war. No paperwork. No questions."

Polly, now fully re-engaged, managed to keep her voice light and calm. "I've learned enough about antiques these past couple of weeks to know that provenance isn't just about pride—it's sometimes about protecting an object. Especially when wartime history gets involved. Looted art can be a legal landmine. And if there's no paper trail..." She set her teacup down.

"Aye. But Geoffrey Clark, the antiques dealer who left the clock to my grandfather, was smart enough to leave a paper trail," Farringdon said. "After Granddad died—and the clock vanished—I went to the police with the provenance. But nobody cared. They didn't do a damned thing about it."

Provenance! In that instant, Polly and her posse sat up straighter. "There's provenance?" Polly nearly shouted.

"The dealer who left it to my grandfather had it authenticated back in the 1970s," Farringdon said, rising from his chair and padding down a narrow hallway. Polly, Tim, and Tiara exchanged looks of disbelief. The cottage seemed to hold its breath. When Mr. Farringdon returned, he carried a badly worn paper document folder, the corners soft and torn with age. He withdrew a paper and handed it to Polly with a kind of reverence as though passing along a burden rather than a prize.

For a moment, no one spoke. Polly scanned the page then looked up. "It's in French," she said, frowning.

Farringdon nodded. "That's the original. I had it translated years ago. I gave the English version to the provenance research team when I first registered it with *Relic or Rubbish*."

Polly's head snapped up. "There's a translation?"

"In a nutshell, the clock came from French nobility," Farringdon said, sinking back into his chair, his fingers steepled beneath his chin. "Then the Revolution happened. Titles stripped, lands seized, fortunes gone. According to the legend, the family didn't go quietly. In their bitterness, they vowed that anything unjustly taken from them would carry a curse. Misfortune for misfortune. Ruin for ruin. Generations later, that clock was one of the few heirlooms that survived—and supposedly, so did the grudge."

He shook his head, slow and grim. "*Relic or Rubbish* said the file disappeared. As if I don't know anything about Cloud storage, for crying out loud." He smiled thinly. "No worries. I still had the French original."

Polly was silently ecstatic. "They think the clock has no provenance at all?" she murmured. "Someone wanted that clock—and they didn't want anyone tracing its history." She exchanged a sharp glance with Tim and Tiara, then turned to Farringdon, her voice all innocence. "Would you mind terribly if I took a photograph? Just for my own notes, of course. I'm learning French," she lied.

Farringdon frowned, and his eyes flicked from the provenance to Polly's face.

"I wouldn't dream of showing anyone," Polly added quickly, sensing his hesitation. "Just one little picture. Here. In front of you."

"Well..."

Polly was already slipping her phone from her pocket.

30

Back at Thistlethorne Lodge, Polly's shoes crunched on the gravel drive as she quickly cut across the forecourt with Tim and Tiara nipping close behind. Mr. Boots, who performed a full theatrical greeting whenever they returned home, got little more than a glance from the trio. He sat indignantly, letting out a meow of resentment that sounded suspiciously like, *"Perish the thought I might matter!"*

As she entered the house, Polly intuitively made a beeline for the library. There, Rosalind looked up, one brow arching at the abruptness of Polly's entry. She tucked a bookmark into her novel and set a mug of tea aside, sensing something significant had happened—or was about to happen. "You look as if you've just untombed Tutankhamun," she said.

"In a manner of speaking," Polly said, her breath tight with urgency. She dropped beside Rosalind onto the Chesterfield settee and pulled out her phone, her fingers flying across the screen. "You speak French, right?"

"*Oui.* Of course. Why?"

Polly thrust the phone into her hands. "Read this."

Rosalind's brow furrowed as she angled the screen. "What

am I looking at?" she murmured, her lips moving as she silently translated the text. The room seemed to hold its breath. After a long moment, she sat back and stared at Polly, her hand tightening around the phone.

"Well?"

"It's provenance—for the automaton clock Arley was appraising when he died." Rosalind blinked, processing. "Wait —how do you have this?" Her tone was half confusion, half dawning realization. She tapped the screen to enlarge the image and scrolled back to read it again, this time aloud:

"Item: one musical automaton clock. Origin circa 1783. Constructed by Jacques Duval, horologist to the court of His Majesty Louis the Sixteenth. Acquired by the House of Montrevault prior to the Revolution. Following confiscation by Revolutionary forces in 1793, the object's whereabouts remained unverified. Believed lost to private hands during the nineteenth century. Resurfaced after the Second World War. Recovered in the Luxembourg region circa 1946. Retained in the UK by Monsieur Geoffrey Clark until bequeathed to Gilbert Farringdon in 1995. Alleged to carry a curse upon unlawful transfer of ownership."

Rosalind's eyes sharpened as she examined the phone again, her fingertip hovering just shy of the screen. "Duval. Montrevault." She murmured the names, almost to herself. "French aristocracy. Pre-revolution." She sat back, blinking once, twice, as if recalibrating her thoughts. She stared at the screen again, the implications crystallizing in her mind. "Polly," she said slowly, "if this is legitimate—and it certainly looks legit—it proves the clock's lineage."

"It also proves Arley was right about its authenticity," Polly agreed. "The clock wasn't just another orphaned antique—it has DNA. A traceable bloodline. A story stretching back centuries." Her eyes locked with Rosalind's. "I'm realizing, if Arley had been able to authenticate it live, on air, that would have become public record. Wouldn't museum curators, legal authorities, and private collectors all have taken notice?"

Rosalind nodded. "And when people like that start asking questions, skeletons have a way of dancing out of their closets and into the light."

Unease crossed Polly's mind. She was almost certain now the clock's provenance hadn't disappeared accidentally. It had been deliberately erased. She repeated one of the lines Rosalind had read: "Believed lost to private hands during the nineteenth-century…recovered in Luxembourg, circa 1946." She looked up slowly, her voice low but pointed. "A convenient gap in history?"

"Or a red flag," Rosalind said. "'Private hands' is provenance code for we don't actually know who had it, or worse—we do know, but we're not saying. And Luxembourg in 1946? That was ground zero for the recovery of Nazi-looted art. If this clock resurfaced there—after the war, without documentation—someone either hid it, smuggled it, or stole it. And someone else probably didn't want those questions asked."

"This is the original French provenance from the antique dealer who left the clock to Mr. Farringdon's grandfather," Polly said, her voice quiet, still in awe of what they had. "Gilbert Farringdon had it translated years ago and gave it—the English version—to Isla Morton for the show's records. But I doubt anyone realized that wasn't the original.

"And maybe—just maybe—Arley caught wind that something wasn't right. The provenance gone missing. The show's sudden hesitation about authenticating the clock on air. Someone trying to pull it from valuation at the last minute."

Polly waited for a response from the others, but when no one seemed to know what to say, she continued. "Arley was the kind of man who tugged on loose threads. If something didn't add up, he couldn't let it go—not just for curiosity's sake, but because he believed in preserving the truth. He didn't chase drama, but if he thought someone was hiding something? He'd dig. Quietly. Relentlessly."

Unable to stop, feeling more confident and certain, Polly was almost not aware she was the only one talking. "He knew the clock was important. And if he suspected someone had deliberately erased its past—wiped the trail clean—he wouldn't have looked away. He would've insisted on exposing the truth. Even if others didn't like that."

Finally, across from her, Rosalind glanced toward Tim and Tiara, almost hoping they'd counter the growing conjecture, to say something that would make the dark logic unravel. But none came. "If Arley had revealed the provenance on air," Rosalind said cautiously, "he might have exposed someone's theft or fraud."

"If the clock's full provenance had come out, and it was maybe linked to wartime looting..." Polly started.

"—It would've been toxic," Rosalind finished what Polly was thinking. "No reputable dealer would touch it. No serious collector would buy it. Especially not if the media got wind of it. War-time theft? Missing records? Supposed curses? It's a perfect storm. The clock wouldn't just lose value, it would become untouchable. Possible lawsuits, restitution claims, scandal—it would poison anyone connected to it."

"And if someone had a financial stake in keeping it hidden— or in silencing anyone who could expose it—then Arley's death maybe wasn't just a sad tragedy," Polly said. Her voice almost a whisper. "What if someone thought they'd destroyed the provenance, but Arley, stubborn and sharp, noticed something scandalous and wouldn't let it go?"

For a moment, no one moved. Polly stared at the carpet, her mind whirring faster than her heartbeat. Even Mr. Boots, sensing the shift, froze mid-grooming. Arley's death was turning out to be more complicated. He had resisted allowing the clock to be pulled from appraisal, even after Isla's orders. He had pushed forward, knowing something wasn't right. He hadn't been willing to stay silent.

A darker thought slid into Polly's mind: Ethan. Too charming. Too eager. Always too close to the fire without getting burned. She didn't want to consider it—especially not with Rosalind sitting just inches away—but a suspicion took hold, cold and heavy. What if Ethan hadn't just been scavenging after the fact? What if he had known exactly what the clock's value was?

A cold knot tightened in her stomach. Polly's memory flicked back to that dinner on the patio, the lazy golden hour when Ethan, all charm and bravado, had let something slip about Arley that he probably shouldn't: *Isla told me he poked his nose into things that weren't his business. Always wanting to cross-check records, dig into old paperwork—all the boring stuff no one cares about.*

He'd laughed then, and a quick, shallow chuckle followed. "*Apparently he was sniffing around old provenance files. Trying to match appraisals to background info. Thought he was being clever. Some people don't know when to shut up and stay in their lane.*"

At the time, Polly had dismissed those words as Ethan being glib—spreading idle gossip, nothing more. But now, sitting in the quiet library, his words unsettled her. Suddenly, Polly saw it clearly: inconvenient people, the ones who asked too many questions or who refused to play along with others' schemes, are sometimes pushed out, quietly discredited—or worse. And Arley? He might have been just *inconvenient* enough.

And what if the clock wasn't the only prize? The realization unfurled in Polly's thoughts, faster now, even darker. What about the other missed valuations? The Victorian lavallière. The William and Mary desk. And the silver tea service Isla had flagged. All pieces that had been stripped of proper provenance, under-appraised, and quietly sold for a fraction of their true worth. Easy pickings for anyone who knew what they were really looking at. Easy for someone like Ethan—or someone working with him—to swoop in, snap them up, and disappear before anyone could ask questions.

A chill worked its way down Polly's spine. Was she standing at the threshold of a much wider plot? She drew a deep breath, steadying herself. This maybe wasn't just about the provenance of an antique—it was about silencing the truth before it could speak.

Around the room, Polly, Rosalind, Tim, and Tiara all felt the same question settle over them. Tim broke the silence, his voice uncharacteristically grim. "Mum," he said, using the word he reserved for moments that mattered, "maybe we should talk to Grayson—just hypothetically. Run it past him without sounding like lunatics. If we're right, he'll know what to do. And if we're wrong—"

Tiara nodded fiercely. "Tim's right. This isn't just some missing brooch or village scandal. It's potentially bigger. Scarier. And a whole lot more dangerous. You might not be able to charm your way through this one, Polly. You always say, 'timing is everything.' Well, the time to protect yourself—and us—is now."

Polly looked at them, seeing the concern in their faces. "But we don't have any real *proof* of anything," she said quietly. "Not the kind the police need to act on. Okay, I have an original French provenance—proving the clock's lineage. Big deal. Otherwise, I only have a trail of things that wouldn't add up in anyone else's way of thinking." She willed herself to stay calm.

"No direct witness. No smoking gun tying anyone to Arley's death."

Across from her, Tiara bristled. "You have clues, Polly." She held up her hand and began ticking them off, one finger at a time. "A missing provenance file—conveniently erased from the provenance research team's system. A last-minute production shuffle that tried to pull that very same clock from the live broadcast. Want me to go on?"

She paused and looked at Rosalind. "And, no offense intended, but we can't overlook a smug, handsome opportunist who started sniffing around the minute Arley's body hit the floor —or before."

Tiara fixed Polly with a steely look. "Where there's smoke, girl, there's fire." Silence thickened the air. "But we obviously can't bring this to Simon for questions and answers," Tiara said, realistic as always. "He's the boss. He might already know exactly what happened. And he's had time to cover his tracks— and polish an alibi."

Rosalind drew a sharp breath. "Simon would never sabotage his own show—not intentionally. *Relic or Rubbish* is everything to him. He built it from scratch. It's not just his career—it's his identity. But he *is* obsessed with appearances. He wants the show to feel clever, cultured, a little provocative—but always safe. He can handle headlines, not scandals. The kind of chaos you can't edit out? That terrifies him." She paused, her voice lower now. "If the clock's provenance hinted at something messy —something real—I can believe he buried it. Not out of malice. Out of fear."

Polly leaned toward Rosalind, her tone quiet. "What we need now is to talk to someone on the inside. Someone close enough to see what goes on but who's not too high up the food chain. An assistant. A researcher. Someone others overlook. They hear things. They notice things. The kind of person others talk around without realizing who's listening—the one who sees the e-mails, overhears the arguments, watches how people really behave once the cameras stop."

Her voice dropped slightly, more reflective now. "You want truth? You ask the person cleaning up the mess, not the one who made it. Every production has them—the ones who aren't in the spotlight but know exactly where it's pointing."

Of course, Polly would know this. She'd lived it daily during her years in show business. She instinctively knew that truth, although guarded by the bosses, sometimes leaked through the cracks. "It's never the star who spills the real secrets—it's the assistant stuck carrying their dry cleaning and listening to every backstage tantrum." Her voice sharpened slightly. "It's the so-called 'little people' no one pays attention to who know exactly where the bodies are buried and who dug the holes." Her tone warmed, but her look was penetrating. "In every show I ever worked on, it was the dresser, the lighting tech, the stage manager. The ones standing quietly in the wings—watching, listening."

Understanding crossed Rosalind's face. "Then definitely don't look to any of the expert appraisers on the show. They have too much to lose."

"Exactly." Polly nodded. "It's probably best to try and find some relatively small potato. I always say, if the truth is hidden behind the throne, it's the janitor cleaning up who finds it."

They sat in silence, each ticking through the staff possibilities: Amelia Cook, who handled scheduling; Marty Graves, the production runner more interested in his phone than the job; Ryan Bell, who carted artifacts to and from the appraisal tables.

"Ryan Bell?" Tim wrinkled his nose. "The guy thinks provenance is a type of Italian cheese. Probably not your man."

Each name rose—and quietly fell. Too loyal. Too clueless.

Too visible. They needed someone close enough to know the rot from the inside—and hungry enough to talk about it.

Polly leaned forward, a glint sparking in her eye. "What about that girl? The one who clashed with Howard Kettering over that seascape. She's on the provenance team, isn't she?"

Rosalind's expression darkened. "Millie Travers? Very unfortunate debut." She paused. "They won't be rushing to put her back on camera anytime soon. She embarrassed one of the big boys. That sort of thing isn't easily forgiven."

Tiara nodded thoughtfully. "She probably knows all the dirt too."

Rosalind added quietly, "And she might be eager to remind someone she's still a valuable member of the team."

Polly smiled. "Then let's make sure that *someone* is us."

Rosalind's phone suddenly lit up on the arm of the Chesterfield. She glanced at the screen and blinked. "Simon," she said, her voice almost bursting with surprise. "Give me a sec," she said to the group as she picked up the phone and moved toward the patio doors.

Polly watched her step out onto the patio. "Simon's calling, so something's shifting. Either he's reeling her back in...or cutting her loose."

31

———————

osalind stared at the phone vibrating in her hand, feeling her stomach twist in anticipation. After a week of silence, Simon was finally calling, and her first thought was that he would make it official: "Thanks for your hard work, but good riddance and good luck."

Until this week of forced hiatus, Rosalind had believed her position on *Relic or Rubbish* was unshakable. She'd been there from the start. She'd helped build the brand. Defined the tone. Shaped the public trust. Her optimism had never been blind...it had been earned. She'd weathered network reshuffles, producer tantrums, as well as low ratings. But the silence from Simon had teeth.

Deep down she had a creeping fear that the show and audience might no longer want her. Rosalind knew how television worked. Yes, she was part of the brand. But if the network thought she'd become a liability? They'd cut her loose with little more than a *thank you* and a politely worded press release:

"We are deeply grateful to Rosalind Fenwick for her many years of dedicated service and outstanding contributions to Relic or Rubbish. *We wish her continued success in all her future endeavors."*

Classic PR—vague, respectful, and emotionally hollow.

Would Simon fight for her if the network winds shifted? She wasn't sure. Maybe he'd be relieved to see her go. He could clear the decks and recast the show with a younger, less costly face—someone half her age with twice the social media followers. Over the past week, she'd silently rehearsed her response to just such a call from Simon. In one version, she'd take the high road —dignified, composed, even gracious. In another, she'd torch the building on her way out. *You've reminded me that in television, the expiration date for women is printed in invisible ink until the lighting and her age makes it visible. I hope whoever you cast next knows how to pronounce "Baroque."*

And yet, now that the moment had arrived—now that his name glowed on her screen—every practiced line vanished. She swiped to answer. "Simon," she said, her voice bright but neutral, "lovely to hear from you."

The conversation was short, and when it ended, Rosalind set the phone gently on the patio table. She didn't move. Just stood there, staring out at the garden, her thoughts swirling.

The French doors behind her creaked open.

"Fortification," Polly said, offering a seemingly ever-present flute of champagne. "Verdict?"

Rosalind gave a short nod. "Good news, bad news, I guess. We start prepping the next episode on Monday. Simon first wants to tape a special tribute to Arley, to air before the next broadcast. Expect a call. He wants you to say something, too. Since you were there when he died."

Polly studied her. "That sounds like the *good news* part. What's the *bad*?"

Rosalind gave a soft chuckle, but there was no warmth in it. "The network is forcing Simon to make some major changes. Staff shakeup. Isla's gone."

"Because of past wrong valuations?"

"That's the narrative." Rosalind's mouth tightened. "A few old missteps being dusted off and polished up for damning evidence."

Polly narrowed her eyes. "And unofficially?"

"He wouldn't go into detail—legal implications—but he suspects Isla's not playing by the rules. Simon's terrified of scandal. Oh, and Millie's out, too. 'Not a good fit for the show's new direction,' he said."

Polly's brow lifted. "The new direction being what, exactly?"

"Safe. Uncontroversial." Rosalind's tone was flat. "Simon wants clean hands and clean optics. He wants the show to be a kind of visual sedative—soothing for viewers in an increasingly chaotic media landscape. History without the hard edges. A calm corner of the world where nothing ever goes wrong, and no one asks uncomfortable questions. And no one dies on camera." She paused. "Anyone with baggage—or bite—is out."

"And Millie has baggage," Polly said slowly.

Rosalind nodded. "Simon didn't say that out loud, of course. But it's clear her ambition—and the dust-up with Howard Kettering didn't help. I suspect Howard had something to do with Simon's decision."

They sat in silence for a moment, a slight warm breeze whispering through the climbing roses. Then Polly said, "If Millie's just been sacked, she might be even more inclined to talk about what she saw behind the scenes."

Rosalind looked out at the garden, her expression unreadable. "Maybe. Especially if she thinks she's been thrown under the bus. People want to be useful after they've been made to feel disposable. It's a way of reclaiming their dignity. If you can't belong, at least you can still matter. Still have something worth offering."

"And right now, Millie has nothing to lose and a lot she might want to prove.

Polly opened her laptop and clicked to compose a new message. She paused, fingers hovering above the keyboard. It had to be the right tone—friendly, sympathetic, but not too obvious. She began to type:

> Subject: INVITATION
> Hi Millie,
> I've heard the news about all the changes at Relic or Rubbish. Every time I thought the world had turned its back on me— professionally or personally—something new always turned up. It will for you, too. I'll be at home in Abbots Clover this week. Rosalind Fenwick is here too, if you'd like to chat with us. We may have a few ideas about where you go from here. Why don't you come for tea? Nothing formal. Just a bit of perspective and maybe the start of something new.
> All the best,
> Polly Pepper

It was bait. A door left ajar. Polly hit Send before she could talk herself out of it.

Millie read the email twice before responding. She'd always heard that Americans could be kind and generous people, and that Polly Pepper had a reputation for being among the nicest stars in Hollywood. But this message was more magnanimous than she expected. She stared at the line, *we may have a few ideas about where you can go from here.* Was Polly offering help? Maybe a job? And Rosalind would be there. Maybe she would ask Millie to join her team. She clicked Reply.

> Hi Polly,
> Thank you for your message. Yes, tea with you and Rosalind

sounds lovely. I'd very much like the chance to chat with you. I can drive down from London tomorrow if that works. Noon?

    Best,

    Millie

She hit Send. And for the first time since being terminated from *Relic or Rubbish*, she felt optimistic.

Millie stepped out of her car and took a deep breath of crisp country air—cool, clean, and faintly scented with the earthy tang of cows from a nearby field.

Thistlethorne Lodge stood before her, like something from a postcard: ivy cascading over stone walls, and leaded diamond windows that reflected the sky like panes of glassy water. Birds trilled lazily from the hedgerows, and bees hummed in the tall lavender. She adjusted her blazer, smoothed her hair, and reminded herself to exude professionalism, and not to come across as too eager.

Tiara answered Millie's knock and ushered her into the sitting room.

"You made it," Polly said, rising from the Chesterfield with a warm smile.

"We're happy to see you," Rosalind added.

"Thanks for inviting me," Millie said as her eyes moved slowly around the room, taking in the tall windows, the gleam of polished wood, the soft, worn elegance of the furnishings. Her gaze landed on the large portrait above the fireplace. "I didn't have an opportunity to see inside your house while we were filming," Millie said. "It's...stunning. And that portrait—who is he?"

Polly laughed, expecting the question. "Everybody asks.

That's the odious Duke of Droitwich. He built this house way back in the seventeen hundreds. A manipulative narcissist who terrorized his family and the village with his flatulent dog."

Millie raised an eyebrow. "Quite the sinister-looking presence."

"Villains are often painted well," Rosalind agreed. "Think Henry VIII. Or Richard III. Tyrants make interesting portrait subjects."

"Tea or coffee?" she asked before Millie launched into what she thought was expected—a light summary of her professional background, a humble but hopeful attitude, and a few self-deprecating jokes that she knew would convey her resilience and pluck. "I've had so much experience as a provenance researcher, I'm ready to move into something where my knowledge can be utilized and more fully appreciated. I'd be open to research, writing, something behind the scenes to start. Whatever you think might be a good fit. I know I'm destined for the camera."

Polly smiled politely but made a mental note: *Destined for the camera? Maybe as a weather girl on a cable station no one watches.*

Millie cleared her throat. "Anyway—I know I'll be of value. Not everyone gets intimidated by competence. The right people will recognize what I offer—and they won't need convincing."

Polly tilted her head slightly. "I'm curious, Millie. Did you see it coming?"

"Being sacked?"

"The way they handled it...it must've felt brutal," Rosalind said.

"Simon didn't even give me the courtesy of an exit interview," she said flatly, her bitterness barely hidden.

"Did they give a reason for the termination?" Polly asked, her voice still easy.

"Not officially. But of course, it's obvious." Millie picked up her tea and took a tentative sip to test its temperature. "It had to be because of that damn Howard Kettering. Pardon my language. Because of that seascape—the one he authenticated on camera. I was supposed to provide background and historical anecdotes about the painting and artist. It was my big break. Then, when I questioned the provenance, he threw me under the bus."

"Classic," Rosalind said, but she wasn't buying Millie's version of the incident. Millie hadn't been thrown under any bus. She'd insulted Kettering's expertise and seniority on-air. It had all been performance. And Kettering, red-faced and rigid, had looked like he'd swallowed a wasp.

"Maybe I kissed up to the wrong people," Millie admitted with a dry smile. "I lowered myself to gofer duties for the so-called experts—fetching dry cleaning, running out for bespoke oat milk, even ironing Ambrose's shirt once because his steamer broke. Arley was picky. He needed strong coffee and hated the swill from craft services. Said it tasted like 'scorched wood shavings.' I found something online I knew he'd like—a special blend. A Blackout Shot. He laughed and called it 'the Dwayne Johnson of coffee.' Thought that was hilarious.

"I wanted him and the other pros to know me better. To realize I'm a team player. I figured if they saw me as someone always ready to pitch in, they might actually start thinking of me as one of their own. See how that worked out? Turns out I'm disposable."

"We all feel disposable at one time or another." Polly tried to commiserate. "Even Arley had detractors."

Millie looked up, curious.

"Surely you saw that," Rosalind prompted. "Yeah, everyone was perfectly polite to his face, but the moment he stepped out of frame? They called him, '*Perfectionist. Over prepared. Scene-stealer.*' Those expert appraisers are a tough crowd."

"You must have gotten that vibe," Polly added. "Especially that day with the automaton clock. Did you notice anything strange about Arley then?"

"Strange?" Millie echoed, her brow furrowing. "Not exactly. Maybe he was worn out. He admitted he was always tired. Maybe he was unwell."

"Unwell?" Polly repeated, prodding.

Millie hesitated. "Nothing overt. He wasn't coughing or anything. But I think he had a situation. They've all got something to complain about," Millie continued. "Ambrose is lactose intolerant but still drinks his tea with cream then blames the caterer when he gets stomach cramps. Diedre's always freezing cold. Her thyroid levels are borderline. Fabian has a gluten allergy. Clara's got arthritis in her right knee. You'd never know it from the way she moves on camera, but she winces when the weather changes.

Polly's expression was unreadable, but her mind did a quiet somersault. She gave the smallest nod, urging Millie to continue.

"And Arley, it was hyper-cardio something. But he was cleared to work—with caution."

Hyper cardio something. Polly was suddenly on high alert, her mind splintering in too many directions.

Rosalind's expression had gone taut.

Millie became aware of the shift in the atmosphere. Her eyes darted between Polly and Rosalind. "Why are you asking me so many questions about Arley?"

Polly gave a soft smile, aiming for reassurance. "We've been thinking about him a lot lately. That's only natural."

Rosalind nodded, her tone carefully neutral. "It's hard not to, isn't it?"

Millie didn't look convinced. Her voice, when she spoke again, had cooled by a degree. "I get the feeling this meeting isn't really about me finding another job...is it?"

Polly held her gaze. "Let's just say we're trying to understand what really happened that day. All of it."

Millie's smile was thin. "What 'really' happened? Arley Kingston dropped dead. Natural causes. The end." She rose, adjusting the strap of her handbag with a touch too much force. "Just be careful. Dig too deep, and you might not like what turns up." She walked to the door, paused, then added without turning, "People see what they want to see, Ms. Pepper. Especially when it hurts less."

Polly almost laughed. The line was pure melodrama, but there was something to it. Denial wore many disguises—optimism, nostalgia, even love.

And then she was gone.

For a long beat, no one spoke.

Then, Rosalind exhaled. "Well. That didn't feel like a reference letter sort of conversation."

Polly didn't respond at first. Her eyes were still on the door Millie had closed behind her. "She seemed to know an awful lot about everyone's health," Polly said finally. "Arley, Ambrose, Diedre...all casually dropped in like she was reading from their charts."

Rosalind's brow creased. "Do you think any of it was true?"

"Don't see why not. Everybody has aches and pains. And some people actually enjoy ill health. She could've made educated guesses based on how they looked or acted or moved. Ambrose's tummy complaints, Diedre's temperature quirks, even Clara's subtle winces. Things most people would dismiss. Millie files them away. If Arley did have a medical issue, and someone knew how to exploit it..."

She didn't finish the thought. She didn't have to.

32

Lush Hour felt oddly adrift without Rosalind, who'd returned to her home in London for the weekend. For the first time in days, there were no *Relic or Rubbish* war stories of Napoleon's chamber pot (later revealed to be a Victorian saucepan) or medieval dental tools unearthed in someone's garden and proved, on closer examination, to be a rusted corkscrew from a 1950s cocktail set. Gone, too, was the retelling of the Royal Doulton hedgehog ashtray—which, allegedly, was once graced by a flick of Princess Margaret's cigarette. (Rosalind agreed that story was vague enough to possibly be true.)

But by evening, Thistlethorne sparkled again—with the surprise arrival of Grayson Jenkins, Elliot Davies, and Terrence Marks.

It hadn't been planned, exactly. In fact, each had made the decision on his own to visit, prompted by the realization that two weeks apart from their significant others were two weeks too long. And in an oddly poetic appearance, they arrived almost simultaneously.

Tim labeled them: "the Boyfriend Brigade." Grayson, the fit policeman; Elliot, Tiara's skinny and hairy romance novelist;

and Terrence, Polly's ever-patient paramour, came with cartons full of Chinese takeaway from a nearby village.

On the patio, champagne was poured and verbal darts tossed—good-natured but pointed—at Polly and company for having gone completely AWOL since the *Relic or Rubbish* filming began. Between the camera crews, the temperamental antiques experts, and Polly's extended role as hostess to television royalty Rosalind Fenwick, there'd hardly been a moment to breathe, let alone entertain suitors. Once the teasing subsided, the conversation veered straight into behind-the-scenes gossip. And Polly was only too eager to spill the tea.

"What's Rosalind Fenwick like in real life?" Elliot asked, eyes gleaming with the kind of curiosity that only novelists and nosy-parkers possess. "Is she as unflappable as she is on telly, or does she ever, you know—snap? Full diva meltdown? They say she's tough as nails but still manages to shed glitter."

"More velvet glove than steel scalpel," Polly assured him. "She's elegant—and surprisingly funny when she lets the armor drop. She commands a room without raising her voice. We've become fast friends."

By the time the first bottle of champagne was emptied, and the spring rolls were gone, the mood had settled into that golden warmth unique to Friday evenings—when the week's chaos gives way to camaraderie among chums. Even Mr. Boots, in a rare display of self-restraint, had curled up under Polly's chaise without demanding so much as a single scratch behind his ears.

And then, as the bubbles and alcohol gently lowered everyone's guard, it was Terrence who—ever the serious journalist, always representing the *Abbots Clover Overview*—tugged on the thread no one else had dared pull. He kept his tone light, almost conversational, but he'd metaphorically withdrawn a notepad from a blazer pocket.

"Arley Kingston?" he asked, his voice mild but deliberate.

"Any update on what actually happened to the poor guy? I mean —other than dying in the middle of a live broadcast, right here at Thistlethorne in front of the cameras, in the middle of appraising an antique clock." He paused. "It's tragic."

Polly hesitated for a beat before delivering her line with saintly composure. "Oh, I wouldn't know a thing. I make it a rule never to interfere in police business. As I *always* say, leave it to the pros."

Even before she got the word "pros" out, the room erupted with laughter. Tiara nearly slid off her chair. Tim clutched his heart in mock alarm. And Elliot let out a strangled wheeze that startled Mr. Boots.

"Oh, please," Tiara gasped, wiping tears from her eyes. "You've practically got a loyalty punch card for meddling in murder investigations!"

"One more corpse and you qualify for a free monogrammed body bag," Tim agreed.

Polly feigned offense. "There is no investigation, because there's no murder, right? Arley died of natural causes. That's what Grayson and the others insist." She turned to Grayson with exaggerated innocence. "Sweetums, you're the one with the badge. Enlighten these philistines."

"Natural causes," Grayson confirmed. "I know it's hard to imagine someone that young—early thirties—but the report was clear. No signs of external trauma. Just—a very unlucky heart. That's what the official report says. And that's where it stands. These things happen."

Terrence had been watching Polly closely—her posture, her tone, the way she absently twisted her ring around her finger. "You believe that don't you, Polly? That Arley's death was from natural causes?"

She shrugged, eyes fixed on the last lazy bubbles rising in her champagne glass. "I believe that's what the report says."

It was the kind of evasive answer that sounded honest—if you didn't know Polly well. But Terrence did. "That's not the same as believing the expert's conclusion."

"I may have a few teensy-weensy innocuous little lingering questions," Polly admitted. "What rational person wouldn't? I mean, there's a lot of fake news out there. But it would never occur to me—*never, I tell you*—to ask our darling Grayson, a pillar of professional integrity and discretion, to reject the educated findings of the crackerjack authorities. Or use his official standing as the lone purveyor of the law in Abbots Clover to procure a copy of medical-clearance forms from *Relic or Rubbish*. Forms that he's surely personally examined and in which he finds zero debateable details."

She turned toward Grayson. "Of course you'd know that Arley and the other *Relic or Rubbish* on-air talent had to take physical exams before filming. That's hardly top secret—right?"

Grayson's expression tightened ever so slightly. "As a matter of fact...I haven't heard of that. And even if I had, I couldn't exactly hand over medical reports to just any ol' looky-loo. They would be private files. There are rules. Laws, actually. Ones I'm required to follow."

"Looky-loo?" Polly echoed, eyes widening in mock offense. "Grayson, please. I'm a woman of refined *curiosity*—not some tabloid hack rifling through people's private trash cans." She let the others share a knowing glance before continuing, lighter now. "And I'm not suggesting you do *anything* unauthorized. Not officially." A beat. "But if a certain diligent officer of the law were to request Arley's medical file—as part of a responsible, by-the-book investigation—well, who could possibly object to that?" She gave him a sweet, pointed smile. "Especially if there's something in those records that someone might not want found."

Tim and Tiara stifled laughs, having seen this move many times before.

Polly went on, her tone smooth as cream. "I mean, purely hypothetically—if someone happened to notice a small but telling detail that others had overlooked, and a certain officer quietly followed up—well, wouldn't that reflect rather well on him? Show initiative? Sound judgment? The kind of elevated qualities a chief superintendent of the Bristol Police Department might take into consideration when he's handing out commendations?" She flashed a mischievous smile. "And, of course, you'd never do anything unprofessional. Just something maybe a little—ahead of the curve."

Tim snorted. "Translation: bend the rules and it's all your idea. Polly had nothing to do with it."

Grayson looked at Polly and muttered, "You are absolutely terrifying."

33

The bell above the door at Bound to Read jingled as Polly and her team stepped into the cozy warmth of the village book and coffee shop. The scent of freshly ground coffee beans was immediate, mingling with the sweetness of pastries and the faint smell of paperback novels. Only two tables were occupied at this early Saturday morning hour—regular customers with their newspapers and dogs. The espresso machine gave a lazy hiss as if even it were easing into the weekend.

Sarah, the owner and barista, looked up and smiled genuinely. "Welcome," she called brightly. "Take a seat. Flat white. Cappuccino. Americano." She rattled off Polly & Co's usual coffee order with ease. Then, with a playful smirk, she added, "Although some of my customers have started asking for an '*Anglicano.*'"

Polly raised an eyebrow. "Oh dear. Is espresso now a matter of national identity?"

Grinning and just short of laughing, Sarah concurred. "A bit of caffeine nationalism, I think. Ever since a certain US blowhard with a delicate ego, a fondness for tariffs, and the complexion of a radioactive cantaloupe started shouting about global trade, a few regulars say they'd feel more comfortable sipping something aligned with the empire than anything with anything 'American' in it."

Tim nodded. "What's next—'freedom foam' in the cappuccinos?"

Polly was smiling at this repartee, but her thoughts were elsewhere. "We were hoping for a quick word," she said.

Sarah gestured toward the nearly empty sit-and-sip area of the shop. "Take a seat." Then she called out, "Charlie, can you cover the counter for a bit?" A faint rustle from the shop's book section was followed by a muffled, "Got it," just loud enough to confirm that her assistant was on his way.

The trio had barely settled in before Sarah returned with each of their drinks—and set down a plate of almond croissants with a wink. "On the house. No better way to start a Saturday."

As Sarah settled into a chair, Polly seized her moment. She retrieved her phone, swiped through her photos, and turned the screen toward Sarah. "Remember this?" she asked, enlarging the image of the takeaway coffee cup she'd found in the tent near where Arley had died. "I showed this to you before. I've learned Arley drank something called a *Blackout Shot*. Ring any bells?"

"Blackout Shot. That's a new one on me." She called over her shoulder, "Charlie? Got a sec?"

Charlie was a tall, lanky guy in his early twenties, all limbs and laid-back energy. His sandy hair was long-*ish*, and he wore a vintage Guns N' Roses tee. "S'up?" he said, with the sunniest disposition this side of a weather report.

"Ever hear of a *Blackout Shot*? A coffee?"

Charlie looked blank for a moment, then gave a short laugh. "Does it come with a paramedic on standby?" He seemed pleased with his own joke.

Polly didn't smile. "Espresso. Cold brew concentrate. Hazelnut milk. I Googled it."

The grin slipped from Charlie's face. "Yeah. I remember making that a few times. When that TV show was here. It was super specific—like, five modifiers deep. Triple espresso, cold brew concentrate, hazelnut syrup, no foam, extra hot. Perfect for someone pulling an all-nighter."

Polly's gaze sharpened. "Do you remember who placed the order?"

Charlie shrugged. "Not exactly. It came through the online app. We just launched it. I'm still working out a few kinks. But I remember it was ordered by *ROR*, which I figured had to be that *Relic or Rubbish* show. Oh, and they used Guest Checkout, so no customer profile, no login or user name recorded. Selected the 'pay at pickup' method. The woman who came in paid cash. No card. No receipt. Just grabbed it and left. Oh, and she was sorta pissy. She also bought a regular Americano and made me swear which was which."

"Can you describe her?" Polly asked.

"Hard to tell. Mid-thirties, maybe? Pale, kind of sharp-featured. Wore big sunglasses—even indoors. She was sort of snappy each time. Told me to be quick about it. Didn't want any chit-chat. I figured she was crew. I've seen 'em running around like they were on fire."

There was a pause as Polly seemed to be completely in her head. Tim and Tiara recognized it. Like a chess player who'd just seen the start of a winning move. And they were right. Questions were circling in Polly's mind, shifting and refusing to settle. *Someone—a woman from* Relic or Rubbish*—had ordered a drink strong enough to jump-start a tractor. And someone had drawn an identifying symbol on a takeaway cup. That much was certain. But was the coffee meant for Arley? Did he order it? Was it ordered for him?*

Charlie had theorized it was made for someone burning the candle at both ends. But something about the specificity of that coffee order—the extreme caffeine content, the takeaway cup— all tugged at Polly.

There were other things too. The coffees had been paid for in cash. Polly knew from experience that on-air talent and production staff usually had expense accounts. For convenience and to keep accounts in order. Lattes, taxis, even throat lozenges for on-camera experts—it all went on the tab.

So why would a *Relic or Rubbish* staffer pay cash? Why would one of them go out of their way to avoid a receipt—unless they didn't want a trail. And the person who placed the order—brisk, impatient, eyes obscured behind sunglasses, an air of authority and impatience. It all seemed odd. And then there was Millie's comment that Arley had been "cleared to work, but with caution." And she'd prefaced that with what sounded like a medical diagnosis: *Hyper-cardio something.* What did that even mean? And again, how did she know about the other appraisers' health conditions? Maybe it was all coincidence. A strong coffee. A weak heart. A stressful schedule and terrible luck. But Polly didn't believe in coincidences. Not when the puzzle pieces were this oddly shaped—each awkward on its own but starting to fit together if you tilted your head just right.

She sat very still, cupping her mug like it might help her hold another thought steady. A theory had begun to form— hazy at the edges, still soft around the middle—but it was gaining weight, pressing in on her like a slow rising tide. She could almost see its shape now. The outlines. The connections. But there were gaps. She needed more. More evidence. More certainty. More time.

But *time* was the one thing she didn't have. Monday's planned taping of the tribute to Arley would be the last natural gathering of the *Relic or Rubbish* team. After that, they'd vanish back into their production offices and London flats. There'd be no reason for Polly to hover on the fringes with a smile and a cup of tea, listening for the offhand comment, the flinch, the slip of the tongue.

Polly had been asked to say a few words during the tribute—not because she'd known Arley well, but because she'd been standing beside him when he died. She wasn't meant to replace the more formal tributes from Simon, Rosalind, or the others, just to add another human moment from someone who'd been there at Arley's last breath. And since the tragedy had occurred at Thistlethorne, Polly had offered to host the taping there. The network had gratefully accepted, relieved not to have to source another venue location.

Still, she knew this might be her last chance to collect evidence. She glanced down at her cup, then drained the last sip. The bitterness clung to her tongue. She stood abruptly. "Lots to do!" she announced brightly. "The crew's arriving early Monday. I've got to write a testimonial—something heartfelt and moving to celebrate dear Arley Kingston. To say farewell."

Her voice faltered slightly on that last word. Because how could she eulogize someone whose cause of death she didn't accept? How could she look into the camera, offer a tender smile, and speak about loss—while wondering if the person responsible for it might be standing just out of frame, watching her? The very idea made her stomach clench.

Polly Pepper had given many performances in her life. She'd played queens and lawyers and wronged women and clowns. But this—this might be her most complicated role yet. She just hoped she'd know her lines when the time came. She turned to Tim and Tiara, her voice bright but her mind already racing ahead. "Come, darlings. I have a performance to write. And a mystery to solve. Maybe bouquets to throw when the curtain falls."

34

———

Monday arrived, and by late morning, the *Relic or Rubbish* production crew had transformed Thistlethorne's main reception room into a makeshift television studio. Electrical cables snaked across the parquet like coils of sleeping vipers, while LED panels formed a soft halo around a well-worn Chesterfield wingback that had been designated the "tribute chair." This wasn't a memorial service but a taped segment to be folded into an upcoming episode of the show. The goal was to capture something intimate and reflective, not ceremonial.

To warm the camera frame, a lit silver candelabrum had been placed atop the grand piano. A tasteful illusion of elegance, curated for a television audience who had grown fond of Arley Kingston, even if they'd only known him through the small screen.

The show's on-air personalities and production executives arrived in waves.

Rosalind Fenwick was the first, her son Ethan (on his phone) trailing behind her. She stepped through the door with her usual poise. Catching sight of Polly in the main hallway, she approached with open arms. "What a strange and sad occasion this is," she said quietly, the memory of Arley's final moments flickering behind her eyes. "Thank you for letting the tributes take place here. He would have appreciated the dignity of it."

She lowered her voice and whispered, "Please forgive the addition of Ethan. He insisted on tagging along, though I suspect he views this more as a networking opportunity than a memorial tribute. I've warned him—no elevator pitches and no start-up talk."

Polly offered a warm smile. "It's actually lovely that he's here." It was the kind of line you said aloud when you needed everyone to believe it—even if you didn't fully believe it yourself.

Director Chad Wescott followed soon after. Tall and lean, in perfectly distressed jeans and a white Oxford-cloth button-down shirt, the sleeves artfully rolled, and collar open. Head-phones looped around his neck like a noose. He paused just inside the reception room, giving the setup a once-over. "Okay," he murmured to the lighting tech, "kill the front left panel—too warm. And someone move that candelabrum. It's distracting."

He caught sight of Polly and Rosalind, and for a moment, the director in him vanished, the human being revealed. His shoul-ders dropped half an inch, and his face softened into something warm. "Well," he said, crossing the room to them, "it's nice to be back at Thistlethorne—though I wish it were under different circumstances." He leaned in to kiss Rosalind on the cheek, then turned to Polly. "Thank you again for letting us do this here. It means a lot."

Simon Belmore, the producer, arrived already mid-panic. He scurried around ranting on his phone. His call sheet had been rolled into a tight paper baton, which he waved in the air as if it had the magical power to fix whatever he was railing about on the phone. He looked around. "Why are we still lighting?" he barked. "We're on a tight schedule, people!"

When he spotted Polly, his phone lowered an inch. "Polly Pepper," he said, not quite smiling, "last time I saw you, you were in my office making a pitch to take Rosalind Fenwick's job. She's not going anywhere." He acted like that was some sort of inside joke.

Polly offered an ambiguous smile. "The future has a curious way of rewriting itself when no one's looking, Simon," she said. "One never knows what's just around the corner."

Simon gave her a look—half wary, half weary—but before he could reply, his phone buzzed again, and he vanished down the corridor, barking about line items, overtime approvals, and why the floral arrangement had somehow doubled in cost.

A chilly breeze—the first whisper of oncoming autumn— wafted into the entrance hall as the next arrival stepped inside. Ambrose Carouthers. His waistcoat was boldly patterned, its buttons straining against his girth. His eyes swept the foyer, pausing on a familiar porcelain form set into a niche in the wall. "Well, well, if it isn't Master Tim's French vase. I suspected it all along."

Before Polly could respond, Clara Montague breezed past with a clipped, "Lovely to see you again..." delivered over one shoulder like an afterthought. She made a beeline for the temporary makeup station—a sideboard hastily repurposed with a lighted mirror, an assortment of powder compacts, and a scattering of blotting tissues. A young makeup assistant hovered nearby, armed with concealer, setting spray, and the slightly haunted look of someone who'd already touched up one too many egos that morning—and here was another.

Then, beyond the lingering veil of Fabian Dupont's cologne, Diedre Paige arrived—tailored in a navy suit, her heels clicking softly against the floor like typewriter keys. She gave Polly a polite nod that served as a greeting and a "keep away" sign.

Martin Hargrove and Howard Kettering weren't far behind,

arriving together in a black taxi and bickering. "It was clearly William and Mary," Martin insisted, jabbing the air for emphasis.

"Please. The legs were cabriole, not baluster. And the veneer was burl, not walnut. That's Queen Anne all day long," Howard sniffed, their antagonism having no end. They barely paused to acknowledge Polly before sweeping into the reception room, their disagreement trailing behind them.

Polly positioned herself near the fireplace—close enough to look involved, far enough to remain inconspicuous. She stood with a casual air, as if simply having a whispered conversation with Tiara. But her eyes missed nothing. Around her, the guests fanned out like wary animals, circling one another. Greetings were clipped, and condolences offered without much sincerity. It was a ballet of egos and subtle one-upmanship—who kissed whose cheek, who avoided eye contact altogether, and who glanced toward the cameras with the longing of a lover. There were murmured commiserations about Arley and just as many backhanded compliments. The banter was a mix of amity and venom in equal measure.

It hadn't been a given that they would all show up. Arley had not been universally loved. Respected, yes. Envied, certainly. But loved? That depended on the hour and whether he'd recently outshone one of them on-screen. Still, they'd all come. For the cameras, yes. For the optics, undoubtedly. Perhaps even for a last chance to position themselves a little closer to center stage—and an invitation from Simon to take Arley's place as a permanent appraiser on the show. Mourning, after all, could be a performance.

Rosalind, to her credit, had convinced Simon that the tribute should include *everyone* who'd worked on the show with Arley, regardless of recent HR history or hurt feelings. "No politics," she'd said. "Just a proper farewell." And whether it was her influence or Simon's desire to avoid a PR problem, both Millie Travers and Isla Morton had grudgingly accepted his invitation to attend.

Near the sideboard where a makeup girl was dabbing powder onto Fabian Dupont's forehead, Polly noticed Millie and Isla huddled with Ethan. The trio stood just out of the main action. Polly, pretending to check the seating arrangement, eased a step closer to them.

Isla's arms were folded tightly across her chest, her face drawn and weary. "I haven't slept in eons," she lamented, low enough to be considered private—though not quite. "Simon hasn't heard the last from me. Just you wait."

Millie gave an exaggerated sigh and wiggled her takeaway coffee cup in Isla's face. "Let's swap. You need something stronger than sympathy. Mine's got an extra espresso shot. It might actually keep your eyelids open through this circus."

She handed Isla the cup and then rummaged in her over-sized shoulder bag. From its depths, she produced a small packet: glossy white with bold red lettering. Millie tore it open and dropped two small, chalky pills into Isla's palm. "Caffeine. Guarana. Ginseng," she said. "Three ingredients. Fuel in pill form. Harmless."

Isla popped the tablets into her mouth and washed them down with a sip of coffee.

With a careless flick of the empty packet, Millie let it flutter into a wastebasket beside the makeup table.

Polly casually drifted to the makeup station. One glance around and then a surreptitious reach. The torn packet retrieved, she slipped it into her pocket. Her thoughts sharpened as she stepped back toward the fireplace. She caught Ethan's voice behind her, low and bitter. "Ol' Simon's going to regret the choices he's made. One way or another." He seemed to be commiserating with Isla and Millie. There was a pause, then, more coolly: "This tribute's a joke, anyway. Let's not pretend Arley was any sort of saint. He made himself a target."

Polly let those words settle in her ears, filing them alongside the others she was collecting and collating. Ethan's tone had carried the smugness of someone certain of a bright future. And the lack of reverence in his voice was striking. She moved a step closer to the fireplace, her profile neutral, the gears inside her head turning.

And now, with everyone assembled—whether out of loyalty, curiosity, or ambition—the production was set in motion.

"Okay, everyone," Chad called out, his voice clear and commanding, "we're starting with a wide establishing shot to capture the tone—soft, reverent, a bit of nostalgia baked in. Then we'll roll straight into the tributes. Phones off, and let's keep background noise to a minimum. If your shoes squeak, stand still."

A hush settled over the room. The usual production chaos evaporated. Not a throat was cleared. No one shifted in their seat. It wasn't just for the sake of a clean take. Whether they'd liked Arley or not, he had died here at Thistlethorne, and now that truth was being acknowledged.

Clara Montague was the first to take her place in the tribute chair, lowering herself with poise. A makeup assistant scurried in to dab at her forehead and smooth a flyaway hair.

"Rolling," Chad called.

Clara sat primly on the wingback Chesterfield and spoke in clipped, reverent tones about Arley's passion for provenance and his "rigorous standards"—which sounded dangerously close to "unbearable perfectionism." Her hands were folded neatly in her lap, her expression the picture of solemnity. Chad nodded approvingly from behind the camera. Simon hovered at the edge of the room, clutching his phone and occasionally dividing his attention between Clara and a text message.

And then, from the distance, the muffled *thunk-thunk* of the brass door knocker on the main entryway door filtered down into the room. Tiara, standing next to Polly, moved silently out of the room. A minute passed before she reappeared and gave Polly an almost imperceptible nod, summoning her into the hallway. Clara continued speaking, and no one noticed Polly's departure.

Grayson in his police uniform, stood in the hallway, his expression unreadable, and his voice quiet and controlled. "You didn't get this from me," he said, and handed Polly a manila envelope. "It's from the *Relic or Rubbish* insurance file," he added. "The physical exam form submitted by Arley's doctor—and other things you'll want to see."

Something in Polly's chest tightened. She said nothing as she accepted the envelope and withdrew the pages. Official letterhead. Clinical phrasing. The neat, impersonal language of risk management. Her eyes scanned the lines, absorbing them almost faster than she could process what they implied—and might ultimately confirm.

She didn't blink. No gasp. Just the faintest tightening at the corners of her mouth—as if she were playing a game of cards and determined not to show her hand. After a long pause, she slipped the report back into the envelope. "You're a very naughty policeman, Constable Grayson Jenkins," she whispered. "And a very good friend. This is more than I could have asked for."

35

Fabian Dupont replaced Clara in the tribute chair. He settled into place with quiet dignity, his silver hair neatly combed, the soft LED lights casting a gentle sheen over his weathered features. He folded his hands in his lap and offered the camera a composed, faintly world-weary smile.

"I used to say—half in jest—that Arley Kingston had the soul of a bloodhound. He could sniff out authenticity—or pretension—from a mile away." He gave a faint chuckle. His gaze flicked—not subtly—behind the camera toward Ambrose Carouthers. Or perhaps Ethan Grant, both of whom stood side-by-side just out of frame.

"Of course," he added, with a little shrug, "when two hounds catch the same scent, they sometimes bark louder than necessary."

There was a pause. Enough to suggest the comment had landed somewhere specific. Polly watched him closely. She recognized the polished tone—but also the jagged edge beneath it. It seemed like a warning bell disguised as wit.

Polly watched as Clara gave a tight-lipped nod of agreement, as if privately seconding Fabian's assessment of Arley. Diedre's brow arched, unconvinced. Ambrose performed an eye roll just obvious enough to be noticed. Polly saw Millie, standing at the back, arms folded, her expression unreadable. Isla stood beside her, whispering something to Ethan—who answered with a slow nod and a smug grin.

The spotlight might have been on Fabian, but Polly saw the entire cast on stage. And she was their attentive audience. As Fabian rambled on, Polly was taking mental notes. Not just of his words and delivery—but how others responded. She studied the faces of the expert appraisers, guests, and production executives. Howard Kettering's jaw clenched tight enough to make his temples twitch. Perhaps it was a reaction to being reminded over and over about Arley's meticulous standards. Or maybe a grudge still glowing hot under his collar, being in the same room with Millie. Diedre's gaze was pinned to the floor, her arms folded in tight defense. Perhaps from remorse, or the weight of remembering a man she'd once privately crushed on, then turned against when he found legitimate fault with her work?

"Arley knew his stuff," Fabian finally concluded. "He challenged egos and corrected others' errors. Yes, that was infuriating to some—but his kind of brilliance always is for us mere mortals in his orbit."

A brief silence followed. Not out of reverence, but uncertainty—unsure if that was finally the end of Fabian's long-winded (and mainly self-serving) tribute. Chad settled the question when his voice broke from behind the camera. "Cut. That's a wrap on Fabian." Then he clapped his hands once, loud and commanding. "Okay, people! Lunch! One hour. Union rules. Cameras roll again at one o'clock. Sharp!"

The crew began to peel away, drifting toward the front door. Craft service trucks sat crookedly along the gravel forecourt, offering a selection of limp sandwiches and watery coleslaw.

The grips mingled with other grips. The appraisers hung out with each other. Someone vaped nearby. Everyone checked their phones.

Polly loitered at the edge of the lawn, quietly observing. She spotted Rosalind eating with Chad and Simon. Fabian had claimed a wooden deck chair, balancing a paper plate on one knee while muttering a monologue into his phone about "funereal lighting choices." Clara stood near the climbing roses, chewing in silence and dabbing the corner of her mouth with a paper napkin. Howard and Martin had retreated beneath a yew tree to reignite their William and Mary-vs-Queen Anne debate.

Polly's eyes settled on Millie Travers and Howard Kettering, locked in what looked like a heated conversation. Polly edged closer, feigning interest in the wildly overgrown topiary that had once resembled a deer—if one squinted hard and believed in artistic license.

Millie and Kettering both looked deeply troubled. "I wasn't trying to humiliate you," Millie said, probably re-exploring their row about how she'd mishandled the on-air appraisal of that Montrose seascape. She seemed to be trying to make peace. "It wasn't personal."

"It couldn't have been any *more* personal!" Kettering's tone was spiked with vinegar. "You got what you deserved. Should have happened sooner!"

"I only wanted Simon to see that I had what it takes to shine on camera," Millie shot back. "That I could take charge of a valuation and hold my own with a seasoned expert. No one gets ahead by being polite and patiently waiting their turn. I needed to prove I could carry off an on-air valuation."

"You carried off my *credibility* is what you did. You're a backstabbing snake in the grass! Pity that's not a trait Simon—or our audiences—values. You threw me under the bus!"

"I didn't throw you anywhere you didn't belong, old man,"

she snapped a little too loudly, her attempt at peace-making morphing into combat. "All you old geezers are on your way out anyway! The network wants to attract a younger audience!" Then, her voice dropped a half-step. "Even Arley's time would have soon been up, and someone would have to step in and take his place. Why not me?"

Kettering blinked. Silence stretched. "What are you talking about?"

Millie's expression shifted. Her eyes widened—mouth half-open before she clamped it shut again. "Nothing. Just—he was a rising star, so maybe he'd have been headhunted by *Antiques Roadshow*—or some place. I could have been his replacement."

"No one could replace Arley Kingston," Howard replied. "He was unique. Don't you get it? None of us would have been offered to succeed him if he left." He spun on his heel and stalked off, muttering under his breath, frustration radiating from every rigid step.

Millie remained frozen. She stared blankly at the half-eaten sandwich in her hand. She knew Kettering was probably right. None of the other appraisers would ever have been invited to be a permanent member of the team. As brilliant as any of them were, they were getting too old, and none of them had Arley's X factor.

From behind a weathered bay tree, Polly took a measured step back into the shadows. Then Tiara came to her side, eyes already narrowed in suspicion. "Thought I'd find you lurking," she murmured. Her gaze dropped to the manila envelope still in Polly's hand. "Want to tell me what's in there? And why I just overheard Grayson on the phone with the detective chief inspector in Bristol—something about requesting backup? I've got a feeling, Polly Pepper. But I trust you to know what you're doing."

Polly's fingers pinched the envelope tighter. It felt heavier now. It carried not just paper, but the weight of the future. Her voice, when it came, was low and steady. "Every show has its climax, Tiara. The curtain's rising on the final act."

The voice of a production assistant cracked through a bullhorn. "That's it, people! We're back! Hustle! Rolling again in ten." Grumbles rose from the clusters of crew, as people began drifting toward the house again with the resigned air of school-children summoned by the bell.

The atmosphere in the main reception room shifted as the crew trickled in, taking last opportunities to look at their phone screens. The chatter dulled to a low murmur as people resumed their places. Camera angles were recalibrated. The makeup girl stepped in to tame Rosalind Fenwick's bangs, spritzing a burst of mattifying mist across her brow. All eyes would be on Rosalind —she was up next. The sound technician adjusted her lapel mic and gave a thumbs-up from behind the boom stand.

A production assistant signaled for the clapperboard.

Snap.

Seated in the tribute chair, Rosalind Fenwick looked into the lens with the poise of someone long accustomed to being on camera.

"Arley Kingston wasn't drawn to television for the spotlight," Rosalind began, "he was drawn to television because it gave him a platform to share what mattered to him: the stories hidden in old things. He had an extraordinary gift for seeing history in everyday objects. Centuries-old portrait art. Furniture. Clocks— especially clocks. He loved to trace their journey to the twenty-first century. He did that with reverence and clarity. He believed that every object has a spirit. A trace of the lives they'd touched.

"He believed that even inanimate objects carry memory and

energy. He treated each piece with that kind of respect. Whether it was an ancient timepiece or a chipped vase. And when he spoke about those objects to viewers of *Relic or Rubbish*, we all listened. And learned. He reminded us that value isn't just monetary—it's emotional. It's historical. It's human."

Rosalind's voice wavered slightly, though she steadied it quickly. "That's why his final valuation segment on *Relic or Rubbish* was so meaningful. The clock he was appraising that evening wasn't just a curiosity. It reflected everything Arley believed in—beauty and legacy."

Another pause. "I remember him saying to me, *'This clock has secrets, and I want the world to see them.'* That was the last thing he filmed. And he didn't get to finish the valuation. Arley was my colleague. In the short time we worked together, he reminded me why I started doing this in the first place. He brought integrity, passion, and a reverence for history that elevated every segment he was involved with. We miss him. Terribly. Goodbye, Arley Kingston."

She didn't rush the final words. Instead, she let them linger —softly spoken, sincerely meant. Rosalind gave the camera a final glance, then rose from the tribute chair with grace.

The silence that followed was reverent.

Now it was Polly's turn to offer her tribute.

36

All the tributes had followed the expected script for these types of things: fond recollections, tasteful sorrow, and just enough personal detail to suggest sincerity. It was performance grief—camera-ready and delivered by pros who knew how to squeeze out a tear and manipulate an audience.

But now, the earlier (mostly fake) reverence was replaced by a quiet fatigue. The lights felt hotter. The pauses and set-ups between tribute speakers stretched longer. People shifted in their seats and glanced at watches and snuck peeks at phone screens. The solemnity that had filled Thistlethorne at the start of the day had been replaced by a collective yearning to just get it over with—then pack up and move on.

Only one tribute remained.

Chad looked around. "Where is she? *Where's Polly Pepper?!*" he called, with the impatience of an accountant who knew the overtime budget was about to be blown.

"Topping up her war paint," Ethan said snidely. "Or fetching her confetti cannon and theme music." It was sarcastic, but where Polly Pepper was concerned, such a grand entrance wasn't out of the realm of possibility.

An assistant scuttled off to check the powder room. Someone else spied into the garden. Tiara leaned against the doorframe, knowing Polly hadn't gone to fix her hair or practice her tribute. When she'd left the room, Polly's expression was the one she wore backstage before a curtain's rise: earnest. She was preparing for a performance.

The tribute chair sat vacant for another few minutes. Then —Polly wafted into the room: unhurried, unapologetic, and still carrying the envelope Grayson had given her. Her gaze swept the assembled, landing in beats on the expert appraisers and behind-the-scenes provenance staff. "Shall we?" she said, her voice composed but carrying something subtle. Not tension. Not grief. *Assuredness.* She walked to the tribute chair and paused. *The final act,* she thought.

Chad moved from behind the camera to her side. "Polly, we've gotta wrap this up. We should have been out of here ages ago. So keep it tight. I'm counting on you." He gave a thumbs-up and turned away without waiting for a response.

Polly serenely slipped into the seat. This was not just her turn to say nice things about Arley Kingston. This was a reckoning. When the camera's red light blinked on, she drew a long breath to calm herself for what she was about to reveal.

"Someone—I can't even remember who—said, 'Arley Kingston wouldn't authenticate a stainless-steel teaspoon from his grandmother's kitchen without three independent sources, a notarized affidavit, and a blood oath from the original owner.'"

That landed like a punch line, and a ripple of soft laughter moved through the room. Polly hadn't intended to be amusing, but humor was her trade. "You all know better than me that Arley wouldn't sign off on any antique valuation unless he'd seen the item with his own eyes, traced every provenance trail, verified every transfer of ownership. If even a single date didn't line up, he'd chase the discrepancy like it owed him money. He wasn't being fussy or intentionally 'stepping on toes,' as some have said. He believed *history* is *truth*.

"I've been thinking a lot about that lately because...I'm sort of that way too. Not with antique clocks or centuries-old snuff boxes. But as an actress, I've always had this itch—this instinct —to dig just a little deeper into a character's—*character*. To ask probing questions of my writers and directors. To peer behind the curtain—especially when I'm told there's nothing back there to see."

She paused, letting the shift toward her life experience settle in. "Over the years I've learned—on stage and off—if you ignore that itch, you're basically allowing someone else to decide what's right or true for you." Her eyes scanned the faces before her. "Some things stay behind the curtain because dragging them into the spotlight would burn everything down."

The room grew noticeably still. There were no whispered cues from behind the camera. No impatient shifting from the crew and production staff. Just the low, collective awareness that Polly Pepper had gone off script. She wasn't offering a tribute to Arley Kingston. She was going for something else. "And I'm glad for that itch," she continued. "Otherwise, I might never have questioned the police or coroner's report about Arley's cause of death. I might have believed their *official* story. Rather than... *murder*."

Murder? A rustle passed through the room as people took deep breaths and shared shocked glances.

Behind the camera, Chad stood with his arms crossed, a deep crease forming between his brows. His instinct was to call "cut," to shut this down before it spiraled out of control. But something stopped him. Maybe it was the way Polly spoke, with calm authority. Maybe it was the look on the appraisers' faces—

equal parts dread and awe. Or maybe, deep down, Chad knew what every good director knows: when real drama presents itself, you let the camera roll.

Polly lifted the envelope slightly from her lap. "We trust *experts*, don't we. And for good reason. They're educated. They have experience. Doctors. Police. Medical examiners. They give us answers no one else can. Sometimes, it's cold and clinical—like a cause and time of death. That sort of thing. They're the final word. End of story.

"But experts can sometimes get it wrong. They're human. They told us Arley Kingston's death was the result of a heart condition. Sudden. Tragic. Don't get me wrong, I *agree*. The coroner's report was clear. Cardiac arrest. These things happen. Even to a relatively young person like Arley. Apparently, Arley had no idea there was anything wrong with him. He thought his persistent fatigue was work-related—long hours of research, travel, deadlines, stress. He didn't know why he had to push through a mental fog each day. Triple espresso shots only get you so far."

She paused just long enough for the silence to press in closer. "It was only because he was required to undergo a routine physical examination for *Relic or Rubbish* that it was discovered: *hypertrophic cardiomyopathy*." She took a breath. "Try saying that ten times fast. I had to sound it out like I was in a spelling bee.

"*Hy-per-tro-phic car-di-o-my-op-a-thy*. *HCM*, for short. That's what it says in Arley's medical clearance paperwork. I Googled it. Manageable...with the right meds. Deadly if ignored—or *exacerbated*." She held up the envelope.

"These job-required physical exams and reports...they're paid for by an employer for an insurer and are usually sent directly to whoever ordered them. In this case, *Relic or Rubbish*. And unless patients tick a box requesting a copy, they don't necessarily see the results. Arley wasn't aware of his condition. Otherwise, he would have taken the diagnosis seriously. You know how he was. Methodical. Exacting. He'd have strictly followed a doctor's orders for treatment."

Her gaze landed on the group of appraisers assembled near the fireplace—some seated, others lingering just out of the camera's direct line of sight. "Other people see that paperwork," Polly continued. "Isla Morton, for instance, head of provenance research for *Relic or Rubbish*. The physical exam reports for on-air talent—Diedre, Clara, Ambrose, Arley—all pass through her office. Her team maintains records and documents related to the antiques presented on the show—and the appraisers. Scheduling forms, appearance releases, that sort of thing."

Across the way, she saw Isla sit up straighter, visibly caught off guard by the mention of her name.

"'Approved/Not Approved,'" Polly said. "A rubber stamp. Those clearance forms—they're treated like any other bit of admin. Barely glanced at, except by the insurer. Filed away." She held up the pages in her hand, her eyes scanning before reading aloud.

Medical Clearance Summary

Patient Name: Arley Kingston

Condition Identified: hypertrophic cardiomyopathy (HCM)

Diagnosis: Confirmed via echocardiogram.

Recommendation: The patient is cleared for professional activities with caution. Due to the presence of hypertrophic cardiomyopathy, it is recommended that the patient avoid excessive physical exertion, high-stress environments, or stimulants (e.g., caffeine, decongestants). Periodic cardiac monitoring advised.

Notes:

- Patient reports general fatigue and occasional shortness of breath.
- No history of prior cardiac events reported.
- Medication and/or lifestyle modifications may be required pending further assessment.

"'Cleared for professional activities.' Signed by Dr. Edmund McEwan." Polly looked up. "It doesn't say Arley *couldn't* work. Just that caution was advised. No urgent warnings. Nothing that screams, *'You're about to die!'*"

"I don't read those reports!" Isla snapped from the back of the room, her voice slicing through the quiet like shattering glass. A hand-held camera pivoted toward her. "They come through my office, yes—but that doesn't mean I study them. They're admin. They go straight into the files. I don't memorize people's medical histories, for God's sake."

Her tone was defensive. Her cheeks flushed. It was anger, certainly. But under that—just beneath the surface—Polly saw the faint unraveling of a woman known for never flinching. Isla Morton looked not formidable but cornered.

"Right," Polly said, her tone calm, almost sympathetic. "You don't immerse yourself in medical histories. Fair enough. But you do immerse yourself in provenance." She turned slightly, addressing the room now. "Because the histories of antiques *is* your business, Isla. You maintain meticulous notes about them. You know the minutiae most people don't see, or even really care about—paper trails, the origin stories, that mourning locket at Pendlehurst Hall for baby James. Producer Simon Belmore even calls you his 'oracle.' And he's sorta not wrong."

Polly's look seared into Isla. "That's why it matters that you and Arley Kingston disagreed over that French automaton clock, his last-ever on-air appraisal. He knew it was important. You disagreed, and lied that Simon wanted it withdrawn until further inquiries could be made." She took a beat. "And—like magic—the provenance file disappeared too. Print *and* digital versions. Erased."

Polly leaned forward, as if attempting to bring the entire group into a private circle. "That's your domain, dear. Your territory. And if something vanished from that territory, you either missed it...or made it happen."

"I told you before, I know nothing about how that file disappeared."

Polly didn't blink. "Even though you told Arley you were 'reducing its valuation' and 'adjusting expectations.' Your words, Isla. Not mine. But you didn't really dismiss the clock's value." She retrieved a printed auction listing from the envelope. "Our redoubtable Abbots Clover constable Grayson Jenkins has done a bit of his own provenance fact-finding. Turns out, that clock is very rare. A significant find, with documented links to the French court of Louis the Fifteenth. We even have the original provenance...in French. Arley was right. And you weren't just wrong—you intentionally tried to diminish the clock. To strip it of value."

Her voice dropped just enough to chill the room. "Why would you do that—unless you knew exactly what it was...and didn't want the world to know."

Isla's eyes narrowed. "You're suggesting?"

Polly's gaze didn't waver. "Lies, darling. Deception. Like the Art Nouveau silver tea set you decreed was a reproduction. And the William and Mary desk you said wasn't telegenic enough for TV. And the lavallière you dismissed. A single mistake can be forgiven. A second invites doubt. A third *or more*—suggests intent."

Silence stretched uncomfortably in the room, waiting for what was next, as Polly continued. "If Arley had exposed a pattern of deliberate under-valuations—you wouldn't just lose your job, you'd be blacklisted from the industry. Your career would vanish. Oh, wait. You *have* lost your job, haven't you?"

Isla's voice was brittle. "You're suggesting I deliberately undervalued antiques that appeared on the show. And maybe— something more sinister? Why would I do that?"

Polly didn't flinch. "Because if an item is undervalued on-air or doesn't even make it to air, it slips under the radar. The paper- work says it's not worth much. No one looks too closely. A buyer gets a bargain. And later—behind closed doors—it can be resold for ten, twenty, fifty times the price by someone who knows its true value."

Her voice steady, each word deliberate, Polly continued, "That type of circumstance doesn't happen by accident. When a valuation is nudged just a little too low. When a provenance file conveniently disappears. When an expert opinion that doesn't fit a convenient narrative is ignored or quietly erased."

She turned back to Isla, her gaze level. "You ran the prove- nance research department. You had the authority to adjust values—subtly, strategically. To overlook a red flag. To suppress inconvenient history. That kind of control doesn't just influence outcomes—it *determines* them.

So yes, I'm suggesting you had something to lose if Arley kept digging—and something to gain if he stopped."

Isla drew in a sharp breath. Her eyes flicked briefly toward Ethan, then away. "You're twisting things," she said, her voice tight. "There's a difference between oversight and intent." Her jaw tensed. "And you know it."

"I'm accusing you of fraud, not murder."

Polly's gaze swept the room. "That odious task fell to someone else. Perhaps someone with a longer fuse and a deeper grudge. The kind of resentment that festers. Someone who doesn't forget...or forgive." She turned slightly, addressing the camera as much as the room. "Diedre Paige, for example. An expert in gemstones. Years of experience. A résumé that sparkles brighter than the diamonds she appraises. And yet—" Polly tilted her head. "—she mistook a genuine eighteenth-century lavallière for costume jewelry. Called it a sweet little trinket, more sentimental than significant.'"

Across the room, Diedre stiffened. Her lips parted, then pressed into a thin, hard line. One hand twitched in her lap, as though debating whether to rise or restrain herself. "That call was based on the evidence I had at the time," she yelled. "And frankly, I find your insinuation offensive."

"Arley saw what you obviously didn't. Or wouldn't," Polly continued. "He disagreed with your assessment of the lavallière. He lectured you about it. Publicly. Of course, you were livid. I would be, too. Adding insult to injury, he was right, and the piece was later discovered to be genuine. You're still spinning that story, saying anyone could've made the same mistake. Arley just 'got lucky.' You'd built your reputation on accuracy, and suddenly a relative newcomer appears and makes you look clueless. Or maybe worse—corrupt."

"Corrupt?" Diedre's voice shrieked, sharp and incredulous. Her eyes blazed. "Are you serious? I've spent decades in this field —decades—building a reputation for integrity and precision. One mistake—one—because I was too busy with other projects and stupidly listened to the dumb provenance team, who'd turned up their noses at it. Suddenly I'm being painted as some backroom schemer tampering with antique valuations? That lavallière was a fluke. A well-crafted fake—or so I was told—that turned out to be the real thing. Yes, Arley got it right. But don't twist that into something sinister just to fit your script."

She folded her arms, chin lifted. "I made a bad call. I didn't do my homework. My bad. But I'm not a criminal. If you're going to throw around accusations, you'd better have more than gossip and grudges to back them up."

Polly shifted her tone—warmer now, almost forgiving. "Not to worry, Diedre. I don't think your bruised pride was a motive for revenge against Arley. It wasn't embarrassing enough for retribution."

Her gaze drifting purposefully. All eyes followed her line of sight until it settled firmly on Ethan Grant. He stood off to the side, one hand tucked casually into his jeans pocket, the other thumbing through something on his phone, a smirk playing at the edges of his mouth. It vanished the moment Polly spoke again.

"Ethan, I need to ask you something."

He blinked, straightening slightly, caught off guard by the sudden spotlight. "Me?"

Polly gave a tight smile. "Over dinner the other night, you told us Isla said Arley Kingston had an *I'm on to you* vibe'. Remember?"

Ethan hesitated and looked at Isla, visibly recalibrating. "No. I mean...not exactly. Maybe someone said something like that, but....everyone knows Arley was poking around old provenance files. Trying to connect dots to things that didn't need to be connected. He wanted to make the other experts look bad, I think. He was a show-off."

Polly tilted her head, pretending to be confused, in need of more information. "What exactly is an *I'm on to you vibe*'? What does that look like? Is it something subtle—like raised eyebrows? Or did Arley follow people around holding a magnifying glass and muttering, 'Elementary' under his breath?"

Ethan gave a lazy shrug. "Who knows? But I hear he was always making voice memo notes on his phone. Lurking around corners. Like, I dunno...maybe a spy."

"You also said about Arley, 'He croaked, so that's the end of that. Problem solved.' Problem? Can you explain what the 'problem' was?"

Ethan's posture shifted—shoulders stiffening, chin tilting slightly upward—as if bracing for a blow. "I didn't mean anything. Just people die. It's sad, sure. Not everything's a conspiracy, Polly."

Polly's voice softened but was still strong enough to be heard in the back of the room. "Some things are, Ethan. Especially if someone with an inside track is being fed information about antiques being undervalued so others can acquire them cheaply."

A flicker of something—surprise, then irritation—passed over Ethan's face. "What are you really saying?"

Polly didn't offer a direct answer. "You're creating a curious business model, Ethan. An online antiques sourcing platform— what's it called again? Oh, right, *AntiqueX*. A not-very-original name for a not-so-original idea. You were desperate for it to be successful. To finally prove you're good at something other than crafting start-up pitches from your sofa, in sweatpants. You exploited your own mother's association with *Relic or Rubbish*. You've coasted on her reputation—and on Isla Morton's access to antiques and provenance files."

Polly rose from her seat and walked closer to the camera. "And Arley Kingston? I think he was asking questions about your start-up. The kind that could make profit margins messy."

Ethan's face was ashen. "You're crazy. You know that, right?"

"Arley was getting close to exposing you, Ethan—and Isla too. He was preparing—what did you call it? —a *'proof of concept.'* A paper trail, a pattern, and a motive. And the night he died, you called Isla. It was moments after the show's live episode ended. Phone records prove it." From Grayson's envelope she withdrew a printout. "—You called Isla—on her *Relic or Rubbish* phone. A company-issued number. Which means it wasn't exactly private. Grayson pulled the records from the show's internal logs—with permission, of course. You didn't think anyone would notice a thirty-two second call at 7:56 p.m., did you?" I suspect it wasn't just a friendly check-in. A casual chat between ex-lovers.

"You had a buyer for the automaton clock—someone who wanted it off the record, no provenance, no public trail. A quiet deal. No questions. And you knew that once Arley appraised it on camera, that door would close. He would authenticate it, elevate its profile, and make it impossible to sell under the radar. The price would go up—but so would the scrutiny."

She stepped closer to Ethan. "You and Isla tried to pull the clock from the lineup before filming. Delay the segment. Bury it. But Arley went on anyway."

A hush followed. No one moved. The accusation lingered like smoke in the room. "And then—just like that—Arley collapsed mid-appraisal. Before he could finish. Before he could say too much. Before the clock could become documented on television." She divided her gaze between Ethan and Isla. "His death couldn't have come at a more convenient moment. For both of you."

37

Ethan's mouth opened, then closed again. His fingers tightened around his phone. Polly's eyes didn't leave him. "Not to worry, Ethan. I'm not accusing you of killing Arley to prevent the clock's provenance from being revealed. But I will say, trying to profit this way from *Relic or Rubbish* doesn't make you a *visionary*. It makes you a *vulture*."

A beat of silence. Then Polly simply turned away. "But this isn't all about you, Ethan—although you'd probably like it to be. "There's also Ambrose Carouthers."

A murmur fluttered through the room, as yet another appraiser was targeted. Ambrose, seated stiffly on a metal folding chair, raised his eyebrows. "You were bound to come 'round to me eventually." He sniffed. "Just be sure you're not confusing drama with evidence."

Polly didn't bother to respond, just zeroed in on him. "You told Tim that one of Arley's most admirable talents was his ability to see what others overlooked. But his asking too many questions could be_what's the word you used—'perilous.'"

Ambrose gave a slow, deliberate shrug and folded his arms confidently. "Sounds like something I'd say. Asking questions *is* admirable—in theory. Socrates made a career of it. But in practice? It wears thin. Too many questions make others nervous. They stir up doubt." He gave Polly a pointed look. "Arley had talent, no doubt. But he also had a knack for pushing too far. And, as I recall, what I also said to Tim was: 'No one likes the class snitch.'"

"And what, exactly, made Arley's questions wear thin?" Polly's voice was cool and measured. "Was it the Ming vase Isla dismissed as a mass-produced knockoff—until Arley traced it to an imperial kiln? The lavallière Diedre misidentified because she couldn't be bothered to examine it herself? Or was it Fabian's William and Mary writing desk—deemed too 'untelegenic' for television—and then Arley connected it to an estate archive?" She let her gaze move slowly across the room. "He didn't just ask questions. He asked the right ones. The kind that made people uncomfortable. The kind that exposed..."

A flicker crossed Ambrose's face—just a brief loss of composure before the mask settled again.

"You knew that some of the appraisals on *Relic or Rubbish* were unreliable," Polly continued. "I think you wanted them revealed too, but didn't want to be seen as a fink informant. You saw what was going on behind the scenes. You were subtly forthcoming about that with Tim. Arley saw the same thing. Items of value being dismissed or sold off quietly for pennies to the pound. A few months later, those same pieces would reappear at high-end auction houses with verified provenance and six-figure sale prices."

Ambrose's voice dropped, almost weary. "You're right. I'm no rat. What I suspected was happening didn't affect me personally." His words hung flat and unrepentant.

"You mean, however questionable the provenance team's conduct was, it hadn't touched you personally. *Your* reputation was intact. *Your* name wasn't attached to any of the questionable valuations. *Your* paycheck still cleared. So as far as you were concerned, if the fallout didn't land at your feet, it wasn't your problem."

Polly's voice didn't rise, but its judgment was unmistakable. "And you didn't try to stop it." She turned, walking slowly back toward the tribute chair. "Arley wasn't just a thorn in the side of the provenance team—or the expert appraisers he contradicted. He was a mirror. A quiet, relentless reminder of every misattribution. Mirrors don't lie. They just make it impossible to keep pretending." She gave a small, wistful smile. "Believe me, I've spent years trying to find one that shaves off ten pounds and subtracts five years. Still no luck."

A ripple of uneasy laughter fluttered through the room—but Polly's eyes stayed sharp. "Truth has a way of showing itself, even if we'd rather not see it. And that mirror—Arley—didn't just reflect mistakes. He wasn't just nosing around for the fun of it. He was gathering evidence. The kind that could derail a very comfortable side hustle that had quietly become a lucrative gig for some of your colleagues. And I get it. I know how meager the pay is for appearing on *Relic or Rubbish*. Fabian said it barely covers travel expenses. He admitted that his own retirement savings weren't enough to keep up his standard of living, and he may one day have to sell his beloved cottage. And you're not consistently invited onto the show.

"I can imagine how it must have felt when Arley, the upstart, the golden boy, not only began sniffing out double-dealing—but was then offered a permanent role on *Relic or Rubbish*. He'd have the spotlight. Financial security. Credibility. Everything some of the expert appraisers had waited years for. Except he got there not by playing politics. Not by flattering the producer or network suits. But by doing the hard work. People noticed. The right people. And another sting for you? He only got the opportunity because *you* bailed on an episode of the show. He was a last-minute replacement for you—and the audience loved him. It was was one of those 'understudy to star' moments, like Leonard Bernstein or Shirley MacLaine or Jennifer Hudson. I always say, 'timing is everything.'"

Polly faced the camera again and continued her monologue. "But someone else had authority over the antiques on *Relic or Rubbish*. Or they were supposed to. Someone who pulled the *Relic or Rubbish* strings. Someone who has the authority to change the on-air appraisal schedule." Her gaze shifted. Direct. Piercing. "Simon Belmore."

Simon's face didn't change, but his body became rigid as though bracing for impact. The entire crew stilled when Polly spoke the name of the all-powerful producer. It was as if a tray had crashed to the floor in a quiet restaurant—forks frozen in mid-air, conversations paused mid-sentence. Every head turned, every breath held. The silence wasn't reverent. It was reactive. Simon wasn't just the show's producer—he was its architect, its gatekeeper. For twenty-five years he'd shaped *Relic or Rubbish* from behind the scenes.

Polly pressed on, her words deliberate, each landing like a chess move. "Simon, you run the show. Every aspect of it. Every appraisal. Every expert's screen time. But you seldom push back when Isla disagrees with an expert's valuation—like the William and Mary desk. You back her. Every time."

Simon's face flushed. "Oh, come on, Polly—that's not how it works, and you know it. Isla's smart. She has an art history degree and a master's in library science—I don't. She has excellent instincts. She knows what works on camera. I trained her well."

Polly raised a hand, silencing him. "You said it yourself—'We do what needs to be done.' Remember? That was your answer when I asked how the show handled valuation errors. Except these weren't *mistakes*." Her tone softened the calm before the storm. "You like Isla. I think you're smitten. But that's hardly any of my business. You certainly trusted her. More than you should have. If she told you an item wasn't worth filming or wasn't telegenic enough, you listened to her and shut it down—no further questions asked."

Simon shook his head, defensive now. "I didn't abdicate my authority to her, if that's what you're saying. I trusted her judgment, that's all."

Polly stepped closer. "You're the producer. The buck stops with you. Every on-air item, every expert opinion, every second of broadcast time—it all funnels through you. When Isla said the French clock was problematic, you didn't question her. You didn't ask for proof. You just gave her permission to pull the plug on it. Or try to. It might have worked if you'd followed the chain of command and told Chad yourself. He'd have followed your direct order. But you were too busy, and Arley wouldn't take marching orders from Isla."

She let that land, then added, "You built this show from scratch, Simon. Every frame, every beat, every valuation—it all bore your imprint. For years, you were the invisible hand guiding it, the curator of what the public saw. But slowly, you let Isla start reshaping the narrative. You gave her more influence than you realized. Let her decide what stayed, what was cut... and what got pushed aside."

Polly looked directly into the camera. "*Relic or Rubbish* isn't just a job to you—it's your legacy. And Arley was enhancing that with his presence on screen. Bright. Telegenic. A natural at making antiques feel fresh and relevant. You originally backed him because he drew viewers." She stepped forward, her tone tightening. "But then he started pushing back—asking questions, digging into missing files, questioning valuations. You thought he was going rogue. That he was intruding on your personal and professional space."

She glanced toward Isla, then back at Simon. "But Arley wasn't *challenging* you, Simon. He was trying to *protect* you and your legacy. He saw something was off in the provenance department. He knew someone was bending the rules. And instead of listening, you called him and warned him to stop asking questions—to tone it down. Told him not to ruffle feathers. That not everyone appreciated being corrected by the bright young star."

Polly's voice dropped, measured and deliberate. "But the threat to your control wasn't Arley. It was the one whispering in your ear. Like Gríma Wormtongue at Théoden's side in *Lord of the Rings*—whispering poison in a velvet voice while wearing the mask of loyalty."

Her voice softened, but each word cut sharper. "You forgot the one thing Arley never did: *provenance* is *truth*. And the truth is, Arley was *murdered*."

A breath. A beat. "Not with a knife or a gun—but with knowledge. Someone here knew his Achille's heel: his heart condition. They knew how far they could push him." She let her eyes scan the room. "Arley's death was a *calculated* act. And that person...is here, hoping no one connects the final dots."

Then Polly calmly said: "Rosalind Fenwick."

A collective inhale swept the room. The grand dame of *Relic or Rubbish*. Polished. Beloved. Had just come under Polly's gaze.

Across the room, Rosalind blinked—sharply—like a spotlight had just snapped on. Her face froze, her well-known poise faltering for half a beat. She straightened her shoulders and her eyes—just for a moment—darted toward the door.

38

---

olly advanced a single step, the gesture loaded with intent. "Rosalind, you're elegant. Sophisticated. You speak French for crying out loud. *'Voulez-vous coucher avec moi, cesoir?'*" She giggled slightly. "Apologies—that's the full extent of my French, I'm afraid. And it hasn't gotten me nearly as far as the song promised. If I weren't already rich and famous, I'd want to *be* you! I realize that could never be. There's only *one* Rosalind Fenwick.

"You recently told me expert antique appraisers' opinions can resurrect or destroy an antique's reputation and value. I'm still learning about your world, but I think what you meant is *expertise* is more than just knowing *facts*. An antique's worth isn't only determined by *what* it is, but by *who says* what it is. One expert calling something fake can tank its value. Another vouching for it can double its worth. Appraisers' words hold a lot of weight. Like those TikTok influencer kids I hear about.

"Because if what was happening behind the scenes at *Relic or Rubbish* were made known—if Arley had lived to lay it all out in black and white—no one attached to the program would walk away unscathed." Her gaze swept across the room. "It wouldn't have been just Isla or Simon or Diedre in the cross hairs. Scandal would've ripped through the entire production like a pandemic. Every appraiser. Every segment where an item was misjudged, undervalued, or pulled from valuation would be brought under the microscope."

Her voice softened but didn't lose its edge. "I said Arley was like a mirror. And some of those on the program didn't like what he was reflecting." She looked directly at Rosalind. "Unfortunately, that includes you."

Rosalind didn't speak. She merely blinked once, then angled her chin a fraction higher, as if shielding herself behind invisible glass. The room caught her body language.

"Arley was about to expose fraud among the *Relic or Rubbish* ranks," Polly continued. "His findings would have totally obliterated the trust this show has traded on for twenty-five years. If viewers stopped tuning in, everything would crumble. Bye-bye credibility. *Sayonara* prestige. *Auf wiedersehen* Rosalind Fenwick."

She allowed that statement to breathe, the air around it thickening. "Also, Arley was set to become a permanent fixture on *Relic or Rubbish*. Not just another expert behind the velvet rope. A co-lead with you. How did that sit, Rosalind? Were you ready to share the spotlight after all these years? Did you maybe think you were being pushed out? The retirement writing on the wall? A little sting maybe? Knowing you wouldn't be the most prominent face of the show anymore? You'd be fading away to obscurity. Or worse—irrelevance."

A slight twitch of unease crossed Rosalind's jaw, but she smiled—tightly. "I realize we have to evolve with the times or get left behind," she said, her voice smooth but lacking its usual velvet. "Television thrives on fresh energy. Arley was young, confident, easy on the eyes—he had what producers want. I could see and understand why they were positioning him for more visibility."

She folded her hands neatly in her lap. "And yes, after twenty-five years as the face of *Relic or Rubbish*, it wasn't fun to think about it all eventually ending. Sharing the spotlight is one thing. Passing the torch is another. I helped build the brand. I *am* the brand." Her eyes met Polly's—steady and measured. Then she glared at Simon. "It would've been nice if *someone* had consulted me before letting the news leak about Arley coming aboard. I learned about it from one of the electricians on the show. You're right, Polly, the crew knows what's going on before the front office does."

Polly nodded, her voice gentle. "Did it feel like a betrayal?"

"It was jarring."

Polly's gaze didn't waver. "And jarring things can have physical effects. I remember your dizzy spell—the one that caused me to take over for you just before Arley died. You later brushed it off. Low blood sugar, you said. Perhaps an electrolyte imbalance."

She let a pause land long enough for Rosalind to recall the explanation she'd given for her withdrawal from the live broadcast that last evening. Then Polly reached into the envelope and withdrew another sheet of paper. "According to your own physical exam clearance form, signed by Dr. McEwan just two weeks ago—you're in excellent health. No history of hypoglycemia. No nutritional deficiencies. No medication that might cause dizziness or any imbalance. *'Cleared without restrictions.'*" Polly tilted her head slightly. "So that dizzy spell wasn't a blood sugar issue. And it wasn't electrolytes or hunger." She set the paper down. "You lied."

Rosalind looked crestfallen. As if she'd disappointed a fan.

"I do think your dizzy spell was genuine, Rosalind. But you lied about the cause. Not because you're a *murderer*. But because you're...a *mother*. I suspect you knew about Ethan's improper connection with the clock. How he coveted it. You panicked. Few

things are more unbearable than seeing your child step know-
ingly into trouble—and being powerless to pull them back. You
were distancing yourself from the clock as much as possible.
From a potential disaster for Ethan."

Polly paused, then added softly: "Because if a sale of the
clock turned out to be fraudulent—or even just ethically questionable—and you'd been part of the appraisal, even peripher-
ally...your name, your reputation, your entire legacy would be
tethered to the scandal. Guilt by association. The public
wouldn't care about nuance. They'd only see the headline: *Relic
or Robbery? Antique Show Shocker!* Your whole career, everything
you built over twenty-five years—gone. Not because *you* did
anything wrong—but because you didn't stop Ethan's
impropriety.

"That clock was more than just a showpiece—it was a potential landmine. A few days ago, after reading the original provenance, you said if the truth about the clock's history came out,
any pending sale could collapse. Wartime looting. Disputed
ownership. Moral and legal baggage. You made it clear—no
reputable dealer would touch it if its provenance pointed to
theft or forced sale."

Polly let the weight of that truth settle, heavy and undeni-
able. Then, like a spotlight shifting on-stage, she turned and
focused on Ambrose again. "Ambrose. I love that quote from
your wise mother: *'Be careful about repeating rumors. There's a fine
line between speculation and accusation.'* A perceptive woman,
indeed. What I'm about to say isn't rumor..."

"Arley Kingston hated coffee. That's true. He made a face
whenever he took a sip. Said he only drank it for the effect: a
rush of much-needed energy. Days before he died, he started
getting the perfect blend. It's been affectionately dubbed a
Blackout Shot. A hyper-caffeinated monstrosity: Triple espresso.
Cold brew concentrate. Hazelnut syrup to cut the bitterness. A

caffeinated drink so strong it would send most people to the ceiling. It came from our local Bound to Read coffee shop/bookstore. But curiously, Arley never set foot in there. Sarah Rodgers, the owner/barista was a fan of his and would have remembered serving him. So who bought the coffee for him?"

She let the question hang in the air for a long moment—then—

"—Millie Travers."

A sharp intake of breath was heard in the back of the room. "What? No!" Millie stepped forward, her voice a brittle roar that cracked at the edges. She looked around wildly, as if seeking an ally—as everyone in the room turned to her. "That's insane. I—! I didn't—this is ridiculous!"

"You made coffee runs for Arley," Polly said evenly. "You bragged about it. Said you knew exactly what he needed. Said it was a *special blend*. 'The Dwayne Johnson of coffee.' Remember?"

Polly let the tension rise. "You ordered a *special blend*, all right. Not one of those ridiculous, twenty-syllable Starbucks mutants my son Tim likes: venti half-caf, sugar-free vanilla, oat milk, extra-hot, caramel drizzle, etcetera." She took a breath. "Gimme a break. Then—for added measure, you dropped in a couple of *CRANK'D* caffeine tablets. The ones you think help with weight loss. Spoiler alert...they don't. You had access to his file, so you knew Arley had a heart condition that could be exacerbated by caffeine."

Millie stood rigid, her face pale—then snapped back into motion as if stung. "This is insane! Sure, I got him coffee a couple of times. So what if he liked it strong? And maybe I use *CRANK'D*. Big whoop! Half my friends do. It's not a crime. It's available online! And I never gave any to Arley. Maybe he saw 'em in my bag; maybe he asked for one—I don't remember."

She looked around the room, eyes darting, desperate for

someone to back her up. "And I didn't even know about his heart condition until after he died. How could I? I'm not a doctor. I don't read people's medical files. I don't even pay attention to half the junk that comes across my desk. I just file it like I'm told." Her gaze landed on Chad. "You know how swamped we were during that shoot. I was juggling three segment changes and six appraisers having meltdowns. Do you really think I had time to sit down and play cardiologist?"

Polly didn't flinch. "That's the thing, Millie—none of us knew about Arley's heart condition. Not then. Not officially. It wasn't made public." Her voice cut clean through the tension. "So it isn't a question of whether you had time to 'play cardiologist.'"

Millie gave a bitter laugh. "If I wanted Arley gone, why wouldn't I have done something easier? Something that didn't require memorizing his medical history and dosing him like some villain in a crime drama?"

Polly didn't raise her voice. She didn't need to. She withdrew another document from the envelope. "This is the toxicology report." She held up the page, letting it speak before she did.

"According to the analysis, Arley had about one hundred eighty-nine milligrams of caffeine in his system at baseline— roughly the equivalent of three shots of espresso."

She took a beat. "But then there's the cold brew concentrate. The lab tested a sample—this one clocked in at over two hundred fifty milligrams." She drew in a steadying breath. "And finally—caffeine tablets. Over-the-counter. The report notes blood levels consistent with ingesting at least one, possibly two, high-dose supplements."

She let the weight of the numbers hang between them. "That's not a casual pick-me-up. That's a cocktail someone meant to brew."

Polly's gaze swept the room. "In total? *Between six hundred forty, and eight hundred forty milligrams of caffeine! In each drink! Over a three-day period!"*

Then, clearly and without hesitation, she said: "That was *targeted! Repetitive! Cumulative!* Arley didn't die from one accidental serving. He died from a calculated pattern designed to push his heart past its limit. Essentially—*you gave him a heart attack in a cup!"*

Polly took a deep breath before continuing, "I did a Google search and found the FDA recommends no more than four hundred milligrams of caffeine a day for healthy adults. More than five hundred milligrams in a single dose can trigger toxicity—even in someone with no known medical issues. But Arley *did* have a medical issue. That much caffeine was a loaded weapon."

Millie tried to speak, but Polly pressed on. "You say you were too busy to read anything about his heart condition. Too frazzled. Too overwhelmed by work. But somehow, you still had time to make all those coffee runs."

She circled the room slightly, keeping Millie in her sight line. "And no, Millie, you didn't have to memorize his medical history. The assessment is only one short quarter of a page. A quick glance would tell you what might tip him over." She raised the envelope again and withdrew another paper. "This came from Arley's *Relic or Rubbish* file. His medical form was sent to the production office by *certified mail* with *return receipt requested.* And, like the excellent archivist you are, you saved the receipt— and stapled it to the report. Look: this is your signature. So we can absolutely prove you handled the report."

"All circumstantial!" Millie spat, her voice rising in pitch. "You're spinning every little detail to fit your ridiculous story. You're desperate to blame someone for Arley's death. It ain't gonna be me!" She took a step back, trembling now—but trying to hold her ground. She scanned the room. "If Arley was drinking too much caffeine, that's on him, not me! You can't prove I had anything to do with it!"

"You think so?" Polly said softly as she reached into the envelope again and retrieved several more pages. "These are printouts from Bound to Read's mobile ordering system. That darling barista, Charlie—he's pretty adorable, isn't he—was kind enough to provide several app logs."

She held up the first page. "This is a screenshot of a coffee order placed at 5:47 p.m. on the day Arley died. The order was placed through the Bound to Read café mobile app—from a *Relic or Rubbish* production laptop. Specifically, the unit assigned to the provenance research department." Polly turned to face the group, her tone sharpening. "IT logs show that the staff login used at the time belonged to *Millie Travers*. And while you didn't use the company expense account, the browser history clearly shows you visited the café's ordering page. The autofill function even retained an e-mail address. Yours. So unless someone else was casually using your credentials and customizing a highly specific caffeine bomb—this has your fingerprints all over it."

Polly held up another screenshot. "Again, no customer name was entered. No credit card used. The coffee was paid for in cash. But like the others, the order included a precise recipe: triple espresso, cold brew concentrate, hazelnut syrup, plant-based milk, no foam. That's not a standard menu item, Millie— you had to build it manually. And that exact same combination appears on two earlier orders made from the same login."

She stepped closer, voice cool. "Even though your name's not on the cup I found, or the orders placed by the laptop, you still left a trail of crumbs." She turned to the next page. "Here's another order. Two days earlier. Same account. Same café. Same custom drink, right down to the hazelnut syrup and the no foam. And again, it was flagged in the app as 'pay in store.' Just like the day Arley died. I have others, but you get my point." Polly placed the papers down like a final hand in a game of cards.

Millie scoffed, her voice sharp with forced composure. "Maybe someone else used my login. It's not like it's locked behind fingerprint recognition. We leave the laptop on the desk. Everyone uses it. You think a drink order proves anything?"

Polly held up the last printed page. "And then there's this. Pulled from the *Relic or Rubbish* production team's laptop. A TikTok search history for something called the *Blackout Shot Challenge*. A reckless little internet trend: triple espresso, cold brew concentrate, hazelnut syrup, a splash of oat milk, and a caffeine booster on top—just to really 'feel the buzz.' People daring each other to down it and video their reactions. History shows you watched the video twice and even took a screenshot of the ingredients—which had been moved to Trash but not emptied."

Polly paced, slow and deliberate. She stopped and turned to face Millie directly. "Harmless fun, right? Not if you have a heart condition. A condition that was flagged in the physical exam report *you signed for*. This wasn't an accident, Millie. This was a series of choices. You researched *HCM*. And the *Blackout Shot*. You assembled the drink three times. You used a work computer with your login info to order it. You paid cash. And on the day Arley died, you marked the cup with an hourglass—*Time's up*—to avoid confusion with your own Americano."

Millie's defensive posture faltered. A tremor of disbelief flickered across her face. She looked at Polly, then Simon, then the others—eyes pleading not for forgiveness but to be understood. She took a breath. "I only wanted Arley sidelined from the show. I wanted to make his heart condition so obvious to Simon and the network and the insurance people they'd have to take him off the *Relic or Rubbish* rotation. Then I could take his place. I thought once Simon saw how great I'd been on camera with Howard Kettering, I'd be offered a chance. Hell, that segment replayed on social media for days. I got interview requests from podcasters. That's why I pushed so hard during that segment with Howard. I wasn't trying to embarrass him. I just...I needed to prove I could hold my own. That I knew my stuff. That I was more than just some provenance pusher quietly managing files in the background."

"I realize you couldn't have predicted the exact moment Arley's heart would give out," Polly said quietly, "that's not how *HCM* works. It's unpredictable. But you knew the risks. You knew his condition, his limits, what could push his heart too far. And still—you made sure the caffeine reached him. Again and again. You loaded the weapon with your own hand. Waiting for it to go off. And when it did, you stood by and let yourself imagine what it was going to feel like to take his place. You didn't just step into his spotlight, Millie—you literally stepped *over* his *dead* body to get there." Polly let the silence settle, heavy and inescapable. "You had the motive—your ambition. And the means—caffeine overload."

"I've been waiting for a real shot at *Relic or Rubbish*—and no one was going to hand it to me." Millie's voice was angry, hardened. "So, yeah, I got an obstacle out of the way. Because no one gets ahead in television with just their charm and talent." She reconsidered. "Well...maybe Arley did."

The room held its breath as Grayson Jenkins, flanked by two officers from the Bristol Police Department, entered the room. "The scene ends and the curtain falls," Polly said.

"I didn't think to delete the search history," Millie murmured, almost to herself. Her eyes dropped to the floor, and her fingers curled into fists as if gripping an invisible regret. "Such a stupid oversight." She gave a humorless half-laugh that quickly died in her throat. "And that sticker on the cup you found...I tried to peel it off, because it was time-stamped. But it tore. Wouldn't come all the way off." She looked up, her voice softening into resignation. "Funny, isn't it? How the smallest things can bring everything crashing down. And that's the first rule of provenance research, isn't it? *The little things*—the overlooked, the ordinary. In the end they're what prove everything."

As the door closed behind them, Polly walked slowly back to the tribute chair and sat. Her voice, when she spoke again, was soft but resolute. "We came here to pay tribute to Arley Kingston. But before I could say goodbye, I needed to know the truth about why he left us at such a young age." She looked around the room—at the appraisers, the provenance staff, the producer—each complicit in ways large and small. "Arley wasn't perfect. He could be maddeningly precise. And maybe just a little smug when he caught someone's error. But he was also principled. He did what was right, even when it made people uncomfortable."

She smiled faintly. "And if that's not worth honoring...then what the hell are we even doing here?"

For a beat, there was only silence—weighted, reflective. And then the room erupted into applause. Not just for Polly, but for Arley. She had reminded them that *Relic or Rubbish* wasn't just about antiques. It was about integrity, legacy, and the stories meant to be preserved.

Polly looked directly into the camera and sat a little taller. "Rest well, dear Arley Kingston. You shook things up, but you reminded us to dig deeper for truth. I imagine you're up there now, surrounded by angels and their golden harps—*and telling St. Peter they're all nineteenth-century knockoffs—and demanding certificates of authenticity!*"

EPILOGUE

Late afternoon sunshine poured over Thistlethorne Lodge, gilding the stone walls. On the patio, Polly Pepper was posing center stage, playing queen bee, surrounded by her loyal drones and courtiers. Tiara glided among them, topping up champagne flutes with the poise of a maître d', while Tim wove through the coterie like a cater-waiter offering a tray of puff pastry parcels oozing brie and fig jam.

Rosalind Fenwick sat pensively on a cushioned wicker settee, listening distantly, her thoughts elsewhere, as Polly recapped how, piece by piece, she'd exposed Millie's deadly deed. Terrence stood just behind Polly, arms folded and eyes twinkling, clearly proud of his clever lover. Elliott sat on a stone garden bench, utterly rapt—as though listening to a long-lost Agatha Christie final chapter—or perhaps taking notes for the plot of his own next novel. Grayson, leaning against the pergola post, gave a low chuckle at every dramatic anecdote, enjoying the performance of a true Hollywood star. Even Mr. Boots, sprawled beneath Polly's chair, blinked with interest, as if waiting for his own name to be mentioned as a main character in a subplot.

Polly lifted her champagne flute and admitted the investigation hadn't been easy. "Of course, it wasn't obvious at first. These things seldom are," she said. "Then, I stopped listening to what my suspects *said* and started paying attention to what they *didn't* say. Truth always seeps through the cracks."

She paused long enough for Tiara to refill her glass, then continued, "Take Isla, for example. Bright, competent, quietly ambitious. My intuition said she lied to Arley when she told him Simon had pulled the automaton clock from the final appraisal spot, pending provenance verification. That was total BS. I sensed it. She made that decision herself. Why? Because she and Ethan needed the clock to vanish from scrutiny. Together, they had plans to flip it for a fortune."

Polly gave a sly smile. "I haven't decided who was using whom the most. Isla was the perfect accomplice for Ethan— overlooked because of her position of authority, and she was grateful for his romantic attention. Ethan fed her vanity like a stray cat he didn't intend to keep. But he didn't stop there. He used his own mother's phone to get the names of high-end buyers.

"And let's not forget the automaton clock itself. That magnificent little monster. Supposedly cursed, remember? I'd scoffed at the idea—just an old superstition tied to some tragic French Revolution aristocrat. But it claimed a whole line of victims. It got Arley...and later, it claimed Ethan and Isla in its own way. Maybe not death, but downfall all the same. So I suppose the curse is alive and ticking."

She looked apologetically at Rosalind. "I mean no offense, darling. These are just the facts. But I knew Ethan didn't kill Arley. He's a hustler, not a hit man."

Rosalind hadn't spoken much, but now she gave a quiet sigh. "Ethan's going to need a good solicitor," she said. "And I'm going to need a long holiday, a bottle of red, and maybe a step-back from the antique world." She swirled her champagne and mused, "I'll probably take some time off to consider my options. Maybe I'll write a memoir. God knows I've got plenty of stories. Or maybe I'll just move to the Hebrides, raise goats and disappear."

"Sweetums," Polly frowned, "you don't strike me as someone who enjoys goat hair in her cashmere."

Grayson spoke up. "By the way, I got a text from the DI at the Bristol Police a short while ago. They've recovered the clock, along with several other antiques, from a secure storage facility rented under Ethan's name. He's cooperating, which bodes well for any penalty he might face. Naturally, he claims he was 'just holding it for authentication.' Call me unconvinced."

Polly glanced at Rosalind. "Roz, trust me, I only ever suspected you of eavesdropping—which you do better than most spies I've met. That's the journalist in you. You grieved, Arley—not theatrically, but sincerely. I trusted you—and still do. I'm happy we're friends."

Then her tone cooled. "But Millie Travers? Oh, we all saw her sparring with Howard Kettering during the live broadcast, smiling sweetly while mentally calculating where to stash his body. I saw it then. A killer instinct. She wanted to climb the success ladder fast, and Arley was in the way. Or so she thought. Here's the kicker: Simon told me this morning that when he spoke to Arley the night before his death, Arley had turned down the offer to become a permanent fixture on *Relic or Rubbish*. He didn't want the spotlight. So, Millie's Machiavellian power play? Completely in vain. She killed him to secure a future he didn't want—and she'd never have."

She let that hang like a humble curtain call, then added, "Oh —and for those keeping score, I've heard the entire provenance staff has been suspended. Rumor has it that the network is considering taking the show away from Simon, replacing the old guard appraisers, and bringing in younger, more telegenic ones. One of the stagehands left their laptop open, and I saw the memo. The word *rebranding* was used five times!"

Tim groaned. "God help us. Influencer-style appraisers shouting, *'Yaasss, Queen Anne!'*—which, for the record, is not a Tudor battle cry but some sort of pop culture internet compliment."

Polly gave him a wink. "With any luck, they'll be too busy chasing social media fame to spike anyone's coffee."

Terrence raised his glass to toast. "To Polly Pepper—the only star I know who can get a televised standing ovation and solve a whodunit at the same time.

Polly gave him a slightly haughty smile. "The so-called experts weren't exactly swarming the premises with forensic test kits, were they. Someone had to do the actual grunt work." She offered a mock curtsy as Mr. Boots let out a low, unimpressed *Mrrow—I've solved at least three hundred mouse murders all by myself, and with far less ego and fanfare.*

"Of course, the *pièce de résistance* came in an e-mail a little bit ago," Polly continued. "The lovely *Relic or Rubbish* crew parked that massive control room truck and generator unit on the front lawn, which was never designed to support the weight of a mobile power plant. The ground sagged and split. Then someone decided the marquee tent needed to be perfectly level, so they scraped back all that turf. And wouldn't you know, they unearthed what the Historic Preservation Society says is 'an item of significant Romano-British interest.'"

She paused, took a sip, and added dryly, "Translation: they found a Roman coin. Probably lodged there since Hadrian passed through to inspect his wall. And now, we're not even allowed to replant the begonias without archaeological supervision."

The sun dipped behind the castle walls. Thistlethorne, ever

the grande dame, stood proud—weathered, storied, and pretty much held together with only centuries-old charm and ivy. Polly raised her glass and made the same promise she'd made after every dead body investigation she'd ever conducted.

"That's it," she said, with dead seriousness. "No more murder investigations. I'm officially retired. Done and dusted."

Tiara groaned.

Tim scoffed, "Every time Polly says those words, I have them embroidered on a throw pillow. I'm up to eight."

Mr. Boots looked her dead in the eye and let out a long *mrrr-ow*—the unmistakable sound he made whenever someone said something profoundly stupid.

Then he coughed up a hairball at her feet.

Commentary, received.

ALSO BY RICHARD TYLER JORDAN

<u>Polly Pepper Cozy Mystery Series</u>

Final Curtain

A Talent for Murder

Set Sail for Murder

Remains to be Scene

A Corpse in the Castle

Shadows at Midnight

Murder and a Missing Manuscript

Murder in Mint Condition

<u>LGBTQ+ Titles</u>

Strangers in the Night

Overnight Sensation

Gay Blades

One Night Stand

Breakfast at Timothy's

ABOUT THE AUTHOR

RICHARD TYLER JORDAN began his career in Hollywood, spending 30 years as a senior publicist at the Walt Disney Studios, where he worked on marketing campaigns for more than 500 feature films. He later turned to writing novels and is the author of the Polly Pepper cozy mystery series, including *Murder and a Missing Manuscript, Shadows at Midnight,* and *A Corpse in the Castle* and several more. He is also the author of the novels *Breakfast at Timothy's, Overnight Sensation, Strangers in the Night, Gay Blades,* and *One Night Stand,* among others. He also wrote the non-fiction book *But Darling, I'm Your Auntie Mame!* Jordan is an American expat writer living in a 500-year-old stone cottage in England. For more information about him, visit www. RichardTylerJordan.com.